The Grove

Jon D. Wilson

Cover illustration by Luisa Galstyan

For Davie, always.

Day One

1

At this time in the morning the airport should really be dead.

Jess had seen 5am from the fun side, the sight of the oncoming dawn cutting through her drunkenness and sending her home in search of the comfort of bed. From a sober perspective it was just plain rude.

Yet somehow there were people wall to wall. They nagged at each other, pointing at shorter queues, and blaming their partners for failing to select the fastest moving one; like it would get them to their destination any quicker. To her horror she felt sympathy for the screaming kids being dragged along on battered Trunkis, the plastic panda and tiger cases doing little to lessen the shock of being awake at such an ungodly hour.

Fuck - even WHSmith wasn't open this early. There had better be an open bar otherwise Dean was going to cop her ire for booking a red-eye flight.

She scanned the crowded check-in queues, looking for the others. This was war and she was not going to into battle alone.

Despite the sea of heads, she was quickly able to spot Oskar, the tall Norwegian boyfriend of her longtime best friend Duncan. They had met as Freshers on their first day at the University of York. She had been trudging back down the steps of her new student accommodation - a warren of cheap rooms that had once been a hotel on the outskirts of the wall - she was lugging another essential box of crap from the car when Duncan had offered her a Wagon Wheel. She had been sold at the biscuit but when he then helped her to cart the rest of the stuff to her room their friendship had been set. Long before Jess's mum had stopped crying (nearly an hour into her long drive down the A1) the pair had hit the local pub. At the same time as her mum opened the front door to her freshly empty nest - breaking down again at the sea of pictures that welcomed her home - Jess and Duncan had downed the first of many tequila slammers.

She wouldn't brave the airport for many people at this time, but she would do anything for Duncan. She waved at them both and pushed her way to the front of the queue, ignoring the passive aggressive tuts from the other impatient tourists surrounding them.

Shreya, Ben, and Dean were all there, standing in line with the boys and rolling their eyes at her. Jess was, of course, the last to arrive. At least no one would have expected her to be on time.

Duncan and Jess may have been the first to meet all those years ago in York but by the end of that first week at uni, the rest of the week's holiday makers had joined their little posse and the group had been set. Over the years, boyfriends and girlfriends had come and gone, but the core of the group had stayed solid. So far only Duncan had managed to tie the knot. She'd been gutted at the time as they had only known each other a few weeks, still in the early flushes of friendship with years of capers ahead of them when Duncan started to mention Oskar.

Oskar who had smiled at him in Costa.

Oskar who had written his number on his coffee cup.

Oskar.

Oskar.

Oskar.

Luckily for Duncan she wasn't the jealous type and had embraced Oskar as the third musketeer.

After three years of university, they had worked hard to ensure they didn't simply drift apart as their lives evolved in different directions and this annual holiday was a culmination of their efforts. Frequent weekends away in the Lake District had led to weekends in Europe which had evolved into an Annual Villa Week. They had essentially been hungover all over Europe.

Miraculously they managed to get through customs in record time and by 5:45am they were sat around a table at the airport bar with six pints in front of them.

'Now we're on holiday!' said Ben, raising his glass.

They clinked glasses and took a deep swig of their beers. There wasn't one of them around the table that would normally even consider a drink at this time of the morning but somehow it had become an essential part of their holiday ritual.

Besides, Duncan had ordered bacon and egg rolls for them all so technically they were dining out.

2

This year, after three successive trips to Mallorca, it had been agreed that a change was needed.

Dean had been quick to offer to find a new spot this year, keen to find something that would fit the bill but that wouldn't stretch his overdraft too severely. The others always made organising these get-togethers seem so effortless, finding picture perfect cottages by a lake or sprawling villas on the edge of beautiful old Mallorcan towns.

The price of friendship had always trumped the extortionate cash cost of a few days away from work. He knew it was just a temporary overdraft of course, he wasn't too worried about the cost as he had known that he was on the verge of a promotion when he had booked it. Fuck knows he deserved it. After the hours he had put in turning that shit hole of a WHSmith's from ear marked for closure to profitable and performing at the top of its size band. Then a few months ago, James Gunn - who happened to manage the largest store around - had gotten drunk at the regional Christmas party and made a pass at his Area Managers wife. It hadn't taken long for the rumours to reach him that Gunn was soon to be looking at other career opportunities and that the store would need a new manager. Dean began to work his arse off to ensure that when they started looking at candidates his name was at the top of the list.

And it was all coming together at just the right time.

Not just for his bank balance, what he had really needed was to prove to his friends - no, to Shreya - that he didn't need their pity.

None of them knew that he had heard them talking about him last year. He'd gone to bed early having gotten slightly too pissed on their last night of a weekend away in the Lakes. Then, in a moment of unprecedented clarity, he'd decided to pop down to the kitchen for a pint of water for the inevitable moment in the night where he woke up, clawing at his throat for moisture. He was just about to turn on the tap when he heard Shreya say his name.

'Bless Dean,' she had murmured. 'I love him to pieces, you all know that I just know there is so much more to him than that shitty little shop in Beckenham. He just seems to be wallowing there with no girlfriend, no prospects, no drive…I don't want to sound like a total cow, but I just miss the old Dean. You know?'

Her words had crushed him.

That Shreya could think he was some kind of loser broke his heart. He propped his head against the door frame, waiting for the others to defend him, but their muttered platitudes proved that they all agreed with her.

None of them thought he was doing anything with his life.

The next morning, he had made his excuses and left early. Driving back down south he had resolved to turn it all around before their next trip, his new determination cemented by Shreya's words still echoing in his head, a nagging loop he couldn't turn off. So, with his promotion on the cards, he had been determined to exceed their apparently low expectations and plan the perfect holiday.

He'd finally found it, sitting alone in his office, long after the store had closed and the last of his team had gone home. The usual holiday websites had been useless, offering up countless cookie cutter holidays, every destination Instagrammed, tagged on Facebook and conflictingly reviewed on TripAdvisor. He had been googling the Canary Islands when he had spotted a link.

Luxury villa on the stunning, unspoiled Isla Manuta.

Further investigation had revealed it to be a small island just an hour's boat ride south of Arrecife. With just over a thousand inhabitants, it seemed that Isla Manuta was looking to tap into the lucrative holiday market and bring in tourism for the first time. The photos of the villa were perfect, and Dean felt a prickle of excitement; it was the right place. Thankfully it had been free the week they had agreed upon and the woman that had responded to his enquiry couldn't have been more accommodating. He had been wary of giving out his card details to a stranger over email, the last thing he wanted was some fucker stealing his card details, giving them another reason for them to pity him. She had been sympathetic and told him cash on arrival also suited her as they weren't the most hi-tech operation.

He'd been expecting some jokes about flying with Ryan Air, but they had jumped at the prices. Seemingly travel snobbery had evolved from bragging about airlines to bragging about price. Still, he had taken the unilateral decision to spend the extra £8 a ticket for them all to sit together.

Now that they were on board the cramped flight to Las Palmas, Dean was glad of his decision. On his first pass down the aisle, Carlo, their bearded air steward, had taken an instant shine to Duncan and Oskar and the special treatment had started. He supplied them with an avalanche of pretzels and when Oskar passed him his card to pay for the drinks he leaned in close, taking the card off him without breaking eye contact. He held the card near to the machine, made a beeping sound and handing him the card back with a wink. Technically it was probably classed as stealing but who ever said no to a free gin? The boys ramped up the flirting with their hot bear-steward, as they called him, and he seemed more than happy to keep syphoning them free drinks.

Carlo had also turned a blind eye when Duncan opened his duty free, topping up their glasses, the ratio of tonic to gin changing rapidly as they flew south over the Atlantic Ocean.

By the time they landed four hours later, they had fully morphed into the kind of group on a plane that they would normally have despised.

3

The air was already hot as they stepped off the plane in Las Palmas. Stepping into the relative cool of baggage reclaim Shreya was already wishing she had travelled in lighter clothes.

It may have been Dean that had booked the holiday, but Shreya was the one in charge on the ground. As a teacher she was used to unruly mobs so herding her giggling friends through the airport was somewhat of a busman's holiday for her. With a little less grace than normal she coordinated the retrieval of their cases, gathered up their passports into her safe keeping and cajoled them towards the exit.

She quickly spotted the kindly older man waiting to the side of the gaggle of drivers, all waving their signs. His weathered face broke into a smile as Shreya dashed over to him, drawn by the handwritten note he was half-heartedly holding up - Mr Dean.

He reached out his hand in greeting but was interrupted by a commotion near the doors. A lady in a dark blue dress yelled as the local police grabbed her by the arms and pulled her backwards, dragging her towards the automatic doors and away from the newly arriving tourists. She shrieked indignantly as they manhandled her, the stack of leaflets she was carrying wrenched from her fingers as she tried to fend them off. The thick sheaf fanned out as they fell, sheets of A5 paper shooting off in all directions when they hit the polished marble floor.

The woman started to cry as she was removed, her anger giving way to defeat. For their part the police were taking it all in their stride, seemingly immune to her protests. Judging by their lack of reaction Shreya guessed that this was far from the first time they had removed her.

Shreya bent down and picked up one of the leaflets that come to a stop by her feet. Three faces stared back at her from the black and white print, sisters maybe or just friends that shared a common look, all three smiling and laughing in the photos. MISSING was written in large black font underneath their happy faces.

'My daughter came here! I know she did!' she screamed as the officers escorted firmly out. 'I need to know what happened!'

The doors closed silently behind her, cutting off her words, leaving the arrivals terminal in an uneasy silence.

One by one people started to move around again, and the silence was broken as the new arrivals pushed the scene from their minds, determined not to let someone else's drama ruin the holiday atmosphere.

A man in a grey service uniform appeared with a cart and picked up the flyers from the floor, scrabbling around for the ones that had drifted away. He spotted the one in Shreya's hand and took it from her, scrunching it up before she could pocket it. He pointed to the doors that the woman had disappeared through and then pulled his finger back to his temple, whipping it in a small circle.

'Esta loca…,' he muttered, pushing the crumbled ball into the black bag on his cart. He pushed it away from them and set off in search of any strays he had missed.

'Mister Dean!'

The voice snapped them out of their trance.

The man with the sign was pumping Duncan's hand up and down, a fixed smile on his face.

'That's me!' said Dean, stepping forward to save his bemused friend.

The man spoke very little English, but they managed to ascertain that his name was Tómas, and he was clearly keen to get them out of the airport and away to the docks.

Tómas either hadn't noticed their lively state or, more likely, had simply chosen to ignore it. He offered to help with their bags but had happily stood aside as they threw them all into the back and slammed the door shut before piling into the small, white, minibus. The pleather seats were already scorching and the air conditioning in the old vehicle clearly didn't work. But, as they set off with the wind blowing through the windows and the rocky mountains looming in the distance, no one really cared.

The airport fell behind them and before long Shreya was the only one still awake, five heads bobbed around her, lulled by the motion of the car and the warm breeze.

She had always loved this bit of the holiday. Arriving in a new place always felt like arriving on a new world, ripe for discovery. This was her first trip to the Canaries, and she had dutifully read up on the islands and their history, but she was still in awe of the dusty landscape that reminded her so much of southern Spain.

Wind turbines dotted the roadside, spinning idly in the breeze that was coming in off the water. Hotels and restaurants flew past on the right as Tómas drove along, flashes of bright blue pools surrounded by identical white stucco buildings, their balconies pointing out to sea. The faded grandeur of the older destinations gave way to newer, glass and steel constructions as they moved along the coast. They promised chic, luxury escapism but she was fairly sure they would just offer up the same views for twice the price.

One day soon she hoped she would come somewhere like this with a husband, maybe a few children. Then the idea of a hotel with kid's clubs and adventure parks would fill her with relief rather than heavy sense of dread she now felt watching them roll past her window. Today it was adventure she was after, something different and unexpected. She prided herself on being prepared but her research into their destination had revealed very little about the island they were heading to. From the scant information she could find online the island had a small local population - less than a thousand people - and, like all the islands around here, it had once been volcanic. Apart from that she assumed it must be self-sufficient.

All told it was definitely not on the tourist map and that was exactly what she wanted. She wasn't exactly expecting Isla Manuta to be some wild jungle adventure but hopefully there would be some spark of excitement, a tale to tell her pupils when she started back at school.

Shreya stared out of the window, watching the sunlight dance on the gentle waves, and wondered if she was looking out towards Africa or the vast expanse of the Atlantic. She tried to work it out from the map in her head but struggled as her focus started to slip, her early morning creeping up on her.

The journey to the docks was less than thirty minutes but by the time Tómas flicked his indicator on for the turning all six of his passengers were asleep.

4

The rush of the wind and the ocean spray soon shook any trace of tiredness from the travelers. Gran Canaria slowly shrank behind them as the boat cut thought the waves, the vast jagged mountains staying in sight long after the beaches and hotels had disappeared into the waterline.

According to Shreya's laminated holiday planner the journey to Isla Manuta was scheduled to take around an hour but after fifty minutes skipping over the waves there was still no sight of land.

Ben watched as she returned to the planner. He was amused to see annoyance written across her face, the disjoint between her plan and reality clearly troubling her.

'Come on Shreya, relax!' Ben smiled at her across the boat.

He was loving the journey and quite happy for it to be longer than they had expected, besides, this was the first time he had ever worn deck shoes in an appropriate setting.

Out of all of them it was clear that had he changed the most since uni. Long gone were his days of DMs, ripped jeans and his favourite baggy jumper. Somewhere along the line he had adopted the casual nautical style that was eternally popular with the City crowd he now moved in - not that any of them had ever been anywhere near a bloody boat.

Somehow, he had become his father.

It had happened by stealth. Death by a thousand corporate events where it was far easier to succeed if you swam with the current rather than fought against it. He was sure that the others found the change in him ridiculous but none of them understood the pressure of working in the city. If Duncan fucked up then the worst that would happen is someone would be missing some vol-au-vents for their event, but if he cocked up at work, important people lost millions.

It wasn't the life he had dreamed of as a kid, hell, it wasn't even the life he planned of when he went to university. His older brother James had meant to be the one to go on to become the successful city boy that their dad could be proud of but apparently his body hadn't been aware of that plan.

From the second that Dean appeared at his door saying his dad was on the phone Ben had known that something was wrong - his dad never called.

All it had taken for was the popping of a tiny blood vessel bursting in his brother's brain for James's life to be over and for his never to be the same again.

Nearly twelve years on and Ben barely recognised himself.

When Dean had called a couple of months ago to tell him the plans for this year's holiday he had almost opted out. The strange thing about friendships is how easy they are to fade. Were he to meet them for the first time now, he would likely have a polite conversation and move on: a nice enough bunch but they wouldn't really have much in common. If it had not been for his brother's death that may well have even happened after that first year at York, but after that call came, his friends had dropped everything to support him, getting him through the hours, days and weeks that followed.

That was a bond he could never break.

The boat crashed into a wave, sending it momentarily airborne, skimming across the surface before it bounced back down. He couldn't tell if Jess was squealing in fear or delight but either way, he was grateful for the distraction from his memories.

He grabbed an iced can from the cooler and passed it to Shreya. 'Come on, put the schedule away and enjoy the ride, have another beer. I mean, who the hell laminates their holiday plan?'

Shreya pouted and was about to justify her organisational mastery when a blast of ocean spray caught the group, covering everything in a fine mist. Shreya's eyes blazed with smug triumph as she raised the holiday plan, wiped it with a towel and gave him the finger.

The alleged hour-long journey crept slowly towards the two-hour mark, and he could see Shreya's irritation mounting. He carefully walked to the back of the boat, arms out to steady himself as they bounced along. With a mixture of hand signals, Tómas' few words of English and Ben's sketchy memories of a Spanish class he had once taken, he was able to glean that their captain was taking them on a wide route to the island. He wasn't entirely sure why - it was either something to do with big waves, big clouds or, more alarmingly, giant birds.

Of course, it was all purely conjecture but he really hoped it was the waves.

When they finally caught the first glimpse of land ahead of them an hour later their excitement was palpable. Three hours in the boat was more than enough for any of them.

The land ran low and long, stretching out along the horizon. A volcanic crater took up at least a third of the island's mass, its circular rim tilting down to the ground like Space Mountain. Unlike Gran Canaria, this island was striking for its verdant appearance. Trees and greenery sprouting from the sandy edge of the beaches up to the highest reaches of the igneous funnel. It was a stark contrast the rocky outcrop they had flown into.

The pleasant breeze of the boat journey dropped as they pulled into a small harbour, the still heat of the island hitting them as they came to rest at the dock. Tómas immediately hopped off the boat and began to tie it down. An attractive, olive-skinned woman in her forties approached them, waving at the group.

'Welcome to our island!' she called, hugging the captain as he tied off the last of the lines. 'I hope Tómas managed to get you around the worst of the swells? It can be a little rough at this time of year.'

At least it hadn't been giant birds.

5

At the sight of the woman Dean stood up and grabbed his bag. He was off the boat before the others had even found theirs.

They watched from the boat as he hugged the lady on the dock, exuding a suave demeanour that they had never seen before. He took her by the arm and guided her onto the boat to meet the rest of the group, putting faces to the names she had been sent weeks before. Christina Duarte had an effortless grace and soon charmed them all. It turned out that she not only ran the new holiday venture, she was also the mayor of the island and had been for many years.

After a few minutes she practically had them all eating out of her hand., so much so that that no one was concerned when she lowered her head, worry written across her face.

'I am sorry to tell you this but the pool in the villa you have booked has had to be drained this morning,' she said looking at the ground. 'I don't know how it happens, but the water took some on some kind of bug? Algae? I know that this is very disappointing. You still want to be swimming, yes?'

The devastated looks on their faces confirmed that this was not what they wanted to hear at the end of their long journey.

She gave the group a warm smile and continued. 'However. I do have another house. It is a little further into the island, but it has a beautiful pool, the same number of rooms and we have spent the day getting it ready for you. If you do not mind the change in plans of course? We haven't rented it out before, but I had help from many in the village to make it comfortable and ready for you if you would rather stay where you can swim?'

Five minutes on shore and Shreya could already feel sweat dripping down her cleavage and several more southern spots.

It was not a difficult decision.

Christina had arranged for their bags to be collected separately, allowing them all to pile into her people carrier for the short drive to the villa. Dean leapt into the front seat and smiled at Christina as she pointed out some local sights on the journey though the small town.

'There are only two bars on the island, and they are both here,' she smiled, pointing out two identical looking buildings next to each other. 'Maybe not enough for one of your British pub crawls but they have cold beer and excellent tapas which I'm sure is all you need.'

Ben looked at the bars longingly and wondered if it was rude to ask her to stop for a swift half on the way to the house. He was still thinking of a cold glass of beer, beaded with condensation when he spotted a strange fountain set back on the road that ran alongside the two bars. He raised his arm and pointed at the gap where he had seen it, but Christina cut him off before he could ask about it.

'Once you are settled you must come back into town, the Main Store is just down this road,' she said, pointing to the left of the car. 'There you can stock up with food and beverages. I hoped you would agree to this other villa and have left some beer and wine there for you already. Both a welcome gift and an apology for the inconvenience.'

It didn't really take much to buy their trust and booze was certainly the right way to do it.

'We are a small island,' she continued 'and for most of our history we have been reliant on only the food we can grow here. We had no real links with the mainland and the boat trip to nearby islands used to be much longer and more perilous before modern engines. To this day most of the food sold there is still from Isla Munata.'

'Well Duncan is your man for that Christina,' said Jess, pointing back at her bearded friend. 'None of us will get a look at the kitchen with him around. Not that we are complaining!'

Duncan leaned forward and wrapped his arms around her shoulders.

'Maybe I'll put my feet up this time let you do the cooking,' he joked. 'Does the shop sell pizza and frozen chips Christina?'.

Jess reached down and grabbed his arm, raised it to her mouth and bit down gently.

'Noooo, we love you Duncan, please cook!' joked Shreya, playing the game, knowing full well he would not be able to stop himself from taking over in the kitchen. 'Besides, you have to make that potato thing that you made in Mallorca, it isn't holiday until we have had that.'

'Patatas Pollenća…' he pouted, trying not to look too pleased that she had remembered, already making a mental list of the ingredients he hoped to find in the shop.

'Is there a barbecue at this other place Christina?' Dean asked. The huge barbecue he had seen in the pictures of the original villa had been a major selling point for him.

'Not just a barbecue, there is a sort of outdoor room with a table and chairs, barbecue, a sink, there is even some lights on a string you can plug in to make it more romantic.'

'That sounds perfect,' he said, beaming at her.

Shreya cracked first and the rest soon followed, laughing at memories of Dean's actual barbecue prowess.

'Perfect for what Dean? You're not going to cook for us, are you?' Shreya challenged.

'I might!'

'Like the time you somehow created chicken-fish?'

'"Chicken-fish?"' asked Christina, clearly confused by such a concept.

'Dean decided to slow cook some chicken on the barbecue but didn't know that if you take the bone out, the meat will dry out. That was the year that Susie came with us, remember, during Dean's bimbo phase?'

They all laughed in the back at the memory of his ex, but Dean flushed a dark shade of crimson.

'She wasn't a bimbo,' he muttered, willing the story to end, 'she just didn't appreciate good food when she had it.'

'Anyway, we are all being very polite and trying to chew our way through the driest chicken you have ever tasted when Susie very politely asked him what kind of fish it was'. Shreya grinned at Dean.

'And look who's talking, anyone remember Gregory?' he asked.

Shreya winced.

On their annual holiday three years ago, she had brought along Gregory, a trainee accountant from Henley. Things had been going well before the holiday and she had been determined to finally take along a partner to one of their getaways. Besides, it had been the right time to take the holiday test. Anyone that could survive a week with her friends had long term potential. Within hours of introducing him to them, however, it became clear that she had made a huge mistake inviting him along. She saw all the quietly exchanged looks as Gregory trotted out the odd Daily Mail reference. When he had proudly mentioned that he had been a member of the Young Conservatives Duncan had nearly passed out.

The night wore on but she had been unable to ignore the constant feeling of discomfort as yet another discussion stalled, people politely muttering about agreeing to disagree. Nor could she shake her own desperate need for him to be anywhere but with them.

Seeing him through their eyes had stripped away all the bullshit she had told herself over the previous months. He wasn't just a little different and a bit of an eccentric, it turns out he was simply a dick. She still didn't know how she had failed to see it for herself, but then again, she also didn't want to pull to hard at that thread.

That night she had taken him to bed early, broken up with him and driven him to the airport before the others even woke up.

Dean deftly steered the conversation away from his cooking prowess by recounting the tale for Christina's benefit.

She laughed in all the right places, but her eyes constantly flicked up to the rear-view mirror, watching Ben as he looked out of the window.

'Not only did the poor sod get dumped and sent home early from his holiday, he also paid for her trip as she used his card to book the flights!' Christina was relieved to see Ben finally laughing along as Dean got to the end of the story.

The car pulled out of the village and memories of the fountain began to slip from Ben's mind. Thoughts of the large white tree surrounded by kneeling figures drifted away as they travelled further inland and soon, he gave scant though to the statues, arms raised towards the twisted trunk, offering up an invisible bounty, their alabaster faces cast downwards in supplication and fear. He even forgot about the fat scarlet tears that ran down their cheeks and into the waters of the blood red water that pooled around the base of the tree.

6

The road out of the village led them away from the open flatness of the island and into the dramatic rim of the volcano.

They passed through the sheer wall of rock that seemed to grow out of the ground either side of them, rising higher and higher until the rock met at the tallest peak in the distance. There were barely moments to admire the incredible view of the crater before the car was swallowed up by dense forest. Daylight vanished around them as they plunged further along the road that cut through the trees - Jonah sliding into the belly of the whale.

The eerie darkness stretched on ahead of them and a silence fell in the car.

'Don't worry,' said Christina with a smile, 'it isn't far.'

Moments later they emerged from the trees and the relief was palpable, the cool of the canopied tunnel once again replaced by the glare of the early afternoon sun on the metal roof.

Christina slowed down and announced their imminent arrival at the villa. Turning off the main road, she drove down a small track, towards a pair of gates set in a long white wall that ran along the edge of the property. A hand carved sign sat to the right of the gates. They had arrived at La Arboleda del Dios.

The gates had been propped open, ready for their arrival.

'The previous owner was a little… unusual, I think. He was very private and so he had the wall built around La Arboleda del Dios. Not that he needed privacy.' She laughed, gesturing all around them. 'As you can see there is no one around to overlook the villa. Although when you are inside the grounds, I think you can see why he made it so private. It is a little haven, hidden from the outside world. Arboreta del Dios, it means grove of the gods.'

'What happened to him?' asked Shreya, silently begging her not to say he had died in the house. She was generally a rational person but felt it was perfectly normal to not want to sleep in a room where some old recluse had snuffed it.

'What happens to us all,' she replied. 'I used to come by his house sometimes and check on him, make sure he was ok on his own. But, over time I could see that he was not managing to look after the house. He was older and it was a lot of work. I offered to help but he wouldn't hear of it. One day, I drive him into the town to get his groceries as normal. He is quiet that morning, but he always was so that wasn't unusual. But, when I got to the shop, I see he is dead, not sleeping.'

Dean shifted uncomfortably in the passenger seat as Shreya visibly relaxed. 'Don't worry though Mr Dean, it wasn't this car,' she said with a wink.

They wound their way along the road leading to the villa and Christina went on to explain that, as he had never made a will and had no family to claim it, his home effectively became the property of the island. It was this that had prompted them to make a foray into the rental market and try to bring some extra income to the island.

'What about the other house?' asked Ben.

'The other house?' Christina gave Ben a confused look.

'The one we *actually* rented. The one with the algae in the pool. Where did that one come from?'

'Oh, I'm sorry, of course. Well, that was standing empty, so we decided to rent it out too. Also closer to town, so better to start with.'

The car stopped outside a sprawling farmhouse and all discussion stopped as they poured out and stood before the rambling villa.

It was picture perfect.

The whitewashed walls of the house were topped with classic Spanish terracotta roof tiles, the sun reflected off the windows which were strewn along the long walls making the house appear to glow before them. A flagstone terrace ran around it, framed at the front by a pergola covered porch. Thick white pillars supported a short roof, its original wooden beams proudly bearing the weight of more terracotta tiles. In the middle stood a large wooden table flanked by benches, a perfect spot for lazy lunches sheltered from the glare of the midday sun and cooled by the stone underfoot.

Christina opened the front door and stepped back to allow the group into the house. Duncan pushed towards the door, but Jess knocked his bag out of his hands and jumped ahead of him, determined to be the first one through the door.

'Children, children,' chastised Oskar, more than used to his role of older brother in their peculiar little family dynamic.

Thankfully the previous owner must have had decent taste for an old hermit.

A large open plan room sprawled out before them, thick, wooden floorboards stretching across the space. The exterior stone walls were equally bare on the inside apart from having had a lick of paint, giving a soft, warm finish to the living area. A large woven rug framed by mismatched leather sofas lay to the left of the door. They were scuffed and softened to the point of perfection and perfectly framed a rustic coffee table sitting in the middle of a bright rug.

In the right-hand side of the room a generous kitchen ran along the full length of the wall. Light grey marble topped the light wooden cabinets below with crockery and glassware was stacked above on open shelves; a copper jug held an assortment of spoons and ladles. It had an effortless and simple charm that would have cost a fortune to recreate back home. Another large table completed the space, this one surrounded by simple chairs with woven seats, cream cushions providing a touch of comfort.

Duncan immediately set about exploring the cupboards and drawers in the kitchen as the others moved through to the long hallway that ran away from the lounge.

Six doors lined the corridor, hiding five bedrooms and a large bathroom. It was quickly agreed, despite Oskar's modest but halfhearted protest, that he and Duncan would take the main bedroom, the largest one with a small en-suite bathroom. Shreya and Jess claimed the two rooms to the rear of the house with views over the garden and a doorway linking them. This left Dean and Ben with the two small, single rooms to the front of the house which were cozy but had little view to speak of and flanked the main house bathroom.

They didn't complain though, their holidays over the years had taught them that they really didn't care what their rooms were like as they rarely go to do more than sleep in them. Besides, it was far more beneficial to let Shreya and Jess think they had been given the better rooms.

7

While they waited for the other car to arrive with their bags, Christina opened the back door and gave them the tour of the outside of the property. They were once again hit by the hazy heat of the afternoon sun as they stepped from the air-conditioned house and out onto the terrace. A large patio of vast flagstones separated the house from a swathe of fruit trees. Had it not been for the line of tall pines growing up behind them it would have been easy to imagine that the orchard ran to other side of the crater, filling the vast bowl with the intoxicating citrus scent that now surrounded them.

Christina explained that the trees before them were the last of the original orchard that had supplied the island with an abundance of lemons, limes, and oranges. Over time the pines had pushed their way back over the land that had once been farmed, slowly claiming it back tree by tree. The previous owner had lost interest in maintaining the land after his wife had passed away many years ago. It was her death that had compelled him to build the wall around the property, sealing himself off from the rest of the world. With his love gone he had simply lost interest in the life, he just existed in his own little world, waiting for the time when he could join his lost love.

It all sounded a bit too Mills and Boon to Jess, but Shreya was sold on romance of it all - ever the romantic trapped in the mind of a pragmatist.

The original orchard must have been a sight to behold as the remaining trees still cut an impressive expanse of waxy green leaves, flecked with bright spots of citrus. Oranges and lemons dotted the dusty ground, gravity having won the battle as they plumped to ripeness and beyond. Christina made them promise to help themselves to as much fruit as they liked and to make use of the juicer in the kitchen.

Shreya ran her hands over the fruit on the nearest orange tree like some princess in a Disney film, but Jess stared longingly at the plump fruit hanging from the trees and offered up a silent prayer to the bacchanalian gods, willing there to be plenty of gin on the island.

They followed the patio around the house, the flagstones leading them to the pool to the right of the garden. The water was perfectly still and seemed impossibly blue in the bright sun. As soon as their host left it would be a scramble to get into that water. Sun loungers were scattered around the pool, inviting them to enjoy the last few hours of sun before the evening set in.

The sound of a car drifted over from the other side of the house, their luggage joining them from the boat as promised.

Christina insisted on leaving one of the two cars behind so they would have some transport to get them to the town and back. Dean wanted to protest but having seen how remote the house was he was glad of her generous offer.

'Don't worry, I haven't forgotten about money Christina, I'll get cash off the others once they have grabbed their bags,' said Dean, eager to settle the debt now that they had arrived at a villa that was, frankly, even nicer than the one that he had booked.

'Please, there is no rush,' she replied, looking a touch embarrassed to take cash from them immediately. 'You must get settled in today and I can pop by tomorrow when you are more relaxed.'

Christina jotted her mobile number down before she set off in the other car and insisted they call her if they needed anything. They waved her off, jumping into action the second her car disappeared around the corner, dispersing to grab their swimmers from their bags and run for the pool.

Shreya pushed her case past the array of half-opened bags and cursed herself as she dragged it into her room to unpack. She had never been able to settle until she had made herself at home in a new place, even when it was just a night away. Only when her things were in order could she begin to relax - she hated it about herself.

An ornately carved armoire stood in the corner of her room, and she took no time hang her dresses and skirts onto the few hangers she found inside it, categorising the rest as best she could in the three drawers that remained.

As with her wardrobe, she had carefully curated selected her beauty essentials for the week, minimising her packing by carefully organising it all into a hanging travel cosmetic bag. Even with her fastidious pre-planning she couldn't just leave the bag on the dresser, she would have to set out her stall fully.

Over the years she had gotten her make up regime down to a fine art, there was no need to compromise on holiday. It just made sense, even if the others took the piss sometimes.

The others were in the pool; she could hear them splashing around already. In a moment of wild abandon Shreya decided to throw caution to the wind and scrap her usual post flight cleansing regimen. A jump in the pool should do the job just as well, besides, they'd been on the go for nearly twelve hours now, she just needed to let go and enjoy herself before the sun went in.

Still, she couldn't resist giving her face a quick scrub and a curl of waterproof mascara.

A flick of eyeliner couldn't hurt.

A final touch of lippy and she was *definitely* pool ready.

There were still a few of her bits and pieces not in their rightful places but she ignored them, quickly changing into a bikini instead and throwing a sarong around her waist.

Stepping into her flip flops she convinced herself that technically she had unpacked, besides, she could always fine tune later.

The sight of the orchard from the kitchen door stopped her in her tracks.

It was simply stunning.

She was a world away from school and it felt incredible. The drudgery of planning for the new term could wait until she got back. No time would be spent thinking about ways to make moody teenagers care about the reproductive cycle of plants; no reading up on the latest advances in science to make sure her best students didn't know more than she did. She was almost glad that this hadn't turned out to be too much of an adventure after all, the idea of a trashy book in the sun was way more appealing now that she was away.

For now, she lived here, in the orchard, life at home was the unreality for a week.

She stepped out onto the patio and breathed in the scented air, casting her eyes out across the orchard before her. As she looked out, she spotted a domed shape amid the spiked pine trees, yet another type of tree growing in grounds of the villa. She found herself drawn to it, the urge to explore bringing her to the edge of the patio, her feet itching to take her into the woods.

The shade of the trees was so inviting, beckoning her away from the heat of the sunlit garden.

'Shreya! Get your arse in the water!'

Duncan's cry was echoed by the others, and she turned towards the pool. Light sparkled on the water sparkled as her friends splashed around, giddy at their first swim of the holiday.

The appeal of a walk in the trees vanished as quickly as it had come.

Resisting the urge to fold her sarong as she took it off, she decided instead to drop it where she stood.

She really was getting adventurous this holiday.

'Let's get this party staaaaarted!!' she yelled and ran to the pool, gracelessly bombing her cheering friends.

8

The lack of booze and the thought of the empty larder finally forced Duncan from the pool.

He had dreaded turning thirty, they all had really. Two years on from the feared birthday and he was now in better shape than he had ever been.

Last year he'd taken stock and really pushed himself into fitness. Weighing up the options of diet, booze and exercise he had quickly worked out that there was only one of them that he was willing to change and threw himself into a new gym regime. The result was that this was the first time on holiday where he was happy to dry off in front of his friends without the usual sense shame and embarrassment.

The irony was that he was attracted to guys with a bit of a belly but had always hated his own. So, just as dad bods had become the new six-pack, he had joined a gym, cut back a token amount on the booze, sort of watched his diet and been amazed that it had worked. Oskar wolf-whistled from the pool as he watched him drying off.

Duncan was also pleased to note that Ben was also watching him in between dives underwater. When they had first met at uni, he had been sure Ben was gay, had been certain that there was a chemistry between them. That first week he had been like a schoolgirl with a crush, hanging out with Ben, smoking fags with him in his room (he'd never smoked before that week) and looking for signs that he was right. Still, nothing had ever happened between them, and he had quickly put it out of his mind when Ben began to work his way through the female population on campus.

That said, there had still been the odd moment when, usually whilst drunk, conversations had turned to sex and Ben had never been shy at asking Duncan questions.

Do you get fucked?

Do you like it?

How does it feel?

Have you never even touched a fanny?

They had both nearly pissed themselves when that little classic spilled out of Ben's mouth.

There wasn't much they hadn't talked about on those nights, usually sprawled on beanbags in Duncan's room, sharing a joint and a bag of Doritos. Still, there were times when the conversation had stalled, and they had shared looks that left Duncan confused and reaching for a cushion to put over his lap.

Despite those moments, any sexual tension - real or imagined - had vanished as the weeks went on. It had been years since Duncan had even thought about those nights but there was something about the sly looks Ben was giving him from the pool that stirred his memories. In the moment Duncan was surprised to find that he was glad of the towel he was holding in front of him.

'Right!' he challenged. 'Which of you reprobates is going to come to the shop with me?' He fully expected a battle as no one usually wanted to be the grown up on the first night. To his surprise though, Dean jumped out of the pool straight away and clapped a wet arm around Duncan.

'I'll give you a hand Adonis, you'll need my help to carry the heavy stuff,' he said, flexing his less than impressive bicep at Duncan. 'Just give me five to change.'

Ten minutes later they climbed into the car Christina had left them and set off. Duncan was happy to let Dean drive whilst he tried to add some actual food to the shopping list he had scribbled down as the others had yelled requests from the pool. He had only got a few bits scrawled down when he became aware that Dean was waiting to talk to him.

'What's up?' he asked.

'Remember that trip we took last year, the one in the lake district?'

'I do indeed, lovely weekend as ever! You buggered off early I seem to remember.'

'Yeah. Well, the last night I overheard you all talking about me when I went to bed. Well, Shreya was doing most of the talking to be fair.'

Duncan started to say something, but Dean pushed on.

'No, it's alright mate, really. I mean, yeah, I was pissed off at the time, but the thing is… she was right. I was stuck in a rut and I didn't even know it.'

'Sorry Dean,' said Duncan, embarrassed. Even though he hadn't said anything wrong he felt complicit. 'You know that it was all because we love you though, right? Even if you can be a big old Tory boy.'

Always resort to humour as a defence, that was his motto.

'Fuck off, I voted Lib Dem last time, I'm evolving! Anyway, it got me thinking and I decided that, if I couldn't just make a relationship happen, then I could certainly get my arse in gear and stop being a manager in a shitty little shop.'

Duncan gave his friend a confused look.

'But aren't you still the manager of a shitty little shop?' he asked.

'Nope. Finally, had it confirmed last week, I've been promoted to manage the Brent Cross branch,' unable to hide his pride as he said it. 'You know, the big one on the High Street?'

'That's brilliant news Dean! I'm so, so proud of you!' Duncan was genuinely pleased. 'They're going to give the store a full refit, it's going to be a brand-new format and they want me to oversee it.'

Duncan happily let Dean tell him the minutia of his new role as they approached the town. He knew nothing about running shops but enjoyed the confidence that took over his friend as he explained about the fine art of retail wizardry that was shaping his new role.

They pulled up in front of the supermarket and the sudden silence made Dean realize that he had been talking, uninterrupted, for most of the journey.

'Sorry Dunks, I'm just so chuffed about it all, so I get a bit carried away.'

Reaching for the door Duncan reassured him that he was happy to hear all about it. His hand was on the handle, but Dean didn't move. He sat unmoving, looking at his friend, something else still evidently on his mind.

Dean's face turned even redder.

He looked down at the gearstick and traced his finger along the lines.

'Do you think Shreya will be impressed?' he asked.

Duncan wasn't used to seeing Dean look so bashful.

'Shreya? Of course she will, they'll all be as proud of you as I am.'

Dean continued to stare intently at him, willing him to understand his real question without having to spell it out. It took a second but finally the penny dropped.

'Wow….'

'Yeah…'

There had always been a spark between Shreya and Dean, several times they had come close to letting it catch but in the end, timing had never worked for the pair. Assorted near misses had scattered their first year of university but, by the second year, they had skipped past the point of romance and into the steady rhythm of an old married couple that had long since abandoned any pretence of romance. Duncan had always assumed that any romantic possibilities between Dean and Shreya had long since faded away but now it looks though they had just gone into hibernation for a decade, waiting for the right moment to be rekindled.

'I honestly don't know if Shreya still thinks about you in that way," he answered cautiously. 'But I do know that she will definitely be happy for you and proud of you.'

Dean's face beamed back at him.

'Wait, you didn't do all this for her, did you?'

'Not just for her, I obviously wanted a promotion and worked hard to get it when I saw that Brent Cross might come up. But I just kept hearing the disappointment in her voice that night, like I had let her down. I couldn't stand the idea that she might think that about me, that I was some kind of failure.'

'She never thought that...'

'I heard how she said it and it just killed me.' The memory of the moment muted the joy on his face. 'But then the more I worked to get this promotion the more I found myself wondering why it mattered so much to me. It took me a while and then I knew. It was because she said it. Turns out the spark was still there; I was just too stupid to see it after all these years."

For once Duncan had run out of words. It was the most emotion his friend had ever expressed.

'Wow. Oh.'

'Yeah, you said that already.'

'Sorry.' Duncan sat back and thought for a second. 'Okay, here's how it seems to me. You are both friends, you are both single and you have both spoken to me in the past about your feelings for each other, even if that was nearly ten years ago. Now that I think back to that conversation last year maybe there was something behind her comments that I didn't spot at the time.' Dean shifted in his seat, listening intently to every word. 'My advice, for what it's worth, would be to tell the rest of them about your promotion tonight and we'll see what happens. I'll find a way to get Shreya alone and see what I can get out of her. You're both my friends and I don't want to get caught in the middle; I know you understand that.'

Dean nodded, tying not to look too eager.

'But at the same time, I could play cupid if Shreya is on the same page.'

Dean broke out in a big grin and grabbed Duncan into a big hug.

'Thanks mate, you're the best.'

'No worries. Now get in the shop and you can buy flagons of the finest champagne to celebrate.'

Duncan raised an eyebrow at his friend.

'Trust me, you want her happy-drunk and champagne is the best way with Shreya. And if I *have* to drink it too then I can cope with that…'

9

Their trip to the shop had been a successful outing and they returned to the villa laden with booze and food. The others were still around the pool, having dragged four loungers into the far corner where they clung to the last triangle of sunlight. At the sound of Dean and Duncan in the kitchen they abandoned the rapidly shrinking glow to forage in the spoils of the shopping trip.

Dean heard approaching flip-flops and quickly hid the supermarket's only four bottles of champagne in the freezer. Jess, with her Robocop like ability to scan a room in three seconds, would have ruined all chance of surprise if she had seen the warm bottles of fizz sitting on the counter.

Back at the shop he had asked Duncan for help to make the right setting for him to share his news later that evening. Duncan had been in his element as he sprang into action, grabbing bags of tea lights and colorful plastic cups from the shelves. From the odd looks the man behind of the counter gave him he was fairly sure the man had never seen a homosexual on a mission to inject unexpected romance into a soirée. He had barely been able to look Duncan in the eye as they piled their purchases onto the counter, instead he quickly packed everything into bags and sent them on their way. Duncan might have been offended had the shopping not been so cheap. In his haste, the guy must have missed off the champagne from the total and he was not about to go back and complain about free booze.

Dean put warm bottles into the freezer to chill quickly, hding them behind a bag of ice as the rabble arrived. The noise level shot up as everyone crowded around the table, rummaging through the bounty.

Oskar stood back and watched Duncan survey the scene, trying to appear calm as the bags were quickly emptied and their contents strewn over the table.

He had learned early in their relationship that when it came to the kitchen it was best to leave Duncan to it. With a cheeky wink at his husband, he grabbed a big bag of crisps from the table and stood well back.

The initial excitement soon calmed, and Oskar quickly distracted the others with alcohol.

'Beer o'clock?' he asked.

A loud cheer was the simple reply. Oskar looked over at Ben, who was leaning against the far end of the marble work top. He flipped a tea towel over his shoulder, popped a can from a chilled six pack and the slid it along the imagined polished bar. Turns out he was no Butch Cassidy - the cold can travelled a few inches, tipped and rolled off the edge.

At least he hadn't popped the tab.

After that he stuck to simply passing the beers out.

When they were all armed with a beer he raised his own can, his Norwegian heritage making it impossible for him to resist the chance for a good toast.

'Cheers my friends. Thank you to Dean for arranging the holiday, Christina for the working pool and thanks to you all for another year of fun, love, and laughter. Skål!'

'Skål!' they all eagerly replied, desperate to swig down the cold beer.

'This would perhaps be a good time for us all to unpack and leave my husband to slave away over a hot stove.'

'Yes, go!' said Duncan, whipping a tea towel at the others as they happily beat a hasty retreat from the kitchen.

Moments later only Shreya remained. She took a seat at the kitchen table and watched Duncan as he began to pull ingredients together.

'Do you want some help?' she asked, picking at the ring pull on her can.

In the time that he had known her Shreya had never offered to help with the cooking. Her culinary repertoire went as far as the Marks & Spencer's Food Hall so if she was offering to help, he knew she must have ulterior motives.

He decided to run with the opportunity and dole out a job he loathed whilst subtly probing her about her decade old feelings for Dean.

'Absolutely,' he said, grabbing a chopping board, a knife, and the potatoes he had just washed. 'You can slice these up for me, tiny slices, as thin as you can make them, please.'

Shreya set about the task, painstakingly cutting slender slices of potato which she then scraped into the large bowl that Duncan had laid out. Slowly but surely the bowl began to fill with identically sized, starchy circles. Across the table Duncan quickly sliced a couple of onions into rings, waiting for Shreya to talk.

He'd moved on to peeling the garlic before she broke the silence. 'Christina seems nice; don't you think?'

He took his cue, watching her closely as he replied.

'She does. I'm so glad that she was able to swap us into a house with a working pool, would have been a nightmare otherwise.'

Shreya kept slicing in silence, so he carried on talking. 'She is so pretty too, she really reminded me of one of those old starlets in the sixties, like Sophia Loren or someone.'

Her brow crinkled slightly at the mention of the other woman's beauty. He held his tongue and started to crush the garlic, letting Shreya stew in silence a bit longer.

It didn't take long.

'Dean certainly thought so. Did you see him fawning after her all the way here? Like he'd ever have a chance with a woman like that anyway.'

Duncan smiled to himself. Either he had been blind to the fact that Dean and Shreya still had feelings for each other, or something had happened to change things dramatically since last they all met up. Suddenly he was eighteen again, his two friends sussing him out for information on the other. He should just drag them both into a room and lock the door until they either fucked or killed each other.

'If I didn't know better, I'd think that someone still had feelings for Dean.'

'God no!'

'Really?'

'No! Well, not anymore. I mean I know I used to but that years ago. It's so stupid but seeing him today flirting terribly with that woman just made me really mad. I don't even know why.'

Duncan clicked on the gas hob and set a large pan on the heat.

'Oh, ok. It's just that it sounds a little bit like jealousy to me,' he said, adding a hefty glug of olive oil to the pan.

Shreya didn't react, she just carried on intently slicing potatoes.

He crumbled fresh chorizo into the pan, the fat of the sausage cracking as it hit the hot oil, the warm smell of paprika and spices quickly filling the kitchen. He decided he could push it a little more.

'Remember that time we snuck out of lectures early and went for a pint at the Union?'

'Ha!' she laughed. 'You're going to have to narrow it down. Pretty sure we did that on a regular basis.'

'Well, on this occasion we had just walked in when you saw Dean at the bar buying Stacy Keener a pint of snakebite and black. She was laughing and had a hand on his shoulder…'

She stopped slicing and looked at Duncan. 'Stacy Keener was a slag, you know that. She'd have mounted you if she thought you could keep it up long enough.' The words tumbled out before she could stop them. 'God, sorry Duncan, I didn't mean…'

'Don't worry, it's true, she really was a slag, although I'm not sure that is culturally appropriate to say these days.' he said with a wink, not remotely offended by Shreya's barbed words. 'She once cornered me at the Reflex, grabbed my crotch and asked me just how gay I really was. Not sure if it was my limp cock or my laughter answered her question.'

'Oh my god,' laughed Shreya.

She picked up her knife and began to slice the last few spuds.

'Anyway. That was all so long ago now. Of course, I used to have a crush on Dean but that all changed. We grew up and we became friends, I haven't thought of him like that for years.'

She looked around, checking they were still alone.

'Ok. So, I hadn't thought of him like that for years. I don't know, just the last few months we have been getting closer. Remember that weekend away last year?'

Duncan smiled to himself at the second mention of that weekend in a couple of hours.

'Of course,' he replied, adding the sliced onions to the chorizo flecked scarlet oil in the pan.

'A couple of weeks after it he emailed me at work and apologised for rushing off on the Sunday, worried that I had been offended. Anyway, after that we started emailing more and more, even called each other a few times. It just reminded me of how I used to feel about him, you know? So today when he was all over that woman, I guess I was a little jealous.'

Duncan was impressed.

He knew Dean had been working to get the promotion, but he hadn't told him that he was waging a stealth battle to win Shreya back at the same time. This afternoon he had been surprised to see Dean being so attentive to their host as he really hadn't thought she was Dean's type. Now though, listening to Shreya talking about her jealousy he could see that his friend had known exactly what he was doing.

The clever little bastard.

Shreya finished slicing the mound of potatoes whilst he added garlic, a generous splash of white wine, some herbs, salt, and pepper to the concoction that was happily bubbling away in the pan. When the alcohol had cooked out of the wine, he took it off the heat he turned to his friend.

'Don't over analyse it,' he warned her. 'The best thing you can do is go and take a quick nap, have a shower, and then enjoy dinner. Don't worry about how you feel about Dean, just enjoy the night.'

She started to object but he cut her off.

'I have spoken! Go forth and chillax or whatever your pupils say these days. I will finish this off and you will come back looking radiant and dressed to kill.'

'Then I must obey! Thanks Duncan, for the advice, and the drudgery,' she said pointing at the perfectly sliced tubers.

She stood up and walked toward the bedrooms. 'And I still love you, even if you did get felt up by Stacy Keener in the Reflex.'

She waved over her shoulder and walked to her bedroom.

Alone in the kitchen Duncan added the contents of the pan to the potatoes and mixed them in the large bowl. He then lay the slices in a large ovenproof dish and tipped the remaining sauce over them before grating some local cheese over the top and sticking it in the oven.

This rekindled emotion between Dean and Shreya was unexpected and he couldn't decide how it would play out. What he did know was that if they didn't deal with their feelings, it would only lead to tension between them and a week of whispered conversations in the group. That would be the worst outcome for everyone. If they were able to talk to each other they would at least have a chance to make it work which was a much better scenario for all concerned.

Best not to think about what would happen if they made a go of things and fucked it up.

One way or another it was going to be an interesting week.

10

The sun had already dipped behind the mountains by the time Dean lit the barbecue.

Just off the pool was a small room, open on one side, which served as an outdoor kitchen. It was newer than the rest of the villa, a later addition to maximise the time spent outside in the cooler summer evening air. In place of the main house's stone, it had smooth, whitewashed walls and a simple terracotta tiled floor. The thick, back wall had a barbecue recessed into the left-hand side and to the right was a wood fired oven built into it.

The barbecue was huge.

Its vast brick mouth housed a large cast iron rack that was raised and lowered with a chain pulley. In days of yore, it could have been a barbaric means of torture but today it merely served to feed hungry tourists.

The walls radiated the trapped heat of the day, keeping the room hot despite the lower temperature outside. Dean opened the windows on either side and felt the immediate relief as a small draft blew through.

He had eschewed his usual combats and comedy t-shirt in favour of trim khaki shorts, their neat turn ups deliberately gripping his thighs, and a dark blue linen shirt. The lady in the shop had suggested a grey one but he had spent a lot of time and money on clothes for this holiday and he was buggered if he was going to have it ruined by sweat patches.

Duncan carried out a tray loaded with meat for grilling. Dean was about to ask him if he had spoken to Shreya but saw him being followed by Oskar, bearing three large gin and tonics, each adorned with large slices of garden-fresh lemon.

'Don't worry,' said Duncan, 'I have clearly told Oskar everything, so you have no need to be shy.'

Oskar doled out the drinks and admired Dean's new couture. 'Looking good there Romeo! You shouldn't have dressed up for me though'.

'Ha-bloody-ha.'

He smoothed down the front of his shirt and checked for any signs of visible sweat.

'Seriously though, do I look ok? The woman in the shop was great but these shorts are uncomfortable as fuck. I miss my combats; they had pockets and room for my bollocks to breathe.'

'You look perfect,' Duncan reassured. 'Combats may feel comfortable but they ain't going win over many ladies, certainly not this particular one.'

Dean looked at Oskar who nodded in agreement.

Appeased he took a slug of his gin and immediately regretted it when he tasted how strong they had been poured. He turned back to the barbecue and attended to the fire.

There was a part of him that was embarrassed at this attempt to assert his alpha-male credentials, but he has spent a long-time googling grill technique, so he wasn't going to quit now. He knew they had been joking in the bus earlier but this time he had left nothing to chance.

Earlier he had even managed to persuade Duncan to relinquish cooking control as he knew what he wanted to cook that evening. His confidence, however, had been quickly thrown upon entering the supermarket. Hours of careful research online had led to a perfect recipe to impress whilst seeming effortless. Perfect, that is, had there been a Waitrose within two thousand miles. Duncan had quickly seen the panic setting in and had offered his help to work out something that would approximate his original plan.

He was pleased with the bowl of marinated chicken joints now waiting to be lowered over the fire on the medieval rack. They were adorned in herbed oil, honey, lemon zest, salt, pepper, and a fiery local spice mix they had found. Links of the fresh local chorizo would take the traditional banger to a whole new level and some skewers of local vegetables completed the lineup for grilling.

Technically he was claiming responsibility for the barbecue, but he wasn't going to refuse his friend's offer to whip up the marinade while he got ready. After all, it was the cooking that really mattered.

Laughter drifted from the kitchen as Jess, Shreya and Ben made drinks. Minutes later they joined the party outside, their approach heralded by the growing sound of Florence & The Machine telling them all that the dog days were over. Ben raised the small speaker over his head, and they all sang along, wailing the words out as they had done since the first time they heard it, in their final year of university.

Shreya sang along, grateful for the familiarity of the lyrics, distracted as she was by the sight of Dean dancing in the corner.

He looked good. Better than she had seen him in years.

It wasn't the clothes that she was looking at though, it was the look on his face. He looked happy and free. He looked like the man she remembered from those heady early days in York. He was elated, yelling along, arms raised above his head with his gin in one hand and barbecue tongs in the other.

Leave all your love and you longing behind,
Can't carry it with you if you want to survive.

She took a sip of her drink.

Then took another.

Finally, a large gulp.

She knew she should have gone for a dress tonight, but it was too late now.

Shreya threw herself into the song and used a slow twirl to quickly undo a button on her blouse and hike her boobs up. She could always blame her low cleavage on the heat.

The euphoric song ended but the mood continued into the evening.

Dean seared the chicken, letting the skin begin to catch as fat dripped down on the hot coals sending flames surging around the meat. He turned it a couple of times, ensuring a good crisp skin, before raising the heavy rack to a higher setting and letting the chicken cook at a considerably more restrained temperature. The drinks continued to flow and by the time he declared his barbecuing to be done they were all well and truly lubricated and in need of food.

Duncan directed them all to the covered dining area at the front of the house.

He had slipped away from the party as Dean was glazing the chicken with a last flick of honey and ensured the table was ready. As they came out of the front door they were greeted by a sea of softly glowing cups, creating the illusion of a string of fairy lights around the table, the soft shimmer of the tea lights flickered against the wooden roof. Further cups had been stashed under plants and trees, lighting the garden, giving a magical feel to their little idyll.

It was gay as hell, and he loved it.

Duncan took a seat and positioned Shreya opposite him, carefully ensuring that the head of the table was clear for

Dean. It was perfect. Dean would be next to Shreya, ready to woo her with his news and newly found barbecue skills, and he would be well placed to watch it play out before him.

Dean appeared through the door bearing the freshly cooked feast.

There was an approving chorus of oohs and aaahs from the table and a short burst of clapping from Shreya who quickly stopped with a giggle when no-one joined in. Duncan saw an embarrassed blush begin to creep up her neck.

Excellent.

Shreya took charge of dishing out her favourite patatas Pollença to the rest of the table as her neck returned to normal. The others took her cue and helped themselves to the beautifully cooked food and passed around a large plated salad.

Out of habit they looked to Oskar for a toast, but he was already halfway through a piece of chicken, the sticky sauce dotting his carefully manicured beard. He didn't even look sheepish as he looked at their expectant faces, he simply shrugged mid chew.

'I'm sorry but this is just too fucking good to wait for!'

In contrast to the slow cooking on the barbecue, their plates were cleared in record time.

Jess used her fork to scrape at a tiny bit of chorizo that was fused to the side of the dish by to a clump of burned cheese. 'Best bit of the meal?' she asked the table, beaming as she snagged the tasty morsel. This was standard questioning after any meal with Jess, who usually chose the most random part of the feast.

'Chicken,' said Ben, to Dean's delight. 'Hands down, pure Gordon Ramsey, well done mate,' he added, toasting his friend with a drumstick.

The sentiment was echoed by the group and Dean enjoyed their praise despite turning a little red. Shreya concurred and apologised to Duncan. 'I still love the potatoes and it is not holiday without them, but Dean did an amazing job.'

Echoing Ben, she raised a chicken bone from her plate and solemnly addressed Dean. 'I, Shreya Gupta, do solemnly promise never to mention chicken-fish again. From this day forth I shall only remember Pollo Manuta.' She half bowed and raised the bone over her head in mock-reverence.

Dean turned fully scarlet as the salute was repeated around the table.

He was on a slight high and decided this was as good a time as any for him to share his news. He looked pointedly at Duncan who spotted his cue and grabbed the empty plates. 'Dean and I will clear, and you bastards can do all of the washing up.'

No one objected as the pair cleared the table and stacked the plates in the kitchen. Duncan gave Dean a big hug and grabbed the bottles of champagne from the freezer.

'So, did you speak to her?' Dean asked hopefully, watching him put the remaining bottles into the fridge and gather up six mismatched wine glasses.

'I couldn't possibly divulge anything, you know how discreet I am,' Duncan said with a knowing wink. 'But what I can say is that you might just be glad you bought this champagne after all.'

Dean took the bottle from Duncan and smiled back as he walked out of the door.

'You're a bloody marvel!'

11

Jess's eyes lit up at the sight of the champagne.

Proper fizz, she spotted, not some crappy cava. She loved champagne, who doesn't but this just proved her suspicions that something was going on.

She had sensed it since the boys had gotten back from the supermarket, but she hadn't been able to get Duncan on his own since. It wasn't anything to do with Duncan or Oskar, she would have known before the holiday if something was going on with them so therefore it had to be something with Dean.

He looked nervous as he opened the champagne, struggling with the foil and casting quick glances at Shreya who was looking on intently. There was silence around the table, everyone waiting for whatever mysterious announcement was obviously coming.

Dean finally opened the bottle, sparking a cheer at the pop of the cork. Glasses were filled and passed around the table. Drinks poured all faces turned once more to Dean, who once again went puce.

He was still looking at Shreya though, Jess noted.

'Urm. Okay, as you know I'm not one for toasts normally, I prefer to leave that to Oskar.' He smiled and tipped his glass at his friend who returned the gesture. 'But I've got some good news that I have been wanting to share with you guys so I figured that maybe I should splash out on some of the good stuff.' He paused and cast another sideways glance at Shreya.

'So, the big news is, well, it might not sound that big but it's a big deal for me…'

'Spit it out fella, I'm gasping!' begged Ben, drawing a laugh, buying his friend a second to compose himself.

'Okay, okay. Well… I've been promoted to be the new manager of the big shop in Brent Cross! It's the biggest store in London and previous managers have gone on to be regional managers so it's a big step on the ladder.'

He started to explain more but was cut off by the volley of congratulations flying at him.

So Proud!….

Knew you had it in you…

Amazing Dean!

The surge of support buoyed him. That his friends were genuinely delighted meant the world to Dean. He looked over at Shreya who was beaming with pride. He wasn't sure but he thought he also detected something else in her face but tried not to read too much into it.

Jess however was watching them both and saw the looks they were trying not to give each other. The penny dropped and she looked to see if Duncan knew already. He raised his glass to her across the table, giving her a knowing smile.

The little bastard.

The night had just gotten a whole lot more interesting. She quickly did the math's and worked out that Ben was likely the only person around the table who had no idea that the Shreya/Dean game was back in play after all these years. Duncan would doubtless have told Oskar, but she would be surprised if Dean had confided in Ben, and she knew there was no way Ben would have spotted any of the subtle tensions around the table.

She made a mental note to have a chat with him later, not that she was a gossip, but she had to tell someone and her options on the island were somewhat limited.

They wasted no time in celebrating Dean's news and were soon cracking their way through the bottles of bubbly. Dean explained about his new job, the refit, the scandal of the old manager and they all let him talk away. It had been years since they had seen him so hyped about his career so happily suffered through the details.

Next to him Shreya was wrapping a napkin tightly around her finger and unwrapping it again. She was no longer confused about whether she still had feelings for Dean or not. She saw Jess watching her fidget and blushed, knowing that she had been caught.

Shreya made her excuses and popped inside to use the loo, fully expecting Jess to follow her inside. She wasn't disappointed.

'You sneaky mare,' said Jess, as Shreya squatted over the toilet. They had lived together for three years so this was far from the first time she has pissed and dissed with Jess.

'I know, I know! I don't know what happened, but I can't help it!'

'How long has it been going on? Has anything happened?'

'God no! I don't even know if he feels the same way. I just… It's Dean, you know, but now it's DeVaan…' groaned Shreya, laughing as she peed.

His announcement about his promotion had tipped the balance and she could feel the butterflies in her stomach for the first time in a long while. She didn't care about the job, he could be a bin man for all she cared, she was just so happy to see him passionate about it. For a while she had almost pitied him as he seemed to have lost his drive and become deeply trapped in a rut he couldn't see. But something had clearly changed, and she was loving the new look, attitude, and vigor he had. Combined with the candles, the champagne… it was sexy as hell.

'Yeah, I don't know what that means, but I do know that Dean and Duncan were up to something earlier and now Dean is suddenly looking like a grown up and cooking like a pro. I don't think you need to be a rocket scientist to work out he is trying to impress someone. And for the record he has been looking at you all night, so I don't think it is me.'

'Oh god, he's dressing well and can cook. He's not gay, is he?'

'Yup, that is the most likely explanation. He has suddenly decided he loves cock and now has his eyes on Ben. That is far more likely than assuming he is trying to impress you.'

Shreya grinned as Jess passed her the toilet roll. 'So? What do I do?'

'Fucked if I know babe, not exactly the best for romantic advice given my perpetual single status. Just remember that he likes you for you and just be yourself. God, I sound like I'm on Loose Women.'

Shreya laughed as she stood up and pulled up her shorts. Jess hopped on the loo whilst Shreya washed her hands.

'Anyway, what about you? Anyone on the scene?' she asked, expected Jess to wave away the conversation as normal.

This time she didn't. Shreya turned around as she dried her hands. 'There is!'

'Can you keep a secret?'

'No.'

'Well tough. If you want to know then you have to. No one else knows, not even Duncan.'

Shreya knew it had to be good if Jess hadn't told him so crossed her heart and waited for Jess to speak.

Her friend paused for a moment, unsure of where to start.

'I was really glad to come away from everything today,' she said. Admitting the next part wasn't going to be easy. 'Ummm, okay. I did something stupid at work and I'm pretty sure it will all have blown up by now, but I haven't dared switch my phone on since we got here.'

'Shit,' murmured Shreya. She perched on the edge of the bath, horrified to see that Jess was on the verge of tears. What the fuck had she done this time? 'Right. Was it Jess-stupid or really stupid?'

'Really stupid.'

'Spit it out, I won't judge.'

Jess really needed to talk about it and the booze made it all seem easier. Stupidly, she also knew that if she had talked to Shreya when this all kicked off then things might not have gotten so out of hand.

'About three months ago I started to see someone, he is a senior buyer for one of the companies we just started to distribute for. It was casual to start off with but started to get more serious. We were having a great time, but I started to press for more, I really wanted to go to Edinburgh and thought it would be a fun tester weekend, you know, to see if we worked on our own in a new place.'

'Let me guess, you didn't know he was married, and he started to make up excuses for not being able to go?'

'Yup, the full cliché. I feel like a twat for not spotting it and then when I challenged him, he threatened to get me fired if I didn't leave him alone.'

'He really didn't know you at all, did he? So, what did you do?'

'Well, let's just say there is a good chance that at this very moment a major fast-food chain currently has no beef for their famous burgers and I'm pretty sure that I won't have a job for long when I get back. I might already be unemployed to be fair.'

Shreya folded up the towel and put it back in the ring next to the sink. 'God, when you do it, you really do it…'

'Don't I?'

'Let's be practical for a minute then. Will someone be working to fix it all now?'

Jess knew that little shit Brian would have jumped at the chance to sort it all out and to throw her under the bus in the process. He had been after her job for months, so she had finally given him the chance to sort out her shit and come up smelling of roses.

'Yes.'

'And realistically is there anything you can do to save your job?'

Given the fury that had driven her she hadn't spent much time trying to cover her tracks, she had just wanted to ruin his big new McContract and hadn't really thought things through. There was no way he was going to take the fall, with her away he would make up some story and they would believe him.

'Nope.'

'Then there is only one thing for it. More booze. Let's get you shitted and deal with this later.'

12

Jess had been wrong about one thing; Ben hadn't been clueless to the drama unfolding around him. He too had seen the looks that Shreya was giving Dean and, in turn, sensed a change in his friend's glances back at her. Please God, don't let this turn back into that whole will-they-won't-they crap he had thought they had left behind years ago. He hoped they would get drunk and just fuck, get it out of their systems and move on. Or get together. Just do something and cut out the bullshit.

The sense of annoyance grew inside him as the evening rolled on.

Dean was back on the career ladder; he was happy and now it looked like he might be about to get the girl. Dean for fuck's sake. Meanwhile he still hated his job in the city, constantly felt like he was faking it wherever he went and hadn't got a one-year plan let alone a five-year one.

Somehow, he still had his job, but he spent half his time wondering when someone was going to catch him out. Every time his boss popped his head around the door and asked for a quick chat, he was convinced he was about to be fired. To top it all off he was still totally single, always finding fault with everyone he dated and ending it before it began.

Maybe he should take a leaf out of Dean's book and just make a pass at Jess.

He shook his head, annoyed at himself for being such a dick. He hated his bitter thoughts but was unable to stop them. He'd been feeling increasingly grumpy since they arrived at the house, but it wasn't surprising after travelling all day.

Then there was Duncan. He'd clearly spend some serious hours at the gym since they last got together. He looked all buff and effortless whilst here he was, getting chunkier by the week, entertaining clients morning, noon, and night. Duncan had Oskar, they'd been together almost as long as he had known them both and it was clear they were happy and in love still.

Ben wondered if Oskar knew that before he had come on the scene, Duncan had often flirted with him, knowing he was straight but still pushing the boundaries, teasing to see if he would succumb one drunken night. He never had though, even if there had sometimes been a strong temptation just to let the lad give him a blow job. He wouldn't have minded letting another guy suck him, a mouth is a mouth, he just didn't want to deal with the fallout afterwards and the confusion it would probably have caused. But today by the pool, he had felt Duncan looking at him as he dried off and wondered if those feelings were still there. Maybe that was something else to get out of the way this holiday.

He caught himself mid thought. Shame flooded him, he wasn't sure how his brain had leapt from hating his job to odd thoughts about Duncan.

He really wasn't feeling himself tonight, in all honesty he just wanted to go to bed and sleep it off, but it was only 10pm and he didn't want to kill the mood for the others.

When Jess and Shreya got back to the table, squawking with laughter, he made his excuses and went inside to use the bathroom. A sneaky shot of something might boost his mood and get him back in to the swing of the evening. He grabbed a glass from the kitchen and snuck to his room to pour himself a slug of the Blanton's Gold Edition that he always stashed in his case for moments like this. He had never really gotten a taste for whiskey, preferring instead the sweet, smoked flavors of American bourbon. It made him feel more like a character in Mad Men than just the average trader, flailing in a City firm, that he was. Besides, with whiskey you don't get a gold, plastic horse on the cork.

Locking the door behind him he spotted that Duncan had lit a candle in the bathroom - ever the sodding host - so he decided to leave the light off. Hiding in the toilet to sneak a drink wasn't very Don Draper of him but the muted lighting helped the illusion. He opened the window and looked out into the garden, taking in the sounds of the island and the murmur of laughter drifting over the roof from the dinner table.

A low hum vibrated around him, the sound of power lines humming on a damp day. He hadn't noticed it before but as he sipped at his drink it became more distinct, creeping up in volume until it had swallowed up the other noises of the night.

He finished the amber liquid with one last gulp and set the glass down.

The noise filled the room around him until he could almost feel it on his skin, making the hairs on his arms quiver with its intensity.

Panic rose inside him as the noise filled his mind, blocking out all thoughts apart from the instinctive need he now had to get out of the bathroom and back out into the cooler air outside. He went to unlock the bathroom door, but his hand froze at the hum of voices in the kitchen. There was no way he could cope with seeing the others right now.

In his desperation to get outside the open window in the bathroom became the simplest solution.

It never struck him as odd that he was sneaking out of the window to avoid his friends. Nor did he question why he silently pulled it closed behind him and then walked in the shadows, staying out of sight of the kitchen as he made his way towards the trees.

Stepping off the patio and into the dark arbor he was unaware of the branches brushing past him or of the soft squelch as he trod on soft, rotting fruits, their sticky juices bleeding into the ground.

Ben was no longer aware of anything.

He just kept moving forward.

Pushing through the fruit trees, then the firs with their sharp needles pricking at him as he walked.

He didn't stop until he came to the clearing in the trees.

At its centre stood bloomed a majestic tree, towering over the tree line.

If someone had told Ben that the gods had woven an orchard together to create the beast before him, he would have believed them. Its trunk was a twisted column of smaller stalks, entwined over centuries until they were one thick mass; roots cascaded outwards making the base twice the width at the ground as it was halfway up. Knots and whorls punctuated its bark like braille until the trunks branched out into a vast bronchial canopy that filled the width of the clearing with its perfect dome of spiked, palm leaves.

The buzzing in his ear changed as he looked on, small individual sounds picking through cacophony until he was able to distinguish the sound of the waxen blades rustling in the gale that had blown up around him since he left the house.

The sound increased in fervour as the branches shook in the howling wind, straining to stay attached to their branches, desperately clinging on to life. The thick boughs swayed under the strain of the tempest; the whole tree whisked into a jarring frenzy of motion despite its vast bulk.

It changed in pitch and tempo until he could hear screams through the storm, desperation and panic replacing the numbness that had led him to this place.

The chaos was deafening.

He dropped to his knees, clasped his hands over his ears and yelled, unable to hear his own shouts over the howling storm.

He knelt there, praying for help, begging for it to stop, needing it to end.

It ceased abruptly and he was deafened by the silence that followed.

He forced himself to uncover his eyes.

The majestic tree still stood before him, its woven trunk reaching up to the sky. He could almost feel the life in the tree, flowing through the dark roots that spread out all around him, pulsing in the soil below.

It was perfectly still. Not a leaf moved in the still of the warm evening.

He stumbled to his feet and staggered away from the clearing and into the darkness of the trees.

There had to be a simple explanation, but he was fucked if he could think of one. He just needed to get to bed without seeing anyone and get some sleep.

His mind raced as he staggered back to the house. He'd laugh about it in the morning, blame it on the champagne and let everyone reassure him that it had just been really windy tonight. Might be best to lay off the bourbon too if this was anything to go by.

The kitchen door was locked when he got back. Annoyed that he would have to see the others he made his way to the front, taking a second to compose himself and put on a fake smile.

He rounded the corner and found the terrace deserted.

The table had been cleared and the candles snuffed. From the darkness in all the windows it was clear that the others had gone to bed some time ago. He tried the front door, but this too was locked. They must have thought he was already asleep.

The bathroom window was now propped open so, for the second time that night, he found himself climbing through it.

He threw off his clothes and jumped into bed. As he turned over his Apple Watch glowed, and he stared at the display in confusion.

It was nearly 3am.

He had been at the tree for hours.

Day Two

13

The sound of laughter and spoons scraping against bowls woke Ben. He raised his watch to the one eye he had barely managed to open and squinted.

10:30am.

He lay there piecing together the events of the previous night. He remembered being grumpy and half-drunk but after that there was nothing. Maybe he had been more pissed than he thought? Beer, gin, champagne, they had been drinking all day and up for hours, it was no surprise he had crashed out. And the bourbon... that was when his memory became fuzzy.

He sat up tentatively but felt no residual hangover and no evidence of his previous grumpy mood. What he felt was a sense of elation. First proper day of the holiday, a cracking night's sleep and he was ready to go again.

He dug into his case and pulled out a crumpled vest top and some shorts. After some coffee and breakfast, he would *definitely* unpack.

'Good afternoon!' Jess greeted him with a smile, rubbing his cheeks in her palms. 'All that beauty sleep and you are still ugly as sin.'

He grinned at her and suggestively ran his fingers down his chest. 'You know you want to get with this....'

Oskar had snapped to duty at the sound of Ben walking down the hall, so it wasn't long before a hot coffee was placed in front of him. He sipped at the hot foam and thanked the gods for Oskar's skills with even the most rudimentary of coffee making equipment at his disposal.

'So where did you get to last night?' asked Oskar. 'I don't believe the king of the party went to bed first. Did you sneak in a local lady already?' His Norwegian accent drew out the 'a' sound in party making it sound so much cooler than it would if anyone else said it.

Ben took another appreciative gulp of coffee, enjoying the slight scald as he swallowed it down.

'I must be getting old. I honestly don't even remember going to bed. After the food and the champagne, it all gets to be a bit of a blur. Pretty sure I went to the toilet and must have just heard the siren call of my bed and crashed out.'

Something in his mind stirred as he said the last words, but it was gone before he could focus on it.

Siren call. Call.

The more he clung to the words the less sense they made until he heard the word on repeat in his head, call, call, call, call - it lost all meaning and just became a sound.

Oskar snapped his fingers, jolting Ben out of his daze. 'I think you might need another cup of coffee…'

Ben was lost in a thought, his head tilting to one side as he concentrated. He laughed and nodded in agreement as he sat down at the kitchen table.

Jess grabbed the chair next to him and looked pointedly across the room at Shreya and Dean who were walking past the window outside. 'You missed all the fun,' she teased, relishing the thought of sharing the gossip with her unobservant friend.

'Don't tell me they finally fucked?' he asked, the sight of the pair reminding him of their closeness over dinner last night.

'You spotted that?' Jess asked incredulously, deflated at having her gossip spoiled but equally impressed that Ben had actually paid attention.

'Wasn't exactly hard to miss, was it? I didn't see it coming though I have to say, did you?'

'Nope. But my sources have revealed that they have been chatting a lot recently. This is basically When Harry Met Sally.'

He stared at her blankly.

'God you are so straight. Meg Ryan? Billy Crystal?'

He'd seen it once years ago but only half watched it - there wasn't enough sex or violence for his liking. He vaguely remembered it, but it wouldn't hurt to play dumb.

'Ugh. They were best friends, but it took them a decade to get together…? Men and women can't really be friends?'

'Why not?' he asked, happy to let her keep talking.

'You really haven't seen it have you? When they first meet Harry tells Sally that men and women can never really be friends as the sex part gets in the way.'

'Of course men can be friends with women. We're friends, aren't we? We haven't let sex get in the way of our friendship?'

'Yeah, but we got the sex out of the way early,' she reminded him, blushing slightly at the memory of a drunken fumble after a lock in at the pub next door. It had been awkward and ill-advised, but fortunately they both found the funny side of it all when Ben finally managed to come. They hadn't told the rest of the group about it and Jess had barely thought about it until now.

'Oh god. Don't.' He pretended to look embarrassed, but the truth was that he had thought about it often, normally when he couldn't sleep and needed to get off. 'Ok, so maybe this Harry has a point although I would amend his philosophy to say that they can be friends if they get the sex part out of the way.'

Jess disagreed, 'Nope, it's a good line in a film but bollocks in real life.'

'So, Shreya and Dean… anything happen last night?' he asked, steering the conversation back to the couple of the moment.

'I think Dean has actually got a game plan,' she said. 'He played it all pretty damn cool last night. The clothes, the cooking skills, the promotion; Shreya was lapping it all up and by the time you vanished, she was putty in his hands.'

'So, they did shag!' Ben marveled, proud of his friend's stealth tactics.

'Nope, worse than that.'

'Worse?'

'We all stayed around the table, chatting, and laughing, booze flowing. Duncan, Oskar, and I all took turns listening in and it was all going well. Shreya was getting flirty, Dean was getting flirty, it was clearly Going to Happen. Then Dean stands up and says that he is absolutely knackered and has to go to bed. You could see Shreya taking her cue and getting ready to follow but then he bends down, gives her a peck on the cheek and says he can't wait to carry on talking in the morning.'

'Ha! Brilliant,' said Ben. Dean had turned into a player, who knew?

'What do you mean by that?'

'He played the gentleman! Great chat, respectful, no taking advantage after lots of booze.'

'But he could have shagged her last night, she was totally up for it and definitely not drunk enough that he would have been taking advantage!'

'Yeah, but now look at them.' He nodded his head towards the two of them, talking animatedly and laughing. 'There are clearly no awkward morning after feelings there. If she was pissed off last night at him going to bed, she has already told herself that he has too much respect for her and now she totally wants to shag him.'

Ben paused as he watched the pair walking in the sunlight garden. 'But I fear the reality may be a lot less Machiavellian than that.'

'Don't say it,' begged Jess.

'He may actually love her.'

14

Dean was on top of the world.

Last night had gone better than he had dared hope. He had proved to Shreya that he was the man she wanted him to be and now he was sure that she felt the same way about him too. It had taken every ounce of restraint to go to bed alone last night, but he didn't want to fuck it all up when a little bit of patience could make it all perfect.

He had always thought she was beautiful but last night she looked radiant in the soft glow of the candlelight. He had dated other pretty women but found himself tongue-tied and prone to making a bit of a tit of himself. Last night though they had chatted for hours at the table, and he had been charming, even a little witty if he dared to say so himself.

Had he not found his eyes repeated drawn to her cleavage he could have claimed to have been the perfect gentleman but a few times she had had to remind him to look at her face, not her boobs. He knew she hadn't minded though, if she had she wouldn't have hiked up her bra when she thought he wasn't looking.

The night had been planned to perfection and had played out better than he had expected.

But now there was no plan.

Deep down he really hadn't expected it to really work, so now finding himself sat with her this morning, grinning like some love-struck teenager, he had no idea what the hell to do next. From here on out he was going to rely on being himself and he was worried it wouldn't be enough to carry him through.

The sun was already high above them, bathing the garden in light and heat, the stone floor already too hot to walk on barefoot. Shreya was already starting to gently perspire and was unusually aware of the slight buildup of moisture on her top lip.

'Think it might be time to get my bikini and go for a swim,' she said, needing an excuse to freshen up.

She thought back to yesterday and cringed at the memory of cannonballing into the pool. Today she would have to be a little more elegant.

She slipped on her shoes and walked to the kitchen door, attempting to look sexy as she went, but soon gave in to the fact that even Gisele would struggle to look graceful in flip-flops.

'Back in five!' she called over her shoulder, 'I might need some help with my sun cream,' she added in her most alluring voice.

Hopefully thoughts of lotion would distract him from her less-sexier-than-planned walk into the house. Crossing through the threshold she sped up, aware that she had less than five minutes to create the illusion of being effortlessly pool ready.

Ben and Jess smirked at her from the kitchen table.

She drew her finger across her lips. 'Zip it!' she yelled, before they could interrogate her and waste precious minutes. Their laughter followed her down the hall, muffled only when she closed the door behind her.

Shucking off her shorts and t-shirt, she stared at the array of swimsuits she had packed. In the shop she had agonised over several styles but was now glad that she had ended up buying all three. The vintage 1950s pin up style halter top she had worn yesterday was cute but covered up far too much skin for her needs today. Instead she opted for a striped one - a classic cut bikini that should highlight her boobs and leave little else to the imagination.

She dragged the brush through her hair, pulling it back and up, deftly twisting it into a neat knot at the top of her head. A few carefully placed pins tucked away any straggling hairs and she carefully pulled two strands of her hair out at the front to give her some Khalessi chic. Thankfully she had already put on some natural make up for breakfast and now she was glad that she had had the foresight to bring only waterproof products with her. Some gold sandals and a sheer sarong competed the look.

She stepped back and looked at herself in the mirror.

Not bad for just over five minutes. She turned around, checking herself from all angles, pleased with her efforts.

She gave her nipples a little tweak through the fabric.

It wouldn't hurt to have everything on show when she walked out to the pool.

Oskar had been watching Shreya and Dean since breakfast and could feel the awkwardness growing between them. He had also spotted that he wasn't the only one watching the pair. Jess and Ben had been conspiring over breakfast and Duncan was barely hiding his voyeurism from the pool.

If this was going to progress, they were going need a change of scene and some privacy.

When Shreya went to change, he quickly rooted around the villa and managed to cobble together some beach towels and a parasol from outside. He made a couple of sandwiches with the leftovers and put them into a canvas bag along with a big back of crisps, a couple of peaches, a large bottle of cold water and some napkins. By the time Shreya came back out the car was loaded, and Dean was lined up by the door with a grateful look on his face.

Yesterday, Christina had told them that there were several beaches along the coast that were easy to find and often empty. If they couldn't make it work, alone on a tropical beach paradise, then there really was no hope for them.

15

The four remaining friends hung around the pool in various stages of relaxed bliss.

Ben was trying to lose himself in a Swedish crime thriller but found that he kept reading the same sentence over and over. He finally gave up and put the book down, letting himself just soak up the sun with his eyes closed.

Jess and Duncan were huddled together, talking quietly, and laughing, their magazines unopened at their sides after quickly abandoning any pretense of reading. Oskar watched them from the pool, his arms draped over a day-glow coloured lilo that he had found alongside the parasol he had given to Dean, the sun warming his strapping shoulders.

Jealousy had always been a silent fourth player in the trio's friendship. Not so much on his part, but he knew that Jess had always resented their relationship, particularly as it had developed so soon after they all met. It wasn't Oskar's fault that Duncan and Jess had barely forged their sexless coupling when he had first met Duncan, but he had been aware that she had resented being relegated to the status of second most important person in his life, the plans that had to be changed; an extra ticket sourced for the Po'Girl gig they had bought; a lunch moved to fit around Oskar's shift - nothing dramatic but enough to piss her off.

For her part Jess had never hated Oskar for it either. Far from it, in fact. The problem was that it was bad enough that Duncan had met someone, but he had had the gall to meet a handsome man with a beautiful accent and a personality to match. In fact, he was exactly her type. Insult to injury. Salt in the wound. Slap in the face. You could call it what you like, it had just been a pisser as far as she was concerned.

As their relationship had grown before her eyes, her slightly tortured indignance had given way to a grudging acceptance of his presence in her life; in time a genuine friendship bloomed between the three of them.

Even after all these years, the jealousy still always briefly resurfaced when they met up on holiday, the group dynamic resetting their behaviour patterns. Duncan and Jess would close ranks, drawing together in some juvenile display of fealty - their comments becoming more barbed and their laughter a little sharper.

Oskar knew the signs and left them to it, happily pretending not to notice that the pair were sneaking vodka into their drinks as it tended to speed up the whole process.

From across the pool Duncan winked at him and Oskar knew that the routine was already winding down. He was therefore not surprised when, minutes later, Jess leapt into the pool and wrapped herself around his shoulders and hooked her feet around his hips, beginning the now familiar process of silent reconciliation.

He hugged her arms and blew a kiss back at her.

They were all good.

Ben watched the scene from the other side of the pool, happy to be separate from their mini drama but relieved it was all over. Ordinarily he would have been watching it unfold and rolling his eyes at Shreya and Dean, but this time they weren't here.

It made him see that there were some subtle divisions forming in the group.

Their dynamic had always worked well as they each had their own relationships within it. As the only girls, Jess and

Shreya had always been natural allies and Duncan and Oskar obviously had their pairing. That had thrown Dean and Ben together as the token straight, white, men to laugh off their friends' jokes and watch the football together at the local. His brother's death had drawn the pair together into a deeper way but, as the years had moved, he felt the bond they shared begin to break down as their lives grew apart. These days they had a simple friendship held together by beer and a sense of duty.

They each had their own relationships and history with one another that still shaped their interactions.

If Shreya and Dean got together again then everything was going to change.

Duncan, Oskar, and Jess hung out more than the rest of them, they were tight in a way that the others weren't, but that had never mattered before as the other three had also been a group by default. Now Ben saw that the two cliques were dividing further, and he was not a natural fit in either.

Whatever way the Dean and Shreya situation played out he was certain that things were about to get very interesting.

He smiled to himself and dropped the back of his sun bed, pulling his towel tight underneath him as he lay out flat, happily watching the scattering of small clouds languidly float by.

Whether they worked or not he was happy to stay on the periphery and make the most of this holiday. The thought that it might be the last time they went way together as a group wasn't going to make him lose any sleep. Sometimes it was just time to move on.

He closed his eyes and reveled in the heat of the sun on his skin. A small breeze caught the hairs on his legs and sent a wave of goosebumps all over his body. A wave of chills spread over him, and he felt his balls tighten and his cock twitch. He tried to ignore it but knew what was coming.

He forced his mind to think of other things but the more he tried, the more his body defied him, flushing blood into his vessels, thickening his dick until it was pushing at his speedos. His only option now was to turn over before he got a full-on boner in front of his friends.

He propped himself up on one elbow and quickly rearranged himself, pulling his cock to the side so he could lie down comfortably. He glanced around the pool as he quickly turned over and caught Duncan's eye. The others were all oblivious to the obvious tenting his speedos, but Duncan was watching him closely, his eyes drawn to the sight of Ben's hand moving inside his suit.

Duncan smiled; Ben blushed.

Safely on his front he laughed to himself, embarrassed at being caught with a random hard-on like some testosterone riddled teenager. As he lay there, he also thought about the smile that Duncan had given him. His still hardening cock told him that it would be a while before he could stand up again.

16

'Oh, thank fuck for that,' said Shreya. Dean pointed the car in the general direction that Christina had described the previous day and set off. 'Love them all, but I'm so glad you thought of this, it was starting to feel like Love Island at the villa. Even Ben was staring!'

God, he owed Oskar one for this.

'I know, hardly subtle, were they?'

Shreya turned the radio on and twiddled the dial, looking for some music to distract them. She was relieved to get time away from the prying eyes of their friends but now found herself nervous on her own with Dean, their conversation suddenly less fluid that it had been back at the villa. The static dropped, replaced by some Spanish popstrel singing about her *corazón*. Shreya wasn't sure if the girl was singing about her heart breaking or bursting but the catchy tune at least suggested a positive motivation for her warbling.

The car jolted along the battered old road and Dean kept his eyes peeled for the perfect spot. It had to be secluded, somewhere with sand and no one else around to interrupt them. He didn't exactly have any moves, so he was pinning his hopes on finding an idyllic spot for them to spend a few hours and share the picnic Oskar had made, see what happened.

Shreya pointed out a narrow strip of sand, but he already spotted the perfect place up ahead. Less than half a than a mile in front of them the land jutted out and he had spied a tiny little cove tucked away in a rocky outcropping, a thin line of sand leading up to it from the left. He kept on driving until he was sure they were close to the place he had seen and then slowed down to look for a break in the rocks. A large patch of open ground spread out of the right, just in front of a perfect gap in the rocks. The path between ran upwards, obscuring any view of the sea but he knew they were in the right place.

He pulled off the road and parked up. With the sun nearly overhead, there was no chance of a shady spot for the car, instead he wound down the windows in a useless attempt to keep it cool.

Shreya was already making her way upwards along the path as he grabbed the stuff from the car and set off behind her.

He couldn't help but watch as her arse jiggled from side to side with each step up, the sarong tied around her hips leaving little to his already overactive imagination. He didn't know how the hell she had managed to pack a hat that big into her tiny case, but she looked amazing in it, like a model from the cover of one the millions of women's magazines he walked past every day in the shop. It baffled him that she could be interested in him but, staring at her as she stopped at the top of the path, he wasn't going to spend a second worrying about it.

She was still stood there moments later when he caught up with her. A red sign attached to a chain barred their way.

Prohibido

His Spanish was beyond basic, but it didn't take a genius to work that one out. Ahead of them ran a small, sandy path, twisting its way through the rocks. He hoped it was the one that would lead them to the little bit of paradise he had glimpsed from the road.

'We could always go back to that first beach we saw?' said Shreya, staring at the sign.

'Nah, just you wait, this spot is perfect.'

'Yeah, but we can't go in.'

'Why not?'

She rolled her eyes at him and pointed. 'That's why…'

Bless Dean…

That version of himself was now long gone. *Bless Dean* probably would have turned around, but New Dean was fucked if some circle of tin was going to stop him getting to that beach. He raised his leg and stepped over the chain, then turned and offered her his hand. 'You're not a teacher now, Ms. Gupta. Stuff the rules.'

Instinctively she hesitated, but seeing the grin on Dean's face spurred her across the barricade. Dean took her hand and they triumphantly set off towards the beach, thrilled at their petty crime.

The narrow strip of sand led them along the jagged wall until it rounded the corner and the path opened out and they found themselves entering the isolated cove. Rough cliffs framed a perfect, hidden oasis of golden sand. The crescent beach rounded on the crystal-clear water of the bay, its gentle waves teasing the shore, the sounds of the tide amplified by the acoustics of their naturally walled hideaway. The sun inched its way westward, shortening the last of the shadows which would soon be banished from sight.

Shreya let out a soft groan of joy and wrapped her arms around him. 'Let's stay here forever!'

Blushing was becoming a habit for him.

They set up camp in the middle of the cove - towels rolled out, parasol wedged in the sand and their picnic hidden away in the shade, covered in their other bags.

'Swim first?' Shreya asked. 'Then I'll still be needing some help with my sun cream…'

'Let's go then!' he grinned.

The water was only fifty feet away, so he didn't bother with his shoes. By his fourth step he was already regretting his decision, four more and he dropped all pretense of playing it cool.

'Fucking hell!' he yelled, ignoring Shreya's laughter as he started to run towards the sea. His long strides pushed his feet deeper into the sand as he ran and his yells increased in pitch with every step, only stopping when he was knee deep in the soothing waters of the Atlantic.

Shreya was still giggling as she made her way towards him.

Dean watched in awe as she seemed to float across the burning sand until she reached the water unscathed, the tears of laughter drying on her cheeks. He couldn't take his eyes off her as she stepped to the water, any nervousness vanishing as she pushed through the gentle waves towards him. Months of planning and hoping had led them both to this moment and he was more than ready.

She reached him and gave him a coy smile, suddenly unsure of what to do next. A strand of hair drifted over her eyes as she looked at him.

All his doubts melted away in that moment. He closed the gap between them and pulled her into his arms, his mouth seeking hers.

That first kiss dragged him back in time to her room under the eaves in York, both stretched out on a mattress that had been pushed far into the corner where the roof met the floor. Two thousand miles and far too many years later he was more in awe of her than ever. There was no reason why someone like her should love him but this time he wasn't going to question it. He was no longer an insecure teenager;

he'd fought too hard to get her back and there was no way he was going to let her go this time.

They stayed like that, intertwined, their tongues exploring each other, until a rogue wave slapped into his back and sent them tumbling into the surf.

They floundered in the water, laughing as they scrambled to right themselves against the pull of the tide. The wave surged up the beach and clawed its way along the sand, pulling Shreya's gold sandals back with it as it retreated to sea.

Dean ran through the water and grabbed them as they floated away, taking them back out onto dry sand.

'My hero,' said Shreya from behind.

He turned to see her walking out of the waves, her striped bikini clinging to her body and wet hair wrapped around her shoulders.

He had never felt more like James Bond.

17

Around the pool, their lazy morning slowly turned into a lazy afternoon.

Duncan busied himself in the kitchen to escape the heat for a while, pulling together a late lunch from the few leftovers from last night's dinner and the remains of yesterday's shop. At some point last night, they had moved inside, craving the comfort of the sofas. As the drink carried on flowing and the music had come on, he was glad to have had the foresight to hide what remained of the barbecue in the fridge before the munchies claimed them.

He pulled the chicken from the bones and sliced up the two remaining sausages. After laying out the cheese, pâté, cold cuts, and bread he felt like he should at least have some token green to offset it all. He didn't spend much effort making the salad, with Shreya and Dean out it would only be Oskar that ate it after all.

He unceremoniously stacked plates in the middle of the food and had just popped the tab on his first beer when Ben walked in, quickly followed by the others.

They dove into the food with the voracity of a biblical plague, stripping the plates bare. leaving little more than crumbs and half a bowl of salad. It was widely agreed around the table that doing nothing was exhausting and it made you ravenous.

Ben looked up at the sound tyres on gravel, soon followed by a gentle knock at the front door. Jess hopped up and answered it, relieved to see Christina standing there. She was the only person they really knew on the island and meeting anyone new would have required way more energy than Jess had right now.

She walked in carrying a large vase of flowers but stopped as she saw that they were eating lunch. She tried to apologize the interruption, but this was dismissed, instead they invited her to join them.

Jess was pleased when Christina left her coat on, clearly not planning to stay.

'No, no. Thank you though. I just wanted to check that everything is okay with the villa. Do you have everything that you need?' she asked, looking around the room, her eyes briefly resting on the bookshelves on the back wall.

'It is wonderful thank you Christina,' replied Oskar, 'We couldn't have hoped for a better place to stay'.

They exchanged polite reassurances and Christina looked relieved.

'I also wanted to bring you some fresh flowers from my garden,' she said holding up the vase. 'I always leave some for my guests but yesterday I did not. You must forgive me.'

She crossed the room and placed the flowers on one of the bookshelves, rearranging the blooms now that the vase was in situ. She carefully moved the stems around, bringing the best of the bouquet to the front.

From the other side of the room, they watched her fussing over the flowers, amused by her fastidiousness. She stepped back and admired her handiwork, apparently satisfied that each flower was in its rightful place.

With her wide coat hiding her, no one noticed as she plucked an empty beer can from the shelf and casually slip it inside one of her deep pockets.

She smiled at them, hoping the bulky can was not visible against her hip.

‘Oh, I also need to collect the money for the villa if that is ok? Did Mr Dean leave it for me before he left?’

‘Of course,’ said Oskar, ‘I’ll just get it for you.’

Shreya had insisted on keeping the envelope of cash in her travel folder, along with the passports that she had gathered off them at the airport. It wasn’t that she didn’t trust them, she just liked to be sure things were all together for her own piece of mind. He grabbed the leather case from the drawer in the kitchen and removed the cash for Christina.

‘Thank you, Oskar,’ she said tucking the envelope in her pocket. ‘Well, I mustn’t keep you, I am sure you want to get back into the sun and enjoy the rest of your afternoon.’

She turned around at the door and smiled. ‘Have a wonderful time, you must make the most of it.’

She made a quick flourish of a wave and walked out, closing the front door discretely behind her.

At the table the four sat in a bemused silence, listening to the car as it pulled away from the villa.

“That was… nice?” said Ben, hoping it was a one-off visit rather than a daily check in. They had stayed in several villas before and never had visits from the owners. But after the initial changes to their villa, it probably wasn’t that odd for Christina to be checking that everything was ok with it.

‘Bless her though, nice to bring flowers,’ said Jess, making a frenzied mime of rearranging some invisible foliage. They laughed and looked over at the vase on the far side of the room. ‘I mean, I think they are nice? You can barely see them all the way over there.’

With lunch over there was nothing left to do but drag themselves back to the pool. Jess grabbed the vase before she left and moved it over to the table in the kitchen.

Had she been paying any attention she might have noticed the sticky ring further along the shelf, the only remaining evidence of the beer can that Duncan had drunkenly placed there as he stumbled to bed last night.

The same can that had been covering the front of an old book whose gaily colored spine hid a tiny lens, its glassy eye angled to take in all the open plan living space.

18

The parasol provided some shade from the sun, but Dean still seemed to be worried that he was burning. Shreya had watched him apply sunscreen three times already and they had been there less than an hour.

She angled the umbrella towards him to give him more cover and stretched out in the sun. Only her head and shoulders were protected, the shade stretching just far enough to keep her Kindle out of the glare. Old schoolbooks had their place but on a trip like this her Kindle was worth its weight in gold; she was a fast reader and couldn't afford the space that books would have taken in her luggage.

The idea of being on a beach like this, reading in the sun with the sound of the sea in the background, had kept her going during in the long summer term but now she was finally here she found she couldn't concentrate.

They had kissed.

They had kissed and then nothing.

This was the perfect setting and yet here they were both behaving like nothing had happened, carrying on like normal when it was anything but. She gave up on the novel and set the reader down on her bag.

They were certainly alone here, maybe some all over tanning would help to speed things along.

Hell no.

That was so far out of her comfort zone it was almost laughable. She'd have to think of something though before Dean did get burned and they had to head back to the villa.

Bloody gingers and their sensitive skin. She remembered how he had always resisted his colouring at university, secretly using Sun In to lighten it, passing himself off as dark blonde despite his fiery roots. These days he kept his hair cropped and it suited him, as did the couple of days' growth on his face rather than his usual clean shave. She loved old Dean, but new Dean was… so much better.

He'd be coasting along for years but now he had picked up a big promotion at work, revamped himself and apparently learned to cook. They had known each other for fourteen years; something must have spurred him to action, but she was struggling to work out what it was. She might have understood it more if she was seeing someone else, but they had both been single for most of that time, stable in their lives and jobs, nothing had changed.

She turned onto her side, propped herself up on her elbow and asked him a question without thinking.

'Why now?'

'Why now what?' he replied.

'You know exactly what. Why now, after all these years?'

He sat up and dragged his legs underneath him, cross-legged and now fully under the shade of the umbrella. He thought her question over and then looked at his watch.

She watched him take the food out of the bag then arrange it out on the towel, killing time while he formulated an answer. There was no rush, so she grabbed one of the baguettes and unwrapped it. Leftover barbecued chicken, lettuce, mayonnaise with a hint of lemon and a grinding of salt and pepper. He'd *definitely* had help with this excursion.

With nothing left to district him he looked up from the picnic and smiled at her.

'Because I was scared it would be never,' he said.

The next few hours flew by far too quickly for her liking.

They kissed, laughed, talked, and then kissed some more. Neither one of them had pushed it beyond that which worked for her. Sex on the beach sounded romantic but she didn't want to spend their first time - well, their first time *this* time around - worrying about getting sand in all the wrong places.

The heat of the early afternoon drove them into the sea several times over and they clung to each other as the water pushed and pulled them in the warm drift of the tide.

After their third dip in the ocean, they lay down together without drying off. Dean ran his fingers up the curve of her hips, tracing a line between the drops of water. He kissed the back of her neck and could taste the salt already drying on her skin. The heat of the sun through the parasol pushed against them and he let his arm rest on top of her as they fell asleep together, spooning in the shade.

They slept long enough that the sun had moved further down the beach, lighting up the walls behind them. Shreya opened her eyes first and spotted a flash of light amongst the rocks. A quick glint and then it was gone. A moment later she saw it again, a short spark as the sun hit something reflective. She sat up, shielding her eyes, and waited for the next sparkle. It came again as Dean sat up next to her.

'What is it?'

'I don't know, just something flashing over there.'

The rocks had looked like a flat wall when they had been covered in shadows, but in the full light of the sun they saw that there were pockets of gloom in the cliff face, small caves lining the walls.

'Still feeling heroic?' Shreya asked with a cheeky grin.

They shoved on their shoes and dashed across the sand until they stepped up onto the solid rocks. Shreya led them to the opening where she had seen the twinkling. A locket hung from a notch in the rock, a small golden heart on a thin chain that swayed gently in the breeze. The heart was split into two halves, twin images stored behind tiny sheets of glass. A dark-haired older lady smiled out of one, a cheeky faced boy in the other. The pictures were faded but the family likeness was unmistakable, a mother, forever staring at her young son in the other frame.

Dean went to touch it, but Shreya batted his hand away. He started to ask why but stopped when he saw her staring into the cave and his eyes followed hers.

The cavern was deep and dark but there was enough light to see what had rooted her to the spot.

Bones were piled up in ornate towers all along the inside of the cave. Some were squat and simple, others had been painstakingly constructed, intricate shapes created out of femurs, tibias, and fibulas. Ribs were fanned out into circular patterns, smaller bones secured the structure and provided artistic punctuation to some of the grander creations. Tiny notes were pressed into gaps, rolled up and tied with ribbons; photos hung from some, other had toys and jewelry incorporated into their design.

But there was one thing they all had in common.

From all around the cave bright red skulls stared out from the centre of each design, the taller the tower the more skulls they contained.

Dean switched on the torch on his phone and shone it around the cave.

They weren't just red, they glowed as he swept the beam around. Bright rubies, glistening like perverse toffee apples at a macabre fair - the white of the bone still visible through their garnet shells.

‘I think it might be time for us to go,’ said Shreya, frozen in the shadow of the cave.

Dean took her hand and pulled her gently away from the spectre before them.

Neither said a word as they grabbed their things from the beach and retraced the steps back to the car.

‘What the hell *was* that?’ Dean asked, loading the bags back into the boot.

In the warmth of the sun, the shock of the discovery was already withering away, and Shreya found herself thinking about Paris. A few years ago, she had volunteered to support two of her friends on a Year 6 trip to the French capital, part of which had included a tour of the famous catacombs. The kids had giggled and joked their way around the strange collection of bones, laughing in the face of death, but Shreya had been moved and humbled by the experience.

‘In some cultures, the bones of the dead are celebrated rather than hidden away. Sometimes cemeteries just get too full. It happened in Paris. I can’t remember the full story, but basically, after centuries of burying their dead, the city just ran out of space. They had to empty out all the graves and do something with the millions of bones that left them with. So, they took them and stacked them up in some old mines that ran under the city. Then later someone had the idea to rearrange the bones into something more monumental and they created a kind of artistic tomb that people could visit.’

‘And that is why we never trust the French.’

‘To be honest, it was kind of amazing. They build chapels out of stacks of bones, they turned skulls into art, shaped them into hearts and designs.

'So, you think that was something similar?' asked Dean as he turned the car around.

'Similar… but not the same. That felt more like a shrine, like people still visited it and made offerings.'

He eased the car back onto the tarmac and set off back towards the villa.

'Well, promise me that you will never leave me in one of those places with my skull all vajazzled, ok?'

'I promise,' she said with mock solemnity.

They picked up speed and the roar of the air through the windows chased away any last vestiges of their find in the caves.

19

They had been on the island for over 24 hours and Oskar was starting to get itchy feet.

He loved their holidays but could only really settle once he had gotten a sense of the local area. They had driven through town briefly on the way to the villa but that hadn't been enough to appease his need to explore the streets.

Shreya and Dean had arrived back at the villa a little quieter than he might have expected but they were still grinning and a little bashful. It hadn't taken much for him to persuade them to head into town early in the evening and go for a walk around before getting a few drinks and some food at the bars Christina had pointed out.

Jess was about to have one last dip in the pool but spotted the look on Shreya's face. Instead, she retreated to the kitchen, grabbed a bottle of cava and took Shreya back to their rooms. Throwing open the door between the two they set about creating just the right look for her to wear tonight.

Shreya had packed too carefully for the holiday, she knew that now, trying too hard to avoid a huge suitcase for the week. Vogue had told her that if she wanted to avoid excess baggage charges, she would need to create a "capsule wardrobe" for herself that would cover a multitude of occasions. So, she had taken their advice and rolled, not folded, her clothes, wearing her one pair of jeans on the plane to save space and all her jewelry.

Stupidly though she had ignored the advice not to forget a "wildcard party dress", a preparation she had deemed a step to far for a getaway with old friends to an up-and-coming island paradise. The fashion bible, however, had not warned her that her old crush from years ago would roar up like a phoenix from the ashes and demand the perfect outfit to seal the deal.

Jess opened Shreya's wardrobe and they set to work while her friend recapped the afternoon she had spent at the beach, leaving out the part about the random mausoleum - there would be plenty of time for that later.

After a few changes they both agreed on a kitschy vintage print playsuit. The pattern reminded Jess of her Nana's old deck chair but somehow Shreya made it look effortlessly chic.

Jess turned up the legs ups to make it just slutty enough to still be decent, paired it with a chunky belt, some of her own earnings and finally a pair of red wedge espadrilles to finish the look. Shreya turned in the mirror and was delighted with the result. Somehow, they had turned her planned shopping look into knock out evening wear.

Dean didn't stand a chance.

Shreya was pleased when Dean was the first to follow her into the back of van and took the opportunity to wiggle her way between the seats in front, hoping her the shortened jumpsuit was riding up her legs sufficiently. One look at his face as she sat down confirmed that it had.

Score one for the playsuit.

By five o'clock they had set off and were heading back down the rustic road into the Old Town. Again, they fell silent as the car entered the shadows of the tunnel as the road through the trees, little light penetrated through the thick canopy of leaves and the temperature change was instant. Halfway along Oskar found he was holding his breath as they sped through the dark, something he hadn't done since he was a child, scared of the long dark tunnels that ran through his homeland's mountainous roads.

In the dim light they could see that the forest was tightly packed, the rotting trunks of fallen trees nourishing the ground around the stronger specimens that had forced them out. Despite its size, it was easy to imagine that there were sections of the island that had never seen human life, pockets of jungle forming a haven for all the island's native creatures.

There was a palpable sense of relief as they emerged from the trees and saw the first signs of civilisation.

The chill of the forest was replaced by a welcome bloom of heat as they emerged once again into daylight. They came to the outskirts of the main square and Oskar parked at the side of the road. There were only a few people in the square, but they all turned to watch the interlopers arrive. In a town like this there was no space for secrets, so everyone knew exactly who they were as they poured out of Christina's familiar car.

Several businesses lined the small square. In addition to the two bars and the supermarket a pharmacy, a salon and a general store provided the inhabitants with all the core essentials. It wasn't late in the day, but all the shops seemed to have closed already, red signs with *Cerrado* gracing their doors.

At the far corner was a larger shop which seemed to be the only one still open. The owners were clearly not big fans of merchandising, in place of displays large tables pressed against the glass, covered in an assortment of products. Jess and Shreya spotted it immediately and made a beeline across the square. They were no strangers to junk shops and were eager to see what treasures they could find in this remote island outpost.

Jess pushed the door open, triggering the bell on the door.

A lady's voice rang out from the back of the stop, 'Momentito por favor!'

They had been prepared to be disappointed but were amazed to find the shop to be a veritable Aladdin's cave of treasures.

Much of it was filled with furniture and housewares, their modest prices simply indicated with a neat, handwritten label. If they had been looking to furnish a house this place would have been perfect, it was heartbreaking to see so many things they would love to buy if only they had the means to get them home. There was original set of pots and pans that was almost identical to some designer ones that Shreya had seen in John Lewis a few weeks ago. Even factoring in the cost of a new suitcase and the extortionate Ryan Air baggage fees it would still have been cheaper to buy them here. Plus, they were vintage.

Furniture was piled high, chairs balanced on top of beautifully carved tables, side boards groaning with old clocks, vases, and bric-a-brac, hoarded then discarded by generations of families that had lived on the island. Everything had passed through several sets of hands before finally finding its way here to the shop. Nothing was wasted. Rails of clothes lined the walls, dresses from every era proving that even in the middle of the Atlantic fashions had come and gone. Jess knew she could spend hours going through the rails and promised herself she would come back on her own before the week was out.

At the far corner of the shop there was a large dining table that held a collection of more modern items - hair dryers and straighteners were laid out alongside sun cream, hats, towels, and bikinis. Scores of books with bright coloured jackets were stacked in precarious piles.

Shreya's well-trained eye caught a little flash of metal coming from a counter at the back of the store and she made a beeline for it, excited by the swathe of costume jewelry that was laid out along the top.

A golden mesh necklace called to her immediately. She picked it up and expecting it to be light but was surprised at the heft of it. She passed it around her neck and managed to fix the clasp at the back. The thick mesh formed an elegant V shape that hung suggestively over her cleavage, the sides tapering out to a delicate band at the neck. The cold metal quickly warmed to her touch, feeling like she had always worn it.

Jess saw her and dashed over to her. 'That is amazing! You have to buy it.'

'I know. Oh my god, I love it,' Shreya squeaked, unable to tear her eyes from the small mirror on the counter. 'If this were gold it would be worth a fortune.' She looked at the other pieces on the counter, no price tags were visible on anything, but she knew she would be prepared to spend good money on it but, based on the rest of the shop, she didn't think it was going to be too unreasonable.

'You jammy cow,' said Jess, scanning for other treasures before Shreya could snap them up.

She reached for a jade necklace as an elderly lady pushed her way through a beaded curtain that covered the archway to the back of the shop.

The lady stopped at the sight of the two tourists, clearly not expecting to find strangers in her shop. She glanced over at the phone on the desk and sighed. Reaching over the desk she knocked the headset back into the cradle and looked at the girls. Before they could say hello, they were startled by the shrill ringing of the phone. The old lady answered it and turned away from them. A heated but short exchange ensued before she replaced the handset and turned back to them.

'I sorry,' she said, walking out from behind the counter to walk her customers to the door. 'We close now. Mañana, we open again.'

Shreya clutched her hand over the necklace and tapped the older lady on the shoulder. 'Please. We can go but I need to buy this necklace. Please, it's important,' she implored, 'how much is it?'

The old lady turned, a sad sigh escaping her as she looked at Shreya's hopeful face. 'We close now,' she repeated.

Shreya's face fell as she reached up to undo the clasp, but the lady placed a hand on her arm, her cool papery fingers giving her a brief squeeze. 'But you take necklace, pay tomorrow, ok?' She smiled sadly at Shreya and turned to the door.

'Nooooo… really??' Without thinking Shreya threw her arms around her lady's shoulders, delighted at the turn of events. 'Are you sure? I will come back first thing tomorrow, I promise!'

She hugged her, trying to get her thanks across in the most universal way. Her hands were gently batted away, and they left the shop, calling back their thanks and promising to return in the morning.

'That was… overly kind of her,' muttered Jess as the door closed behind them.

'It was nice! She's just being welcoming.' Shreya couldn't take her hand away from her new necklace.

'Of course, it was just a little surprising I guess.'

'You're just jealous!'

'Fair point.' Jess smiled at her friend but couldn't help looking back over her shoulder. The old woman had been watching them walk away but quickly drew the blinds when Jess turned around.

Inside the shop she stepped away from the door and made her way to the rear, past a small pile of suitcases and a table offering up an assortment of backpacks and handbags. She drew her fingers across her heart and then down, offering up a silent prayer at the thought of the pretty young girl and her excitement at her new golden trinket.

They should never have been in the shop.

There would doubtless be trouble about that, Christina would take it as proof that she had been right all along and would be forcing them all to have those stupid phones with no buttons that could send messages to everyone at once.

Still, she was glad she was able to bring some joy to the poor girl. Maybe the necklace would bring her some happiness for a short while.

There would be no money coming back for it though, nor did she want any.

The girl had more than paid the price already.

16

Whilst the girls were browsing in the shop the others had abandoned the square in favour of the backstreets that surrounded it. Five minutes of walking through identical residential streets and it became apparent that they would soon be heading back to the main square.

Duncan and Oskar dawdled along the street, happy to have some time alone as Dean and Ben strode ahead. Duncan gave his husband a peck on the cheek having quickly checked the street around them. He was unsure of local reactions to two men kissing but was trained to assume the worst. He had never been one for public displays of affection but often couldn't help groping his man when they found themselves alone.

He wasn't stupid, he knew that he had simply been conditioned to limit his affections to those moments when he had the least chance to offend or draw attention undue attention. Today he chose to think of it as more romantic – just two more lovers stealing a kiss as they wandered around the empty streets of a sunny, foreign town.

Oskar smiled back at him and took his husband's face in his big, Viking hands and drew him in, kissing him deeply, his tongue hungrily seeking his. Duncan responded but couldn't shake the fear that every door would suddenly be flung open, villagers spilling out of their homes brandishing stones and flaming torches.

He pulled away from the kiss, casting a quick look around to confirm that no one had seen them.

He blushed at his prudishness and Oskar gave him an understanding smile but walked on, the mood broken. Oskar would never challenge Duncan for his fear of standing out, he had spent too many of his years feeling the same to ever judge his partner. Everyone always assumed that growing up as a gay kid in Norway would have been a breeze as everyone knows *how liberal and forward thinking those Scandinavians are.* On paper they were right, but as with most things in life, the theory was often very different from the reality.

Oskar's own coming out to his parents in his early teens they had been relatively easy. They had been understanding and very accepting of his sexuality, their only real concern had been that he didn't let this make him stand out from the crowd.

Janteloven was just a way of life.

It had been drilled into him since he could remember. The importance of the group was everything, the individual was merely part of a wider collective and anyone seen to put their head above the parapet was quickly brought down by those around them. He had been brought up not to think he was any more special than others, that he wasn't smarter than anyone else, that he wasn't better at anything than anyone else.

On their second date Duncan had joked that Oskar could win the Nobel prize and not want to tell anyone; Oskar had joked back that the real irony was that the Nobel prize was Scandinavian at all, but the joke went over Duncan's head. He tried to explain but quickly discovered that Norwegian jokes are easily lost in translation.

To be fair he had been relieved when Duncan had called to arrange a third date.

They walked along the cobbled streets in silence, the shadows slowly sliding down the walls around them as the sun disappeared behind the mountains once more.

Duncan was annoyed with himself, feeling he had spoiled the moment.

He slipped his hand into Oskar's, giving it a gentle squeeze. 'I love you, you know. More than anything.'

'I know you do, and I love you too. You big poof.'

Duncan moved in a little closer as they walked, hoping to get the moment back and was pleased when Oskar bumped his shoulder into his. If he couldn't be romantic in public somewhere like this, then there was no hope for him. Besides, after their stroll through the streets it was clear that not one door was likely to open.

Ahead of the boys Ben stopped at the opening to a small square.

It was the same spot that he had glimpsed twenty-four hours earlier as Christina drove them from the boat. Today though, the centre of the square was draped in a giant blue shroud, as if Christo had snuck in overnight and wrapped up the fountain and declared it art.

He walked across the cobbled street, staring at the shiny tarpaulin dome that now graced the square. Thick ropes crisscrossed the woven plastic, anchoring the sheets to the fountain below, tightly knotted to ward off prying fingers and eyes.

Ben reached out a hand and traced a finger over the edge of the blue material, feeling the resistance of stone against the wrapper. He pushed harder, probing the hidden shapes, a blind man trying to see the sculpture below. But he didn't need to feel the thin, flat ellipses to know what was there. He had forgotten all about the statue, but it had come to back him as soon as he stepped out of car - the strange white tree surrounded by prone figures, blood red water flowing from their eyes.

Another memory of a tree flitted in the back of his mind, painfully close, but still dancing out of reach when he tried to lock on it.

'What're you doing?' asked Dean, slapping a hand on his shoulder from behind.

Ben jumped, snapped out of his trance.

'I saw this from the car yesterday,' he said, pulling his hand back from the white tree he knew lay beneath.

Dean looked down the road to the square beyond. 'Can't say I did but I was probably more interested in the bars to be fair. You'd have thought a big blue dome would have caught my eye though.'

'That's the thing though, it wasn't covered when we drove past.'

'Really? That's weird. I wonder why they covered it?'

'No idea,' said Ben.

There was no reason for him to be suspicious, but he couldn't shake the feeling that the fountain hadn't been covered, it had been hidden. He had tried to ask Christina about it when they drove past, but she had talked over him – and now it was under wraps. It felt like too much of a coincidence. He had seen countless fountains, in squares all over the world, they were almost always celebratory; dolphins shooting water from their blowholes; mermaids gazing enigmatically out over jets of water; plump children pissing in a pool. The fountain he saw yesterday was flat out creepy, there was no other word for it.

The more he thought about the tree the more familiar it felt, he could almost hear waxen leaves rustling in a gale.

When had he heard it? The sound was so familiar, so overwhelming but there hadn't been a storm recently. Still, the memory of being terrified tugged at him. Despite the heat of the evening a chill run down his spine.

Dean grabbed his arm and pulled him away, distracted by the sight of Shreya and Jess waiving at them from the square. They pointed at the two bars and Dean gave them a quick thumbs up.

'Come on, I think it might be beer o'clock,' he said.

Ben was happy to be led away from the shrouded fountain. With each step he felt the dark cloud that had descended over him start to dissipate. By the time they joined the girls he was almost back to normal, the sensation of the fear was gone, but the memory of its grip over him still lingered.

Approaching the two bars, they had been unsure of the etiquette as to which to choose given the odd situation of having the only two bars in town right next to each other.

Shreya took the lead.

Opting for a neutral stance she led them to a table on the square that straddled the fronts of both. There was no way to tell where one ended and the other began as each had the same white plastic tables, bleached a light shade of yellow by the sun with matching chairs. Cushions had been laid out on each chair, given the quietness of the town though, it seemed more than a little optimistic.

Their confusion was compounded moments later when they were approached from either side by what appeared to be the same man. The men wore matching jeans, short-sleeved white shirts, and similar glasses. Each had a small towel draped over their forearms, one on the left, one on the right, it seemed to be their only distinguishing feature.

Twin bars for twin owners.

It was weird as fuck.

'Good evening,' said the twin on the right. 'I am Matheo, and he is Mathias. You are not surprised to hear we are brothers.'. He flashed the table a handsome smile, immediately putting them at ease.

The twins explained that they originally run the bar on the left, but when the owner of the hardware store next door had retired last year, they had taken it over to expand their business. Rather than knock through, the twins had kept them separate but operated them as one entity. It was only on closer inspection that Shreya noticed that the one on the left had a long bar running down the left whereas the one on the right had fridges lining the opposite wall.

As Mateo chatted it became clear that he was very much the front man for the bars, his brother, on the other hand, was obviously more comfortable behind the scenes.

Oskar ordered a large draft beer, and the others quickly followed his lead, happy to sample the lone tap that graced the bar. Ben, as ever, spent a little while scanning the menu before settling on a bottle of craft IPA that was brewed by a brewery called Drago in Las Palmas. He could sense the others rolling their eyes, but he didn't care, he liked what he liked, he couldn't help it if his tastes were a little less pedestrian.

Jess watched the waiter head back inside, admiring the way his jeans clung to the tight rump below.

'I could watch that arse all day,' she said once he was out of earshot. Duncan, Oskar, and Shreya all nodded.

'Definitely not on our team,' said Duncan, smiling at Jess, 'maybe there is scope for a holiday fling for you yet!'

There is a kind of alchemy that occurs when ice cold beer is added to sunny squares in foreign climes. Even the most basic blend of water, barley, yeast, and hops is transformed into a tall glass of chilled, bubbling nectar, fit to grace the table of any ancient god. The local beer on Isla Manuta was no exception. The cold beer hit Dean's empty stomach quickly and he was already enjoying the rapid onset of his beer buzz, so he threw back the first round in record time.

Ben took a little longer, savouring the amber nectar he had decanted from the dark brown bottle. Jess picked up the empty and squinted at the label - a sketch of a dragon wrapped around an unusual looking tree growing out of a mound of earth, thick sheaves of wheat framing the image. She guessed it was probably a small brewery that used one label for all its beers as IPA had been stamped into a white shield at the bottom in black ink, Spanish words below.

"…Allí dónde la sangre del dragón fue derramada, creció un árbol"

Mateo arrived with another round of drinks, giving Jess the opportunity to flirt a little. She pointed to the bottle, asking him if he could translate.

He read the label and smiled.

'Ah, it means *there where the blood of the dragon fell, a tree grew.'* he looked back at Jess, his eyes dropping briefly to the low cut of her neckline. 'It is from the old legend of the Drago Milenario in Tenerife.'

'What was the legend?' she asked with a smile, spotting the way his eye had dipped. Maybe the holiday wasn't going to be a dry spell after all.

He looked mildly panicked at the idea of explaining an old legend in English, but Jess grabbed a chair from the next table and dragged it close to her. She flashed him a coy smile and tapped the cushion.

'Es muy complicado' he said with a grin.

Jess turned away from the table as he sat down, giving him her full attention. Careful to keep his eyes on hers, he started to explain. 'There are many stories about the trees but most famous is that Hercules had to kill Ladon, a dragon who guards the gold apples. *Los Trabajos de Hércules*?'

'The Labours of Hercules!' yelled Shreya, to Jess's annoyance. How did she know everything?

Shreya clocked the look on Jess's face and turned away – two may be company but five other people staring at them around the table was more than a crowd. Duncan had also spotted Jess making her move so distracted the group into a trip down memory lane.

Mateo relaxed as the conversation moved on around them, no longer the centre of attention.

'Okay, so... Hercules must steal these apples and so he has to kill the dragon.' Mateo raised his hand to his neck and made a chopping motion. 'He cuts off his head and the blood it goes everywhere, all into the ground. Where the blood falls, they say the Drago tree, it grows.'

'So why is a Canarian myth based around a Greek hero?'

'Why do you think it is a myth?' he replied. He stole a glance at the kitchen and was glad to see that Mathias was nowhere in sight. He leaned in and dragged his index finger down Jess's arm, letting the nail drag softly along her skin like a knife. 'When you cut into the Drago Tree the dragon's blood still pours out of the wound to this day…'

Jess gave a nervous laugh and leaned back, rubbing at her arm to ward off the goosebumps that were already popping up. It wasn't the story that had her on edge though, it was him. They had barely spoken and already he seemed far too comfortable, happily breaching her personal space – the pressure of his touch still burned on her arm.

'So, are these trees just in Tenerife?' she asked, forcing a smile - he might be a little creepy but there were two bars on the island and five more nights still to go. 'No, you can find them hidden in all the islands. Long ago when people have come from L'*Espagna* they found people already living here. Now they say that these people were called the *Gaunches* but there were others before them. The first people they worshipped the tree and gave gifts to keep balance. The new people say they are primitive, and they make them work, slaves you say.'

'Fuck' said Jess, 'so what happened to them?'

'Many died, but some survived. We were protected as the conquistadors came to understand the island...'

'Mateo!' yelled Mathias, cutting his brother off mid-sentence, waving him back inside.

Mateo jumped to his feet, flustered to have been caught in the act of flirting with a customer. He turned curtly and retreated inside; his head dipped in contrition. Mateo may be the front man of the enterprise, but it was clear who had the upper hand.

'That was a little intense,' said Shreya, turning around as the waiter vanished inside. 'Not that I was earwigging or anything...'

'Ben, you are now my official boyfriend whenever that man is around.'

She repeated the waiter's tale as they passed the bottle around, staring at the odd little label.

'Bit dramatic for a bottle of beer though, isn't it?' asked Dean, turning it around in his hand before passing it Oskar.

'This tress is about as creepy as he is,' said Oskar.

'Weird thing is, I'm sure this tree is the same as the one in the statue.' Ben said as the bottle was finally placed back in front of him.

'What fountain?' asked Oskar.

Ben was still trying to describe what he had seen yesterday, and their earlier discovery that it had been covered, when Mateo returned with another round of drinks.

'Isn't this the same tree as the one on the fountain?' asked Ben as Mateo placed the drinks in front of each of them. The look on the man's face showed that he equally hadn't expected to be asked the question.

'Fountain?' he asked, looking confused. 'My English, I'm sorry.'

Ben pointed to the square behind the bars, the blue shroud visible from where they sat.

'Fountain,' repeated Ben, certain that the man knew what he was being asked but was stalling for time.

'I ask my brother; he speaks better than me.' He grabbed his tray and crossed to the other bar before anything else could be asked of him.

The others went back to chatting. Ben ignored the banter around the table, instead focusing on the two men conferring at the back of the bar. Mateo gestured to their table with a tip of his head and Mathias looked over, catching Ben's eye. Mathias gave him a terse smile, unable to disguise the concerned look on his face.

After a brief discussion Mateo picked up two bowls of crisps and headed over to their table. He placed them down and smiled at them all, any trace of concern hidden from his face.

'Ah! La fuente?' he asked, ever the charming host. 'I think it is the same, yes. We had to cover it today, the children play in it but there is yesterday disease in the water, makes you very sick if you drink.'

Ben wasn't sure why he was being lied to but there was no doubt that he was.

'There seems to be a lot of water problems on the island at the moment,' he said, challenging his answer. 'We couldn't go to the villa we booked as there was a problem with the water in the pool there. Maybe they are linked?'

Mathias smiled back at him. 'Maybe.'

The change in tone in the conversation was clear around the table and they watched the stalemate in silence. Shreya's eyes darted between them, trying to understand the change in atmosphere, unsure why Ben was suddenly worried about trees and water borne diseases. She hated this kind of macho bullshit. There was no need for Ben to be having a standoff with the man – unless... God, she hoped he wasn't jealous of the attention he had been giving to Jess.

Thankfully Dean didn't have that streak in him, or if he had she had certainly never seen it.

The stories Mateo had been telling Jess about the old customs on the island had piqued her interested and she wanted to ask more about them but given the turn in mood around the table. It could have to wait for another time. Instead, she reached forward and took a crisp from the bowl. 'Thank you so much for these, I love plain, salted crisps when I am away, they really taste like holidays don't they?'

The waiter smiled at her, grateful for the tacit interruption.

'My pleasure, please enjoy.' he said.

He cast one more look at Ben before turning on his heel and heading back inside and out of sight. Unknown to the men inside Ben could still see them from his spot at the table, reflected in the mirror behind the huge selection of spirits.

Mathias was angry, his arms flying as he shouted at his brother who was holding out the phone to him. He snatched the phone from his hands and glanced up, catching Ben's eye through the looking glass. Caught, he turned and ducked through a curtained doorway, clutching the phone to his ear.

Something going on. He had no doubt that the fountain had been hidden from them; he had never been meant to see it in the first place, he was sure of that now. The statue had been grotesque, even from the quick glimpse that he'd had, but covering it up ran deeper than an act of civic pride in front of tourists. You only hide something that you are ashamed of, something that would make people ask questions if they saw it.

Something that they didn't want tourists to know.

Although the more he thought about it the less evidence there was of any actual tourism here. They hadn't seen any other holiday makers in their walk around the town, no one else had shared their boat journey to the island, in fact, he had barely even seen any locals since they arrived.

The few people they had seen milling around the square when they arrived had all since disappeared, back to their homes and out of sight.

The square around them wasn't just peaceful, it was dead.

17

Oblivious to the apparent tension in the air and Ben's distraction, Dean gazed at Shreya, his head tilted in confusion. Something was different about her since they had left the villa, but he couldn't figure out what it was. He wasn't exactly famed for his attention to detail, in fact it was an area that he had had to heavily focus on in his bid to be promoted at work. Through sheer will power he had forced himself to become a "completer finisher", some bullshit phrase that had stuck in his mind after the last management training seminar he had attended. He was great when it came to the ideas and creation aspect (which had apparently made him a plant) but had no interest in making sure every detail was in place. Not exactly what they were looking for when they were looking to give someone the keys to a shop which turned over millions of pounds a year.

Retail is detail.

God, he hated those courses.

The necklace… had she been wearing that when they set off? Thinking back, he didn't think he remembered her wearing it in the car, he was sure he would have noticed the gold mesh around her neck if she had been. But he wasn't sure and didn't want to risk her thinking that he hadn't noticed what was clearly an expensive bit of jewelry.

Jess had clocked his confused looks at Shreya and waved her hand subtly at him as she reached for another crisp. She caught his eye and slowly lifter her hand up, pressing the open palm to her breastbone, mimicking the necklace around

Shreya's neck. Shreya was talking to Duncan, unaware of the clandestine game of charades going on across the table.

New? he mouthed back at Jess, tipping his head slightly at the hand Jess still held to her chest.

She nodded in the affirmative, and raised an eyebrow, tipping her head towards Shreya.

Go on, ask her…

He took another long gulp of beer while he waited for her to break off her conversation with Duncan, not wanting to be discourteous and interrupt. He would normally have just barged in but was still trying to be on his best behaviour, wanting to do everything right. Oskar put his hand on Duncan's leg, and he turned to his husband, giving Dean the break that he needed to swoop in.

'Shreya, you weren't wearing that necklace when we left the house.' It had somehow ended up sounding like more of a blunt statement than he had planned. 'Were you?' he added.

'Do you like it?' she beamed.

Running her fingers across the shiny links of the golden mesh she recounted the story of finding the thrift shop and how she had begged the kind old lady to let her buy it before she closed the shop.

'So, you haven't even paid for it?' he teased. 'You basically mugged an old lady for her jewelry?' He hoped this was coming out as jokily as he intended. Thankfully the sly look of indignation on her faced reassured him that he was still on safe ground.

'No! Well, technically yes… I mean I haven't paid for it but I'm going to go back tomorrow when the shop is open again and I'll pay her then like she said.'

'Trust me, that is what all shoplifters say,' he joked. 'It looks amazing though, really nice with your dress thingy.'

'Dress thingy? Thanks Dean.'

'Well, I don't know what it's called do I? Is it a romper suit? Some kind of dungaree? Don't get me wrong, I love it, I just don't have any idea what it is."

He knew he should have kept it simple. Just compliment her on the necklace Dean, then move it, fashion is not your strong suit. He wished he had thought this through first.

'You're right Dean, she does look beautiful,' said Jess, coming to his rescue. 'I think it was very sweet of the lady to let her wear it tonight. Anyway, it's not exactly like we can do a runner off the island, is it?'

Duncan had barely finished his pint before Mateo appeared out of his bar, keen to take another order from the only customers.

While the others had been talking Oskar had decided that he was going to attempt to be somewhat responsible and make this his last drink, aware that he had to drive them all back to the villa. But his request for a diet coke was met with scorn by his friends.

'I don't think you have to worry about being stopped by the police out here Oskar,' argued Jess.

'You can have a few, mate, it's not even that strong,' said Dean, backing her up.

'It's not a long drive, hon, we can take it slow on the way back - I doubt we'll have to worry about anyone else on the road.' Even Duncan seemed to have decided that this was no time for caution.

Peer pressure never normally worked on him but this time he was tempted by their reasoning, eyeing up his now empty glass and already regretting his attempt to be sensible. Mateo returned moments later, placing another beer in front of them all, no diet coke in sight.

'Tonight, is no problem, you get home safe I guarantee. Drink, have fun!'

For once Oskar was very glad to have the decision taken out of his hands.

There was no menu at the bars. Instead, Mathias crafted local specialties from his kitchen in the second bar. They gorged themselves on fried fish that had been caught hours before, grilled bread with a local spicy vegetarian pate called almogrote, salty baked new potatoes served with mojo and pimientos de padron. The plates of salty, spicy, fried food complemented the cold beer perfectly.

The sun slowly set behind the square as they finished off the last of the blistered peppers, bathing the buildings in a warm rosy glow as a full moon rose high in the night sky. Mateo had become more confident as they praised his food and thanked him profusely for the feast, he had created for them. After another round of beers none of them could really work out which brother was which. Even Shreya had resorted to calling both brothers Matty, a rare departure for a woman who never forgot a name or a face.

Dean was telling them how the vacancy at the Brent Cross store had come about, the original tale now somewhat stretched and embellished for full comedic effect. Ben joined in with the hilarity, but his laughter sounded hollow although his friends were too far gone to notice that it always rang in a beat too late. He had lost track of the conversation, just managing to nod along, mimicking mirth well enough to seem engaged. He had never managed to fully shake the sense of disquiet he had felt at the covered-up fountain, the feeling further exacerbated by Mathias' shallow lies.

Then there was the necklace.

He had seen one exactly like it at one of his firm's gala dinners. They held them sporadically, raising money for local and national charities, trying to prove that bankers aren't wankers but failing spectacularly every time. Their gaudy displays of wealth were always more memorable than the not-insignificant sums they raised for the poor and needy who barely warranted a mention.

The reality was that none of the attendees gave a shit about helping Syrian orphans or raising money for further research into a cure for cystic fibrosis, they were there to show off their own wealth and success. He watched them bid for prizes they had no use for just to bolster their altruistic credentials. Now he remembered one such recent event where there had been a silent auction, the attendees bidding for a raft of riches; a holiday to Barbuda, dinner with a minor royal, the chance to have an X-Factor winner sing at your home, all the usual crap.

There had also been a Tiffany necklace that looked remarkably like the one now gracing Shreya's neck.

He had rolled his eyes when the host had valued it at five thousand pounds but clapped along with the rest of the room when one of the Vice President's wives had won the bidding at over twenty thousand.

He had oohed and ahhed with the others when Shreya had leaned forward to show it to them, asking her if she minded him touching it, joking with Dean that he would, of course, be a gentleman. The mesh of the necklace had been heavy against his fingers, its solid links uniform in colour with no signs of tarnish.

It was either a very expensive fake or Shreya had just been given five grand's worth of Tiffany jewelry on trust.

They all commented on how kind the old lady in the shop had been, but Ben just wanted to scream at them - WHY? Why would she do that??

As darkness descended with the setting sun, the only light in the square came from the two bars and a handful of shuttered windows. The only sound that of the raucous laughter of the six tourists ricocheting around the quadrangle, piercing the heavy silence.

In their enjoyment of their evening the others remained oblivious to the void surrounding them. Even the most pious of villages are not silent on Sunday evenings, bells ring in praise of the lord and footsteps sound against the cobbles as the devout head to church for a second dose of absolution.

Ben was glad when Mathias and Mateo finally came out bearing a tray of shots and the offer of a lift back to the villa. It was clear from the state of the group that Oskar was no longer able to drive.

They settled their bill and tipped the pair heavily before piling into the back of Mateo's red Jeep. He pulled away from the curb, waving at Mathias and promising to be back soon. They held onto each other in the back of the truck, laughing as it bounced around, seemingly hitting every bump and turn in the road.

Only Ben watched the square as they drove away. He saw the lights coming on behind closed shutters, a door opening, then another as people emerged from their homes as the six strangers were driven out of town.

The soft ringing in his ears returned, the gentle buzz increasing in volume as they sped away from town.

18

The evening had been fun, but Jess was glad when Mateo dropped them off and didn't hang around. After the close attention he had given her earlier she had half thought he might make a move, clearly though his brother had made an impact and she watched with relief as his Jeep sped out of the gates. Despite the bizarreness of the bars and their owners, it had been a great night. She'd more than drunk her fill and even managed to ignore the eerie silence of the square around them.

Ben had been the only one of the others who had seemed to notice the absence of locals in the town. Several times she had spotted him staring around the square, an odd look clouding his face. Dean and Shreya had barely looked away from each other so there was no chance they had been aware of the world around the table. She hoped they would fuck tonight, just do it already so they could all move on. Of course, she was happy for them. It would be selfish not to be, but that didn't mean that the simpering, doe-eyed looks weren't starting to get on her tits. Duncan and Oskar hadn't been any better, but then they were always partly in their own little universe, so it was no big surprise that the lack of people in the square hadn't jarred with them.

Fewer distractions from their happy little bubble. - lucky fucks.

Perhaps she shouldn't have any gin tonight, she thought, if she was already at the maudlin stage it wasn't going to improve her mood. Or maybe it was just what she needed - push through and get shit-faced. She grabbed a glass from the cupboard and measured out a healthy three fingers of gin, then another. When she was done, she took the drink outside and walked to the pool.

The lights around it cast a low glow, but the pool was left in darkness, the moonlight barely penetrating the glassy water.

She sat down at the edge and lowered her legs into the cool water. Almost immediately the old fear surfaced in her mind, but she pushed it back down. At twenty-nine she was too old to think there was a shark circling below, eyeing up her tasty toes - Steven Spielberg had a lot to answer for.

She drained her drink in two big gulps, grateful of the cold in her belly and the hit of the booze. Beer was fine but liquor was quicker, isn't that what they said? Maybe it was wine is fine. Either way having both was sure to work the best. She liked a beer but, after a while, she became immune to the buzz, the bloating and constant pissing tended to sober her up.

Gin could always be counted on to seal the deal.

Music started up in the kitchen and Oskar stuck his head around the door.

'Hey Lolita, you want a drink?'

She held up her empty glass, rattling the ice.

'More booze please!'

Moments later her glass had been refreshed and they were all around the pool, five sets of feet for the shark to choose from. Only one set was missing - she hadn't seen Ben since they were dropped off.

It wouldn't be the worst thing if he had gone to bed, he had been a buzz kill so far on the holiday. Crashing out early last night and then his oddness at the bar tonight. She'd half expected him to back out of the holiday this year, in some ways she had almost been disappointed when he finally did say yes.

Duncan joined her poolside, ever the mood-setter, had somehow materialised packets of glow sticks. He passed her four, each loaded with a small plastic connector.

Who the hell brings glow sticks on holiday?

Of course, it was the perfect though. If Duncan knew anything it was how to elevate the moment. She snapped the first one, relishing the crunch of the tiny glass capsule at its heart as it released the magic trapped inside. She squeezed it all the way up and down until it crunched no more. After much, careful deliberation she settled on bracelets and anklets then watched, mesmerised as she swirled her feet in the pool, making yellow and green infinity signs with her feet.

So intent was she on crushing the tubes and adorning herself she hadn't heard Duncan get up. She jumped as Duncan's naked body flew past her, squealing as he soaked them all with a graceless cannonball. He laughed as he his head broke through the water, ignoring the cries of *tosser* and *twat.* He grinned at them all, his neck lit up by a necklace made of three of his glow sticks, a glow at his waist revealing the juvenile placement of the fourth.

He was clearly delighted with his backlit junk.

She had to admit, the water looked tempting but there was no way she could be bothered changing into her costume now. Nor was she ever going to get her chuff out in front of her friends. Peeing in front of Shreya was one thing but she would have to have been a lot drunker to strip in front of Dean.

As a compromise she got up and flicked the off lights around the pool and a small cheer went up. Safe in the darkness she stripped off her clothes in record time and jumped in, the glow sticks around her wrists and ankles marking out her star jump into the pool.

It was bliss. The pool was still warm from the day's sun and the salt water lifted her gently to the surface. They splashed around like kids, dunking each other and skimming their arms across the surface, pelting each other with great arcs of water.

At least, three of them were.

At the other end of the pool eight glow sticks were clustered around the steps, casting off just enough light to see that Dean and Shreya were moving along to the next level. Jess grabbed Duncan and Oskar, turning them around to look at the glowing dance macabre in the corner. The glow stick that had been moving up and down underwater stopped.

The sudden quiet in the pool had broken the spell for the lovebirds in the shallow end and they giggled, two teenagers caught in the act.

Jess was relieved and grossed out in equal measure. 'Get a room!'

'Got one thanks!' said Dean. He swam over to the metal steps and climbed out, turning away to hide his erection. Shreya followed; Jess could see her trying to cover her rock-hard nipples in the moonlight.

Lucky cow.

She watched them gather up their clothes and run into the house, giggling as they went.

They'd better go into Dean's room; she really didn't want to hear them shagging tonight.

The windows in Shreya's room stayed dark and she offered up a silent prayer of thanks.

19

Ben didn't remember going to the tree.

He didn't remember anything before he was here.

He had no recollection of leaving the others; no memory of his walk through the orchard or of taking off his clothes.

But here he was.

Naked.

Kneeling in the profound silence of the trees.

He knew he had been here before but had no memory of when or even where he was.

Nothing existed outside of the giant arbor before him.

Before the overwhelming sense had been one of terror.

It had challenged him, demonstrating its might, striking fear into the core of him.

Testing his worth.

Tonight, was different.

The tree was majestic and proud.

He gazed up at its thick branches in awe, feeling the life flowing through every part of it, coursing out beneath him and out into the forest, radiating out through the vast underground network that gave life to the island.

It was hungry, that was why he was here.

The energy of the tree changed as he knelt before it. Dim spots of light began to appear on its branches as clusters of tiny fungi began to glow, the brighter green light of their caps punctuating the faint light of the mycelium webbing that coated its mighty body.

It was the most beautiful thing he had ever seen.

A single cap began to fluoresce brighter than the rest, drawing his eyes upwards to the branches above his head.

It pulsed with light, burning bright in the dark sky, its green light paling to bright white as energy surged through its gills.

He heard a soft pop as the fungus released its precious cargo, and the mycelium network went dark. A single glowing spore drifted down from the darkened tree, moving slowly towards him.

A sudden yearning overwhelmed him as watched it drift closer.

Instinctively he opened his mouth, pushed out his tongue and waited for it to descend.

It burned his tongue, but he didn't flinch.

This was how it had to be.

It was inside him now, chemicals surging instantly in his blood, probing at his body and mind.

In an instant it was everywhere, *he* was everywhere, tapped into the vast network that hid the real power.

The network was the island, but this tree was its beating heart, it had been for centuries.

Long before the orchard.

Long before the town.

It had weathered hurricanes and storms, withstood the waves as tsunamis had washed over the land, living far longer than it had any right to do.

The spore was within him now; its need was his need now.

With one last look at the tree, he turned and walked towards the villa.

20

Oskar was shit-faced, something that his husband rarely saw.

Normally he was quite restrained around alcohol, something he attributed to his Norwegian upbringing. Duncan had always been fascinated by his heritage and was baffled by the concept of their strict control on alcohol. He'd been 14 when he bought his first bottle of White Lightening from the shop down in town, the one everyone knew never checked IDs.

Control had never really entered it for him.

He was quite enjoying watching his husband drift in the pool, eyes drooping, trying to battle his drunken need to sleep. He swam up behind him and wrapped his arms around him.

'I think it might be time for someone to go to bed" he whispered into his ear.

'I'm fine. Just five more minutes, the water is so nice.'

'Promise you're not going to fall asleep and drown?'

'I promise. But even if I did you would save me.' He grinned back at Duncan, charming as ever despite his pissed state.

Duncan pushed back in the water, drifting away but keeping a careful eye on Oskar. Two minutes later he watched as Oskar's head dip forward, saltwater washing over his face and flushing into his nostrils.

His head jerked up, shocking him out of his stupor.

'Ok... Maybe you are right - it is time for bed.'

Oskar walked along the floor of the pool, slowed down by the resistance of the water and his own exhaustion.

Practicalities had gone out of the window in their drunken excitement at skinny dipping. Oskar grinned at Jess who made no attempt to hide the fact she was watching him get out of the pool. He grabbed his clothes and clutched them to his crotch in a half-hearted attempt at modesty, still dripping as he made his way to his bed.

Tomorrow they must remember towels.

Duncan decided to stay in the pool a while longer, give Oskar a chance to bumble around and fall asleep. He loved him but on the rare occasion he got drunk it was easier to let him fall asleep first.

He dived under the water, pushing his way down into the dark until his chest was brushing against the bottom as he explored the silent depths. He reached the end wall and followed it up, breathing out until his head broke the surface. Wiping the salty water from his eyes he saw that Jess was also out of the pool, drying herself with her discarded top.

'Nighty night poodle, I'm done too. Looks like the party may have died.'

'It's not over 'till the fat lady sings,' he said.

'In that case, good niiiiiiight!'

He laughed as she bowed and backed away still blowing kisses to her audience of one.

'Don't drown!' she yelled as she disappeared back into the house.

They were clearly reaching an age, he thought. It could barely even be midnight, yet everyone had already crashed for the night. This must be what happened when you hit your thirties. He could forgive Dean and Shreya, though he doubted either one of them would be getting much sleep tonight.

He ducked under the water once more, swimming the length of the pool in one breath – hardly an impressive feat given the size of it. At the end he turned around, leaning his head over the edge of the pool and allowing his limbs to float up. Considering his head was resting on the concrete it was surprisingly comfortable. He decided to give Oskar a few more minutes to fall asleep, then he would head to bed too.

The gentle lapping of the pool and the warmth of the air and water was bliss. Despite having felt wide awake a few moments ago he started to feel his mind lightly drifting in the calm of the evening.

Not asleep, but not fully awake either.

Sleep was calling him, but he couldn't shake the feeling of being watched. It nagged at him, tugging him back from the edge and forcing him to open his eyes. Righting himself he turned to look at the villa, expecting to see Jess or Oskar coming to send him to bed but there was no-one.

It must be time to go in if he was spooking himself.

The thought of bed was appealing now that he was alone, the party now well and truly over.

A sound in the trees behind the pool startled him. He didn't want to look around, suddenly picturing himself as *that* character in the film - the stupid one that stayed alone, in the pool, naked and defenseless.

It never ended well for that guy.

He turned around, determined not to leap out of the pool and run screaming into the house. There was no masked psycho wielding a buzzsaw. Instead, he was relieved to see Ben step out of the trees and walk over to the pool.

Stark bollock-naked Ben.

'Jesus! You scared the shit out of me!' he said. 'I thought you had gone to bed?'

Ben looked at him and shook his head. 'No.'

'Decided to join the skinny-dipping party?' He gestured at the empty pool around him. 'I think we can just fit one more in.'

Ben walked to the end of the pool, stepping onto the metal ladder and slowly lowering himself in. Duncan could have sworn he saw Ben's cock growing as he slipped under the water. He swam over to Duncan with his head above the water, never breaking eye contact. Duncan sensed the vibe and decided that now he *really* should go to bed before something happened that he would regret tomorrow.

His legs didn't move though, he just stayed in the pool, watching his friend's slow approach.

Ben stopped swimming as neared him, barely an arm's length between them. Duncan willed himself to move, to say something to break the tension of the moment. The glow stick around his cock and balls tightened as they stared at each other.

He had to get out of the pool.

Had to behave.

Ben seemed to sense he was getting ready to go and leaned back in the water, stretching his legs out, brushing his now hard cock against Duncan hand.

'We can't…' said Duncan, but still his hand opened and wrapped around Ben's girth.

Ben groaned and put his finger to his lips. He wrapped his other hand around Duncan's, pushing it up and down. Duncan's feeble attempt at resolve crumbled and he tentatively tugged at his friend. It felt sleazy and wrong.

It felt so good.

He'd come so many times thinking about getting Ben off, he'd never imagined it would be in a pool though, not with their friends just meters away, with his *husband* asleep inside. He reached under and cupped Ben's balls.

He had to stop.

Ben once again seemed to sense his doubt and moved to the edge of the pool and lifted himself out of the water. His bounced his dick up and down, inviting Duncan to put his mouth around it.

Every remaining ounce of resistance dissolved into the water around him.

He put his hands around Ben, sliding them down to his arse and wrapped his lips around the head, running his tongue under the foreskin, tasting his cock. He angled his head to take more of it in, pushing down and drawing his cock to the base. He choked but kept it in his mouth, sucking and running his tongue along the length.

He couldn't breathe but he didn't care.

He prided himself on his oral talents, it wasn't like it was on his CV or anything, but he knew he was good. Ben was never going to have had a blow job like this.

There was no tenderness though as Ben grabbed Duncan by the hair and lifted his mouth almost off his cock before shoving it back down, forcing it all into Duncan's throat. He gagged, choking on the thick head, retching up bile and beer. He had no time to get used to it before his head was pulled of his dick again and pushed back down. More bile and beer. Ben used his mouth, repeatedly slamming his cock down Duncan's throat, his balls tightening as the pressure built inside of him.

He tried to get Ben's hands from his head but couldn't focus enough to get a grip, struggling to catch his breath as his throat was repeated raped. Ben tensed. Duncan's head was pulled up a final time and held in place. He gulped in as much air as he could, breathing around the cock still throbbing in his mouth. Ben was close. In desperation he closed his mouth around it, sucking his cock again, desperate for it all to just be over.

Hands clamped tightly over his ears, blocking off the sound of the world around him. Ben pushed his head down slowly, sliding his cock deep into his throat and holding it there. It twitched in his mouth before pumping blast after blast of cum down his throat.

He swallowed desperately, trying not to choke on the thick seed that was flowing into him.

Ben held Duncan's head in place as his dick softened in his mouth, wrapping his fingers around the base, pushing out one last shiny bead of cum.

Done, Ben got to his feet and silently walked back into the dark embrace of the trees.

He no longer thought about his former friend in the pool. no longer remembered infecting him.

All he knew now was his need to return to the tree.

Duncan sank below the water, letting the cool water wash away the taste of rape, his tears flowing silently into the salty water of the pool.

21

Jess woke up suddenly, startled awake by a dream she was already forgetting. Something to do with work. Her boss had been chasing her. Whatever it was it was too early in the holiday to be having back to work dreams. God knows she had enough to worry about when she got back, but so far she had managed to repress it pretty well and she wasn't going to let the silent, morning hours amplify it now.

She turned her pillow over to feel the cool underside against her face. A quick press of the home button on her phone confirmed it was still the middle of the night, not even 4am. She could get back to sleep, she just needed to close her eyes and drift off again.

Her brain had other ideas, flooding her mind with random, unconnected thoughts and images. The more she tried to push them away, the worse they became: recurring lyrics from songs; work, her single status; work; how she was going to get out of Christmas with her family; work… work, work, work. The thoughts went on and on until all possibility of sleep was gone.

Resigned to being awake she opened her eyes and lay there, staring at the ceiling fan that whirred above her head. Perhaps she could hypnotise herself back into slumber? Across the room she became aware of the strip of light that still shone under the bedroom door. Frugality had been drilled into her from such an early age that even now, thousands of miles from home she was still found herself annoyed at the waste of energy and annoyed with Duncan for not switching it off when he went to bed.

Did he go to bed? Of course, he did. He would have followed behind her once he got bored of being the only one still swimming. Her brain was churning now. It was irrational, and she knew it, but her brain started to churn again. Thoughts of her friend floating face down in the pool, his face already bloated in the warm water. Sitting down with Sue and Bryan and having to admit that she had left their son alone in the pool and gone to bed.

Yes, he had been drinking she told them through tears, *but I never thought…!*

No, that's always been your trouble Jessica, you don't think, do you Jessica? And now our boy is gone.

I'd do anything to bring him back!

By the time she had gotten as far as imagining herself breaking down during his eulogy she knew she was going to have to get up and check on her friend. He wasn't dead in the pool, he just wasn't. He had been soberer than most of them and was a strong swimmer.

What would she wear to his funeral?

She got out of bed, a slave to her imagination. She shrugged on her silk dressing gown and stepped out into the hall, wrapping it tightly around herself as she blinked at the sudden brightness of the house. All the doors in the hall were shut so she crept down the corridor.

The back door was closed but she pushed down on the door handle, willing it to be locked. Her heart sank as it clicked, and the back door opened out. This still didn't mean he was dead.

It didn't.

The pool was dark, barely lit by the moon which had now moved across the garden, once again fleeing to the west.

There was no body floating on the surface. She let out the breath she had been holding since she stepped outside. He wasn't dead. Well, he wasn't floating there anyway. She peered into the dark water but couldn't see anything in the gloom. Maybe that was enough, she had checked, and he wasn't dead. She could go to bed knowing he was ok. But she was lying to herself. She would lie there in the darkness, still imaging the worst. She needed to see the bottom, needed light.

She turned back towards the house but stopped. Duncan was asleep on a lounger in the corner, still naked, curled up into a tight ball. It was mild out, but she knew she couldn't leave him there all night. She went over and sat down on the edge of his makeshift bed, ran her fingers over his shoulder and whispered his name, not wanting to scare him. He didn't move as she gently shook him.

Then his eyes snapped open.

'It's okay babes, it's only me. You fell asleep.'

He turned his head towards her, staring at her intently but making no attempt to move.

'Come on, bedtime, you must be freezing.'

He grabbed her by the wrist before she could stand.

'Ben did it,' he said.

'What did he do?' she asked, trying to keep a straight face. This was far from the first time he had babbled at her as she woke him up. 'Ben did it,' he repeated, tightening his fingers around her wrist.

'It was just a bad dream hon.' Her hand pulsed from his tight grip, it hurt. Her amusement morphed into fear as he stared at her, unblinking, still trapped in a dream state. She tried to pull her hand away, but he held fast, tightening his grip. 'Come on,' she pleaded, forcing out shaky laugh, 'let's get you to bed and you can forget all about it'.

His eyes were glassy, unwavering, and devoid of any emotion. 'He gave it to me. Now I must give it to you.'

Jess pried her nails under his fingers, but Duncan's grip was too strong, he kept squeezing, crushing her arm in his hand. 'Stop it! You're freaking me out… That fucking hurts!'

She leapt up from the lounger but was still tethered by the hand on her wrist.

'Duncan please!'

He rose, pushing her back by the wrist as he did so.

He towered over, his newly gained muscle adding to his power, dwarfing her as she crouched in pain. His body turned suddenly, yanking her down and forwards at the same time. She twisted, instinctively trying to ease the pain as she fell, and tumbled forward, falling where Duncan had lain seconds before.

She sprawled there dazed, her dressing gown flapping open from the tussle. Duncan stepped either side of the lounger, straddling her.

He was hard.

This isn't happening she thought. The thought of Duncan trying to rape her should have been laughable, but terror welled inside her, freezing her to the spot.

Her Duncan would never want to fuck her. He wouldn't attack her like this. It made no sense but somehow this wasn't him.

Her instincts took over and she knew she had to get away.

She screamed as loud as she could, but he wrapped a hand over her mouth, muffling her cries. Jess bit down, her teeth closing around the fleshy ball of his thumb. At the same time, she thrust her legs up, striking his balls with her shin.

He should have collapsed and rolled the ground in agony but instead he simply staggered back, slightly off balance from the force of the kick. Jess drew her legs up and pushed them into him with as much might as she could muster. He went back again but this time he went down as his foot caught the edge of the sunbed behind him.

She gagged at the taste of blood. Her tongue brushed against the morsel of flesh still rolling around in her mouth.

Jess spat it out, swallowing down the vomit that threatened to follow it.

Duncan looked up at her from behind the lounger, for a moment she saw fear in his eyes.

'Run!' he pleaded.

She didn't need to be told twice. She scrambled to her feet and ran for the villa, not looking back at the sound of chair legs begin dragged across the patio.

'Jessicaaaaaa…'

Her friend was gone again, replaced by whatever the fuck it was that seemed to be inside him.

She yanked the kitchen door open and slammed it shut behind her, screaming for the others as she turned the key in the lock. She flipped the switch by the door and the garden was flooded with light.

One by one they ran from their rooms to find Jess staring put at the night.

Duncan sneered at her before slipping out of the light and disappearing into the darkness.

Oskar reached her just as her legs crumpled. She fell into his arms sobbing, Duncan's blood all over her face.

23

Across the island a handful of locals huddled around three small monitors.

They watched the man lower one woman onto the couch as the darker skinned woman appeared in shot, carrying a bowl and a cloth. There was no sound, the equipment was too basic, but the panic and fear on the faces of the holiday makers was palpable.

Christina reached for the phone and sent off a text as the drama unfold on the old black and white screens.

At the villa Mateo's mobile vibrated in his hand.

IT'S TIME

The message was simple, but he knew what it meant.

Batch 4 were infected.

Day Three

24

Oskar couldn't listen to Jess.

'This is crazy Jess, why are you making this shit up?'

Jess stared at him. Blood smeared her face as she sat on the sofa shaking. 'I d-don't know what happened. H-h-he was asleep out there and when I tried to get him to g-go to bed grabbed me and shoved me down…' Shreya pulled Jess tighter in her arms and stroked her hair, trying to calm her down. 'H-he was going to rape me!'

He shook his head back and forth, as if the motion would somehow expel the words from his mind, sending them scattering back across the room and back into Jess's mouth. He was still drunk and none of this made any fucking sense. Where the hell was Duncan? He had to go and look for him.

'It's all lies,' he said, 'I don't know why you are lying but you *are*.'

'He did it Oskar.' Her words were so quiet he barely heard them.

'This is sick; you know? I mean, I know you always wanted him for yourself, but this is *sick* Jess.'

'No!'

'You have always been jealous and now you are trying to… I don't know what the fuck you are trying to do. Just stop it, ok? Where is he?'

They just had to find Duncan, and this would all stop. Then they could all go to bed and work it all out in the morning. He just wanted to slip into those crisp white sheets, wrap his arms around Duncan and fall asleep, let this all be some terrible dream.

Dean moved to the back door and wrapped his fingers around the key but stopped as Jess yelled. She leapt out of Shreya's arms and ran to the door, pushing him away as he tried to put his arms around her.

'Okay, okay!' he muttered, backing away from her, away from the door. He walked away from Jess and took her still warm spot on the sofa, his hand wrapped around Shreya's. They had to go and look for Duncan, but Jess's reaction had made him hesitate. He knew she could be dramatic, but this was different. She was terrified and covered in blood. By the way she was guarding the door now she obviously had no intention of letting the go outside. They would just have to wait until they could work out what was going on.

Oskar walked to the kitchen, still half-drunk and needing something to do. He needed coffee.

He found a jar in the back of a cupboard and heaped spoons of instant coffee into mugs, making six out of habit. Jess repeated her story as the kettle boiled.

She had found Duncan asleep outside. He was naked. She woke him up. He told her Ben gave it to him. Then he tried to rape her.

It just didn't make sense.

Oskar looked around the room and only then did he notice that Ben wasn't there either. He abandoned the coffee making and walked down the hall to Ben's room. The bed was made, his case lay full on the floor by his bed, yet to be unpacked. He checked the bathroom but that too was empty. A quick search of the rest of the house revealed that neither man was inside.

'This is a joke, yes? Some weird prank to scare us?' Oskar already knew that it wasn't, but he willed Jess to own up, for the other men to walk through the door laughing. He would laugh along too, he swore he would, he just longed for relief that moment would bring.

But he knew that wasn't going to happen.

Shreya cleaned Jess's face with a wet cloth, hugging her friend as she wiped away the blood. Dean had fetched some clothes for her from the bedroom and Oskar and Dean turned away as Shreya helped her get dressed.

'What the fuck is going on Oskar?' Dean asked.

He had no answer. The kettle clicked off and he went to finish his task, grateful for the distraction. He found sugar cubes in the cupboard and added them to the mugs.

The coffee was strong, hot, and sweet.

The four of them held their drinks in silence, two cups left untouched, cooling on the side.

Jess was playing it all over in her head. 'It wasn't him. That wasn't Duncan out there.' She paused to take another sip of coffee. 'He was cold. Cruel. His eyes were dead. It was like he had been hijacked or something.'

The others sipped at their drinks, unable to process her words.

Oskar still refused to believe that Duncan had attacked Jess, but he had to understand.

'You say he said that "Ben did it… he gave it to me". What does that mean?'

'I have no idea. Oskar, you know I would never…'

'I know...,' said Oskar. 'Duncan would never try and hurt you Jess, he loves you. I don't know what is going on but if what you are saying is true then he is out there somewhere, alone and hurt. He needs me. I can't sit here; we've got to find him.'

He looked to Dean for support and could see him nodding. 'Ben must be out there too. Whatever this is, we just need get them back inside.'

'We can't go out!' Jess looked at them both, wide eyed and frantic. 'Something is going on out there, we have to stay inside and keep the doors locked. If they come back, we can talk to them, but you are *not* going out there.'

'What about going for help in town?' asked Shreya.

'We don't have a car; we were driven home remember?' replied Dean. 'We'd have to walk for the best part of an hour, through those woods. If there is something going on out there, then we'd be totally exposed.'

'So, we wait for daylight? Is that all we have?' Shreya looked at Dean, tears welling in her eyes as the bleakness of the situation set in.

Oskar went to the window, pressing his head against the glass, willing his lover to appear. There was still time for this to be a mistake. He just couldn't explain how Jess had become covered in blood. He turned back to them and saw his phone charging in the wall.

Of course, he should have thought of it before.

'Wait. Dean, didn't Christina give you a contact number?' he asked.

Dean didn't answer, just ran to his room, returning seconds later, clutching his iPhone. His thumb scrolled down the glassy screen.

'Got it... fuck, no signal.' He walked around the room, raising his phone to the ceiling, pacing in front of windows looking for any trace of signal.

'Try opening a window, that can help the signal get through sometimes,' said Oskar.

Dean dragged a chair over to one of the large lounge windows and pulled the top of the window down. He craned his head towards the top, holding the phone close to his face. No signal. He stood still, waiting for a miracle.

He yelled as one bar appeared quickly followed by the Vodaphone logo. He tapped on Christina's number and waited for it to connect but the line was silent. Instead of a ring tone he heard a recorded Spanish voice.

He didn't understand the words, but the tone of the message was clear. The number he had dialed had not been recognised. Please check the number and try again.

'No. No. No. No! I know the number is right, I've texted her on it.'

Shreya dashed to her room, returning moments later with her copy of the itinerary. She handed the laminated sheet to Dean who compared the two numbers.

'They're the same. It's been disconnected.'

Despite his awkward position he managed to open Safari, trying to access the internet before he lost the tentative connection to 3G. He brought up his history and scrolled down until he found the link to the villa. The blue bar appeared at the top of the screen, barely moving as it battled with the weak signal. He'd almost lost hope when the screen changed, turning white with the message that the server could not be found.

His heart sank.

He clicked on another link in his history, praying for there to be an issue with the signal but he was shortly greeted by an amazon page.

'The website for the villa has gone too,' he said, still staring at the phone.

They sat in stunned silence.

'It can't be gone,' said Jess, shaking her head. "It must be the signal or something. It can't just have vanished."

"I tried to open another page and that worked.' He looked around their room, their faces stared back at him willing him to be wrong. 'The site I booked the holiday through is gone.'

Oskar sat back, dragging his fingers through his beard. "Why would someone delete the website; it makes no sense."

They sat there, each lost in thought, none of them good.

Jess cast her mind back to their time in the town a few hours before. She'd assumed that it had been deserted because it was a Sunday evening but now, she wasn't so sure.

'It was so quiet in the square tonight, did no one else notice that?' asked Jess. 'We were the only ones out apart from the twins. Why was that? Not one single person walked through that square.'

No one answered.

Shreya barely heard her as she poured over the trip itinerary, looking for anything that might help, something they had missed. Dean had created the PowerPoint for them all, still keen to look organised and mature. It was a complete guide with flight details, contacts for Christina, copy and pasted descriptions of the villa and photos dragged from the website, enlarged so they could daydream about their holidays as they counted down the weeks and days.

She looked at the photos again, staring at pictures of a villa they even never set foot in.

The rooms weren't vastly different to the ones they had here, nor any of the other villas they had stayed in for that matter. They were always taken from the same angles, trying to make them look as big and airy as possible. Generic pictures on the walls, local scenes depicted in watercolours, easy care leather sofas, shiny clean kitchens and blue pools reflecting the glorious sunshine.

Her eyes flicked back to the image of the lounge on the itinerary. The quality of the image wasn't great, so it wasn't easy to pick out the detail of the painting on the wall, but something wasn't right. She stared at the image until it dawned on her.

'Look at this. The lounge of the other villa has a picture of that Cathedral in Palma on the wall.'

Dean took it off her, getting close to the page. 'Looks like it, so?'

'So why does a villa on a tiny island in the Canary Islands have a painting of a building on another island thousands of miles away?'

'Maybe the owners bought it when they were in Mallorca?' offered Jess.

Oskar sighed, knowing where Shreya was going with her question. 'Or maybe the photo is of some villa in Mallorca.' He looked around the room, it finally dawned on him that they had been conned from the outset, herded into this house in the middle of nowhere and have never once questioned it. 'There never was another villa on the island, was there? We were always going to be brought here.'

'They hooked us in, got us here and then deleted the website.' Said Shreya, following his logic. 'Oh fuck, we don't even know where we are.'

'What do you mean?' asked Dean.

'We flew to Gran Canaria then got on a boat with a total stranger. The itinerary says the crossing to Isla Manuta is an hour, but our trip took three times that.' She paused as the pieces of the puzzle slipped into place. 'If they have lied about everything so far then we could be anywhere.'

'No.' Dean shook his head. 'This isn't some big conspiracy. There is going to be a simple explanation for all of this, okay? We just haven't worked it out yet. Besides, even if you are right, deleting the website doesn't erase it. There is always a trace, there were emails, payments, all of that would lead someone to where we are.'

'No there wasn't,' said Shreya, 'we paid cash for the villa as Christina told you there was a problem with the online payment. She only gave us her number after we got here and anyone with any skill can hide an email trail.

Oskar stared at the flowers on the table. Shreya was right. Right now, they didn't know where they were and it seemed as though they had been lured to this island, wherever that may be, for reasons unknown. All of that together meant that they were in a shit load of trouble. No one would trick six strangers onto an anonymous island in the middle of the Atlantic for anything good.

He cast his mind back to Christina's visit the previous day. He hadn't thought anything of it at the time but now something struck him as odd. That fact that Christina had brought them flowers wasn't strange, what was weird was where she had put them. Why would she not set them down on the dining room table? You don't bring over flowers and then hide them away in a dark corner of the room. It was Jess that had moved to them to the table in front of him.

He got up and went to the shelves, trying to remember where Christina had originally put them. There was a faint circular depression in the thin layer of dust on one on of them. He grabbed the vase of flowers from the table and returned them to the shelves; the base of the vase lined up perfectly with the depression in the dust. The others watched him as he looked around the bookshelves, silently reenacting Christina's movements - turning anti-clockwise as she had done, then turning back to face the shelves.

Further along the shelf he spied another ring in the dust. He ran his fingers over it, feeling the still sticky residue. Something had been here before she placed the flowers.

A tiny pinprick of light reflected off the spine of one of the books as he moved.

He grabbed the thick tome with the bright spine and pulled it from the shelf.

Thin wires ran from the back of the tome and disappearing behind other books. He carefully opened the pages and found a small camera nestled into a hollow carved out of the pages, its tiny lens carefully pushed through a hole in the binding. He ripped it out of the book and held it out to show the others.

'They're watching us.'

25

Dean stared at the tiny device in Oskar's hand.

If he put his mind to it, he was sure he could explain everything that had happened so far, weave a magical tale that would explain the weirdness into one complex comedy of errors. He wanted them all to be laughing and telling the story over and over for years to come as they holidayed together.

But the camera broke that narrative.

Casting his mind back he thought he could remember seeing Christina pocket something as she had deposited the flowers, but he hadn't thought anything of it at the time. One of them must have put a can down that first night after they had moved inside from the terrace. It had blocked the lens and Christina had come in to move it, restore their eye in the room.

There was no hilarious anecdote to gloss over that.

They all sat in dumb silence, processing the latest turn of events, trying to work out the one big question. Why was this all happening to them? For the first time Dean really started to worry about Ben and Duncan. When it had all just been a big misunderstanding, he had been annoyed with them but now concern gnawed away at him.

'When did anyone last see Ben?' he asked.

'He didn't go to the pool,' said Jess. 'I don't think I saw him after we got home, I went straight to the kitchen and then out to the pool. I just assumed he was being a lightweight again and had crashed early.'

'Okay. So, we got back and went for a swim, all apart from Ben who seems to have vanished from that point. Shreya and I went inside first and that was all we knew until we heard Jess screaming. What happened in the middle?'

Jess cast her mind back, barely four hours had passed but it already felt like a lifetime ago. 'Oskar went next,' she said, remembering the pang of jealousy she felt as Duncan smiled as he watched him get out. 'You were falling asleep in the pool, so Duncan told you to go to bed.'

'I barely remember that.' said Oskar. 'Those shots at the bar got me too drunk. I remember getting back to the house, maybe being in the pool and then nothing until I heard you scream. That's it.' He willed himself to remember but nothing came, just the blackness of drunken sleep.

Their eyes turned to Jess. She flushed.

'I don't have much more than you lot. I stayed in the pool for a little while longer and then went to bed. Duncan carried on swimming. I fell asleep but then woke up and got it in my head that I had left him drunk and swimming so went to make sure he got to bed. That's when….'.

She fell silent as she remembered what followed.

Dean got up and paced around the room. They had lots of bits of the puzzle but no way to piece them together, no sense of the scale of it. Somehow though he was sure it must have started with Ben. He'd been quiet all holiday, but Dean hadn't really paid much notice. It had been obvious that something was up when they were in town earlier. He'd been odd about that covered statue then had sparred with the waiter. He should have checked on him, found out what was going on, but he had been too focused on Shreya and her new necklace.

In fact, looking back he had been so wrapped up in Shreya since they got here that he had pretty much neglected Ben from the outset. It had been easier to let Ben tell him he was fine than challenge him when he suspected his friend wasn't fully there with them. Had Ben even gone to bed early on that first night? They had just assumed he had, but he was never the first to crash on holiday, he could always be relied on to keep things going until the early hours. They had no reason to doubt he was lying until he went missing again tonight.

It still didn't explain anything, just raised more questions without answers.

'Ben was….'

Dean was cut off as the power went in the house and everything around them went black.

There was no crash or pop, just instant darkness. The air conditioner clicked off, leaving them in a silent, black void.

Dean felt his way back to the sofa, reaching out for the table in the darkness. 'Everyone stay still, let me grab my phone, we can use the torch to find some candles and get some light back in here.'

He felt the edge of the table and groped around until his fingers hit the familiar cold glass. In the total darkness of the blackout his phone cast a surprisingly bright beam around the open plan room.

They dug around in the kitchen, finally finding the second bag of tea lights that Duncan had bought and a lighter. Spread out around the room they drove the darkness back into the smallest of corners. Tonight, the soft warm glow felt out of place, a mockery of the mood they had created on that first night here.

They regrouped around the kitchen table, once more sitting in silence now they had some semblance of light back. Dean reached for Shreya's hand under the table, holding it tight, not wanting to let go. He had only just got her, and he had no intention of letting go now.

Across the table he spotted that Oskar was staring out of the window, his eyes wide, mouth moving in silence.

Dean didn't want to look but knew he had to.

There was nothing to see at first, just the darkness outside the window, sunrise still an hour away. It was pitch black out there. Apart from… apart from a soft yellow horseshoe, like some primeval bioluminescent jellyfish, drifting in the dark abyss. What the hell was that? It drifted closer to them, the neon glowing brighter, lighting up the pale skin around Duncan's neck, his eyes staring blankly at the group huddled around the table.

He put his hand up to the window, spreading his palm out on the glass.

Jess grabbed Oskar as he started to move towards his lover, trying to hold him back. He shrugged her off and walked forward, raising his hand to match Duncan's on the glass.

'Let me in,' he whispered from the other side, tilting his head towards Oskar. He wanted to as well, he would have run to the door and pulled Duncan inside were it not for the look on his face. He knew that the British liked to say that you wear your heart on your sleeve, but Duncan truly wore his on his face. He could try to hide his feelings from Oskar, try to protect him, but his emotions were always written across his features, betraying his attempt to hide a smile or a frown.

The face looking back at him was empty, completely detached from any emotion. A mask of his husband worn by someone or something else.

When Oskar didn't move Duncan tilted his head the other way, craning his neck to look around him, seeking out the others, probing for someone weak enough to open the door to him.

'Jessssica, let me in…' he said.

Oskar took his hand off the glass slowly, reluctantly breaking the contact. Whatever was standing on the other side of that glass was no longer his husband, but still he couldn't bear to let him go.

'That's not Duncan,' he whispered.

Dean stepped forward and gently led him back to the table.

'We can't let him inside,' whispered Jess. 'Remember that he said he had to give it to me, I have no fucking idea what *it* is but I'm pretty damned sure it is the same thing that has done this to him.'

Outside the window the Not-Duncan was pushing at the glass, trying to find a way in, testing for movement. It repeated the probing along the length of the window before going out of sight behind the stone wall.

Shreya ran to the kitchen door and turned the key in the lock. She found herself face to face with the Not-Duncan, who stared through the glass of the door as she backed away, key in hand.

'Doors and windows!' shouted Dean.

No further explanation was needed. Dean took his phone and ran to the bedrooms, checking all windows were locked. Oskar followed him around, closing all the wooden shutters as they went. He grabbed wire coat hangers from the wardrobe and gave them to Shreya and Jess, telling them to secure the shutters any way they could.

The Not-Duncan followed them to every window, watching as they locked him out. It smiled at them, the action forced and inhuman, like it had worked out the mechanics but not the emotion that went with it. The smile gave way to a maniacal grin as it watched them race from room to room. In a thin, flat voice it began to sing.

Heathcliff, it's meeeeee your Cathy, I've come home now.

Two years ago, Duncan had sung the song at Karaoke in Pollença. He'd fucked it up with aplomb and brought the house down. Tonight, the sound was terrifying. Its voice mournful and full of malicious intent as it circled the house, looking for a way to get inside.

With the bedrooms secured they dragged sofas to the front and back doors, creating a further barrier between them and the outside.

The Not-Duncan's voice retreated, growing quieter as it gave up its quest to get into the house until they could no longer hear it.

Dean grabbed the cushions off them and threw them onto the floor. They added duvets and pillows from the bedroom to the pile, creating a soft nest in the middle of the room. He grabbed a knife from the kitchen and hid it behind him as he came back to the centre. 'Come on, let's huddle up. We can't do anything in the dark so let's try and get some rest while we can. I'll stay awake and keep an eye out, you guys try and sleep.'

Jess wanted to argue but didn't have the energy.

They sat together as the adrenaline wore off. Jess was the first to fall asleep. She tried to fight it, still scared of what the night could bring but her exhaustion took over, dragging her under against her will. She curled up on the pile, glad when Oskar lay behind her a moment later, wrapping his arms around her, each needing the other to keep the demons at bay.

Dean gave Oskar's shoulder a squeeze as he sat down next to him, not knowing what to say to his friend. He placed the knife close by as Shreya lay down next to him and put her head in his lap. He ran his fingers through her hair and tickled the back of her neck. With the night going to shit around him he took comfort in her closeness and warmth. His tickles grew slower, his hand pressing into her back as he drifted towards sleep.

Despite the situation she smiled, enjoying the weight of it pressing against her.

When she was sure he was asleep she carefully reached behind her, walking her fingers along the duvet until felt the cold steel handle of the knife. She brought it around and felt the weight of it in her hands, knowing the first watch was now hers.

26

Shreya was sure she hadn't slept yet moments later it was morning and she found herself leaning into Dean's shoulder, the knife lying forgotten on the duvet. Sunlight already streamed through the shutters, adding to the heat in the already warm, airtight room. With no air conditioning and open windows, they would not be able to stay here very long. She was annoyed at herself for falling asleep but was also relieved that nothing had happened whilst she got some rest.

They had to get out of here but where could they go? Christina was the only person they knew on the island and by now it was clear that she was the one that had brought them here, tricked them into this trap. They had no idea who else was involved but it must have taken a lot of people to pull off something like this.

Which meant they couldn't trust anyone. They were going to have to get off the island and find their way back to the mainland on their own.

Panic welled in her stomach as the reality of the situation hit her full force. Her heart started to race, and she felt beads of sweat popping out on her forehead and top lip.

It was all too much. How the fuck had they gotten to this point? Her breathing quickened, and she felt herself losing control, the sense of impending doom blocking out all reason in her mind. She finally gave in to the truth that she had been denying since she heard Jess screaming.

She knew it in her bones that they had been brought here to die.

Panic surged through her, uncontrolled. She wanted her mum to meet Dean. Wanted to have kids with him. She wanted to do everything now that she had him by her side.

They couldn't die here, she had to get them home.

She took a deep breath in through the nose and exhaled through her mouth, forcing herself into a calmer state as she counted each breath. When she was little and unable to sleep her mother had taught her to count her breaths slowly backwards from eighty-seven, telling her that it was the magic number and that no one could count backwards from it without falling asleep. Now she counted forwards, feeling her mother urging her on, giving her the strength to fight her way home.

She thought about her Mum as she counted. Ten. Thought of the love her parents had always wrapped her in. Twenty. Her little sister, copying her hair in the mirror and putting on her bangles when she thought Shreya wasn't looking. Thirty. Her dad making fish and chips every Friday because that is what British people do. Forty. Her parents driving her to York, so proud of her for getting into university. Fifty. Meeting her friends that first day. Sixty. Meeting Dean. Seventy. Dean. Eighty. Dean. Eighty-Seven.

She opened her eyes and looked around at the others, still sleeping in the nest he had made for them all.

They may have been brought here to die but that didn't mean they were going to.

She got up slowly and tiptoed to her room, grabbing her rucksack from the cupboard and filling it with essentials; sun cream, her mini first aid kit, spare clothes, her mobile phone, anything small and light that might come in handy.

. She pulled on a pair of denim shorts, a t-shirt and ditched her flip flops in favour of socks and trainers, knowing she was going to need to be dressed practically for the journey ahead.

Back in the kitchen she opened the drawer where she had put the travel folder and added it to the growing pile in her rucksack.

It was too light.

She knew what was missing even before she checked, her fears confirmed when she flipped open the folder.

All six passports were gone. *Fuck.*

She went back to the living room and woke the others up. 'We have to go, now, it's still early and they won't be expecting it.'

'Who won't be expecting what?' asked Jess, still half asleep.

Shreya turned to Dean and looked him in the eyes. 'We have to get off the island, you know we do. I don't know why but we were lured here, and no one is planning on us leaving again.'

'Babe, we don't know that.'

'Yes, we do. On top of everything else that is going on, someone has taken all of our passports. They clearly don't expect us to need them again.'

Three blank faces stared back at her, still processing her words. 'You know I like to keep them all safe in my folder,' she said, holding up with empty case.

'Christina,' said Oskar. 'I took the folder out of the drawer yesterday when she had asked for the cash for the villa. She knew where all six passports were and must have driven by last night when we were all in town.'

Faen, he cursed to himself, he had practically given them to her.

Shreya knew there was no time to wallow. 'Get a rucksack if you have one and grab anything that might be useful. We need to find a way off the island, and we need to do it alone. If we can get to the harbour, we can steal a boat and find our way to another island, maybe even back to Gran Canaria.'

They ignored the fact that not one of them knew how to sail, for now there was no other plan.

'What about Duncan?' demanded Oskar. Shreya's plan was all well and good, but it didn't include his husband. 'He's sick and been out there alone all night and now you want to leave him and Ben behind, just run away? Duncan would never abandon any of you and you know it. You lot can run if you want but I need to stay and find him.'

'Oskar, we have to…'

'Shreya,' said Jess, waving her friend and Dean towards the bedrooms. 'Why don't you and Dean start to gather the supplies you talked about?'

Dean took the cue and grabbed Shreya by the hand and pulled her gently out of the living room. When they were alone Jess sank down on the sofa, sidling up next to Oskar.

'You know I love him too Oskar, he's like a brother to me. He would want us to get away from here and I think you know that.' Oskar shook his head at her, unwilling to listen. 'Remember that time at uni when we got tickets for Alton Towers and got all giddy planning our trip?' she asked.

'Stop it Jess, you can't change my mind.'

'Remember?' she persisted. 'Duncan hired a car, and we planned our strategy for the day, which rides to hit first to avoid the queues. You guys decided that we would swap around with each ride so that I wasn't always on my own? Then the night before, you were late finishing work and so you grabbed yourself a takeaway from that god-awful Indian takeaway down the road - the one that we had all warned you about.'

'The Spice Grills,' he muttered.

'Fucking hell, the name alone should have been a warning. You got so ill that night and we couldn't do anything to help, you just locked yourself in your bathroom and made us turn the volume up on the TV. We decided to cancel the trip, but you wouldn't hear of it. Duncan wanted to stay but you made me promise to drag him to Alton Towers in the morning as there was no point in us all staying home when there was nothing we could do to help you.'

'This is nothing like that Jess and you know it. We're not planning a day out at Alton Towers; we are talking about leaving him behind while we run away.'

'You saw him last night Oskar. You know that isn't Duncan anymore. The Duncan we know, and love would never attack me or turn on any of us. I don't know if he is still in there or if he is gone but I do know that we can't help him right now. The only thing we can do is get away from here and get help.'

His shoulders shook gently, and Jess leaned into him, wrapping her arm around his chest. They sat like that until Oskar took a deep breath and wiped his eyes with the back of his hand.

'We said we'd never leave each other,' he said.

'But this time he would be telling you to go. He loves you too much to put you in danger.'

'Fuck.'

'I know'

Oskar kissed the top of her head and pushed himself up from the sofa.

'We have to go before I change my mind,' he said.

27

Five minutes later they were all back in the kitchen. Shreya handed out knives, bottles of water and any food they had been able to cobble together. They hadn't planned on survival when they had done the shop so were reliant on a jar of Nutella, cheese, crisps, some stale bread, and jar of gherkins. They split the meagre supplies between their bags; Bear Grylls wouldn't have been impressed but it was the best they could do.

The four of them gathered by the front door and hugged, each one fighting back the emotion as they steeled themselves for what lay ahead.

Oskar and Dean pulled the sofa back from the door, lifting it as they moved it, trying to avoid making a sound. If they were going to make a run for it, then it had to be quick and quiet. The Not-Duncan was still out there, maybe even Ben, and no one wanted to have to face that.

Jess and Shreya looked out through the slatted shutters, checking the route to the gates was clear. Outside leaves fluttered on the trees in the early morning sun but everything else was calm, no sign of the others.

Bright sunlight streamed through the door as Dean eased it open, blinding them as they emerged from their darkness of the villa. They edged forward onto the terrace, tightly huddled together, each one looking in a different direction to ensure they weren't taken by surprise.

Their confidence grew step by step as they left the villa behind them, walking more surely towards the gate at the end of the drive. At this side of the house the orchard thinned out, trees giving way to an expanse of thick, tropical grass that ran to edge of the property's wall. They could see the route ahead was clear and picked up the pace, eager to break free of the confines of the walls.

'Wait,' said Shreya, looking ahead to the exit.

No one had bothered to close them since they had arrived but now the heavy metal gates were firmly shut, a thick chain looped through them with a padlock hanging down from it.

They had been locked in.

'No, no, no, no....' Jess mumbled as she crumpled to the floor.

She had believed they were going to get out of here but now they had fallen at the starting line.

Shreya walked up to the gates and tugged at the chain. Someone had known they would flee the house and had been ready, locking them in before they could try. With every passing moment, the layers of planning that had gone into this were revealing themselves. Nothing had been left to chance, no move unwatched since they got had arrived.

Last night the drinks had come thick and fast, those free shots had been so welcome at the time, accompanied as they were with the offer of a free lift home. But now they had no car to batter through the gates with, no car to escape to the harbour in.

Nothing had been left to chance.

She looked up, noticing the barbed wire strung across the gates for the first time. The tops of tall white walls that ran along the perimeter of the villa were sparkling in the early morning light, sun reflecting off shards of glass set into the concrete.

How had she not spotted that before? The barrier around the property had never been there to keep the rest of the world out.

It was there to keep them in.

Footsteps and the sound of whispering voices carried over the wall.

'Hey! What's going on?' she yelled. 'Who's out there?'

The voices stopped and, for a moment, there was silence. Then the footsteps crunched once more on the gravel and Shreya raised her knife in their direction.

Christina appeared around the barrier, walking slowly up to the gates she stopped an arm's length from the ironwork.

'Good morning,' said the matriarch, politely nodding to Shreya. 'I am so sorry, truly I am. I hope you understand that this gives me no pleasure, but sadly there is no other way.'

She looked past Shreya and gave a sad smile to the other three prisoners, still the hostess even when the gates were barred.

Jess rushed forward, reaching through the bars, pleading with their captor.

'Please Christina. Please. We won't say anything, just let us go home.'

'No, I'm sorry but you cannot leave here now. This place is an ancient place, the sacred heart of our island. The fates have chosen you and here you will stay. We are all forever grateful for your sacrifice.'

Some of the pieces were coming together in Shreya's head, snippets of the conversation with the waiter last night.

The first people they worshipped the tree and gave gifts to keep balance.

'You are one of the first people, aren't you?' Shreya demanded. 'The original tribe that lived here on the island?'

A look a fear flickered over Christina's face, barely a second, then she regained her poise. 'Very good. My family is all that remains of the original people, that is why I must do what we have always done.

'Why did you bring us here?' demanded Dean. 'What has happened to Ben and Duncan?'

'You will see soon enough,' she replied, looking down the path behind them. 'It won't take long now that it has started.'

They turned and followed her gaze.

The Not-Duncan stepped out of the trees and onto the rocky path. Still naked it walked towards them, not even wincing as sharp pebbles pierced the soles of its feet. It just kept walking towards them, a strange smile still fixed in place.

A lone tear ran down Oskar's face as he watched it approach. What had once been the love of his life now filled him with terror. Nothing of his husband remained now.

He wiped away the tear and grabbed Jess's hand.

'Run!'

The spiky grass bounced underfoot as they raced along the wall. When they hit the tree line they pushed in and kept running, not stopping until they were deep into the dark shade of the orchard.

Dean looked behind them and saw no one following them.

No sign of Not-Duncan.

No sign of Jess and Oskar.

Shit, how could they have become separated so quickly?

He looked around, trying to size up their options but saw they were limited. On this side of the orchard the orange trees were densely packed together, having been left to grow unchecked until their branches interlocked into an impenetrable barrier. Lower branches sagged under the weight of the plump fruit, on the lowest the fruit resting on the ground, still attached at the stem. He turned his ear to them, listening for oncoming footsteps or the crack of a branch. Nothing. He dropped to his knees and lowered his head until his cheek lay on the dirt, scanning under the trees, only standing up when he was sure they were alone.

If nothing was following them then Jess and Oskar had been less lucky.

He got back up and watched as Shreya peeled an orange she had plucked from a branch, opening it out and giving him half. He stuffed two segments into his mouth, grateful for the sweet juice and the hit of sugar.

'We need to keep on going, keep moving away from the gate and keep ahead of them,' he said.

Shreya nodded and stuffed another segment into her mouth, chewing it quickly.

'Agreed. We can't get through the trees here, but we need to find a way back to the house. If we are trapped here, then we need to be somewhere we can defend ourselves.'

Dean had always loved her tenacity and determination but overnight she had transformed into an Amazon warrior. Despite their circumstances he had to admit it was hot.

She swallowed her final segment of orange and wiped her fingers on her denim shorts. 'Come on, let's go.'

God, he loved her.

They started to follow the wall once more, breaking into a jog where the trees allowed it. He had no idea how far around the property they had gone, it was hard to gauge with the curved walls and dense foliage. Shreya stopped in front of him, spotting a tiny gap in the orange trees. She looked back and waved him forward before turning and slipping into the gap.

He held his breath, listening to the sound of her feet as she walked around inside the trees. 'This way, there's a path through!'

He let out the breath he had been holding.

Branches scratched at his face as he pushed through the small gap, relieved to find himself in a verdant corridor. Shreya pointing at a path she had found through the trees. 'This seems to head back in the rough direction of the house, we're going to have to listen carefully, any sound that isn't us we stop. Okay?'

'Yes ma'am!' he whispered.

She led the way, walking slowly along the narrow path, trying to avoid brushing against any branches, not wanting to give their position away now that they were back in the trees. They had been going for a few minutes when Shreya pulled up quickly. Dean hadn't heard any noise but froze too. He could hear nothing but silence around them. 'What's wrong?' he whispered.

'Nothing. I just… nothing, let's go.' She set off down the track again, cautiously heading forward but her head kept drifting to the left. He followed her gaze, scanning through the gaps in the leaves, but didn't see anything to catch his eye the way something had clearly caught Shreya's. She pushed forward but her pace was slowing, her attention constantly being drawn to their left.

Finally, she stopped at a gap in the trees that ran off to the left and turned.

'Wait! The villa must be ahead of us, we need to keep going and get shelter,' he whispered.

She kept on walking away from the path, giving him no indication that she had heard him. *Fuck, what now?* He turned off the path, following her along the narrow corridor. They had been going for a minute when he noticed that the trees around them were starting to look unhealthy. Dark spots mottled the green leaves whilst wizened skeletons of fallen foliage coated the ground below them, crunching underfoot as Shreya marched them forward.

He reached out and touched a crisp black leaf. It was so dry it practically crumbled into dust at his touch. Every nutrient had been sucked back out of it leaving just the brittle dust that now floated to the ground.

Up ahead Shreya was now standing in the sunlight, staring at the twisted bark of the great tree that rose majestically over the canopy of the surrounding grove.

The same tree they had seen replicated hours before on the label of Ben's beer.

He stared up at the thick branches of the mighty arbor, a sense of wonder creeping over him, dulling his senses as he took in the scene. This tree was the heart of the island that Christina had mentioned earlier. He could feel it. There was an ancient power flowing around him, making the hairs on the back of his neck stand up.

Shreya hadn't moved since he stood behind her but now her shoulders were shaking, sobs wracking her body as she let out a thin wail. Her cry broke the spell of the tree, and he wrapped a hand around her mouth, trying to muffle her sounds, afraid she would give away their location. He pulled her back to his cheek, whispering into her ear, trying to calm her.

As she tumbled back into his chest he froze, for the first time seeing the gruesome tableau before them.

Ben was naked.

Squatting in front of the tree.

His knees were bent out at right angles, arms outstretched with his palms facing upwards in offering.

A thick tube sprouted from his anus, connecting him to a thick root in the ground below. His sallow skin clung tightly to his bones; his skeleton now visible through his mottled flesh.

The tube softly pulsed, slowly sucking all the life out of him, nourishing the mighty tree before him.

Dean walked forward tentatively, peering around his friend's body. 'Ben?' he called out softly, praying for his friend to be dead already.

Ben was beyond their help now and Dean was ashamed that he felt relieved. He knew he wouldn't have had the guts to save him from this slow, torturous death. He walked around his friend, giving him a wide berth as his face came into sight.

Bloody tear tracks ran down Ben's cheeks, but his eyes were cloudy and lifeless. He had died with a maniacal grin on his face, the look of a religious zealot who had finally been called to the ultimate act of sacrifice for their Lord.

Ben's cheek twitched and Dean jumped backwards.

He couldn't be alive.

He stared at the cheek, certain he had imagined it but jumped again as the fingers on his right hands slowly started to move, curling towards his palm. Dean looked to his left hand and saw the fingers had begun to close as well, mimicking the right.

His body was shrinking in on itself, tendons contracting as he was drained. All traces of his blood, water and nutrients being stripped from his cells, desiccating him from the inside out.

He staggered away from the shell of his friend, his stomach clenched, and he threw up, watching in horror as tiny tendrils grew up around the puddle of bile, sucking it all into the ground. He staggered away, wiping his mouth on his t-shirt, and turned back to Shreya.

She was no longer looking at Ben, her eyes were turned up to the tree, arms outstretched, palms raised to the sky.

A small glowing spore drifted towards her open mouth.

He closed the distance between them in seconds, tackling her to the ground, wrapping his arm around her hips then dropping them down to her ankles, forcing her off balance.

She hit the ground hard, her head bouncing off the dry earth below her, blood instantly flowing from a cut to her scalp. He looked back and watched the spore fall to the ground, it settled in the dirt still glowing but unmoving. More tendrils sprung up from the ground, sucking up the blood that was pooling around her head, feeling into the air for the source.

The spore drifted over the ground, tumbling over the surface until its delicate fibres caught a breeze, pulling it back into the air.

Dean pulled Shreya to her feet and reached around for his rucksack, trying to find one of the bottles of water. His sister had spent hours in the garden looking for dandelion seeds to catch so she could make a wish, only to cry when he snuck up behind her and doused them with the watering can before she could catch them. He found one and dragged it out, never taking his eyes off the glowing speck as he popped up the sports cap and squeezed out a spray of water.

The reaction was instant and violent.

Water hit the spore and it sparked into flame sending a tiny plume of steam into the air. It was over almost as quickly as it had begun. A faint burning smell all that remained.

Shreya stood there dazed, one hand pressed to her head to stop the bleeding.

'Oh my god, I'm so sorry!' he said, pulling her up by her other hand. 'I panicked; I knew I couldn't let you breathe it in.'

She looked at him oddly, feeling the strange trance slowly slipping away from her.

She pressed down hard onto the cut on her scalp, the shock of the pain finally clearing her thoughts. Something had been there, a connection building as the light came towards her, she could *feel* it will her on, wanting her to breathe it in.

'I'm sure it looks worse than it is.'

She looked over at the shrinking form of Ben's body. 'Is he…?'

Dean nodded.

He looked up at the tree and could feel it tugging at him, a gentle buzzing noise starting at the back of his mind.

'Come on, we need to find the others and get as far from this fucking place as we can.'

28

Growth was all it had known.

Since the first shoots grew from the rock, the network had expanded. Millennia of life had come and gone, linked together through the ancient energy. Life rose and fell, new growth springing from the rotten mulch of fallen ancestors, the forest ever thriving.

Until the human arrived with steel and fire.

Then it learned survival.

On the other side of the compound the Not-Duncan lumbered after Oskar and Jess.

The Fire inside it was in full control now of the body now, steering its mind and shaping its will.

Time was running out and it needed to pass to a new host, that was now its sole purpose.

The moment the spore hit the host it released The Fire - the parasite's function was simple, push the carriers to spread the contagion to another host before returning to the source. The fungal spores spread the parasite and the parasite helped the spores to source new nutrients.

The hosts were fragile, their bodies violently rejecting the infection within hours unless it either spread or was absorbed. The clock was always ticking.

The Fire searched though the memories of this carrier, identifying both bodies ahead of it in stream of images. The memories with the male involved fluid - saliva, blood, and semen but it found none in the memories of the female. The link with this host was degenerating already, the connection eroding and weakened as the body fought to reject it. It discarded the memories of the woman, focusing purely on the bearded man.

Its name was Oskar.

'Help me… Oskar,' it called after the fleeing pair. The woman staggered on through the trees, but the male slowed, turning to look back at his pursuer.

It had been effective selection.

It raked through memories again, flipping through the rolodex of memories, looking for something it could use to tether the other male.

They step out of the multiplex and Oskar put's his arm around Duncan, drawing him in close. "You told me it wasn't a horror film!" says Duncan, still shaking, "I told you I can't cope with horror! I've never been so scared in my life!" Oskar stops, turns, and takes Duncan's face in his hands and kisses him deeply.

'Oskar, I've never been so scared in my life!' it repeated, copying the tone and emotion from the memory.

Ahead Oskar stopped, looking back at him, searching his face for traces of recognition. It moved slowly towards Oskar, stepping cautiously, trying not to startle him.

'Dunc? Is that really you?' Oskar took a tentative step towards him.

The distance between them closed, the two now alone in the trees as the female still fled, unaware that she was running alone. It needed to win the male over and was on the right track.

More memories.

It could be done mouth to mouth but that carried the risk of rejection, implanting would carry the highest rate of success.

It searched again, trawling for scenes of the men implanting, looking for words it could repeat.

They walk amongst tall pines, hand in hand, Oskar points out an opening in the trees and the duck inside to find a small fort made of wooden pallets stacked up and covered in sheets. Oskar had built it when he had been a boy, he tells Duncan that he had spent hours in here as a child. He drops inside and reaches to the back, pulling out a wooden box. He opens the box and shows Duncan a faded magazine, naked men posing and grinning from the pages. "You dirty little boy" says Duncan and they both laugh.

It senses the growing heat in the memory, watching as the carrier whispers in the bearded one's ear, seeing him remove his clothes, looking over his shoulder as he waits for the carrier who moves towards him.

It looks at Oskar, drawing on the memory, recreating the emotion of the moment.

It pulled the lips into a smile and whispered. 'I'm going to fuck you in your fort.'

The words stopped Oskar dead.

He had been so desperate to believe that Duncan had somehow beaten the thing that had taken him over but now he knew he was gone. He remembered that moment, it had been hot as hell at the time, getting fucked in his childhood hideaway, the place he had dreamed of being with another man, never once believing it would happen to him. The sex had been quick and intense, both coming at the same time. They lay there, their top halves in the fort, bare arses out in the cold Norwegian air. Oskar had tried to hold back the laughter, not wanting to ruin the moment, but the more he tried not the more he started to shake until tears running down his face.

I'm going to fuck you in your fort. They had laughed about that moment for years, whispering it to each other at inappropriate moments, trying to make the other laugh.

Now those same words filled him with sadness.

His husband was gone; he knew that now.

Something else was inside him, controlling him, masquerading as the man he had loved for a decade.

He wanted to kill it, to rip it out of his lover's body and destroy it with his bare hands. Tears welled in his eyes. He knew that he was incapable of destroying the monster before him, it might be an abomination, but it still wore Duncan's face.

He couldn't destroy it.

Behind the mask he could feel it watching him, waiting to see how he would respond.

'I love you baby.' He said, taking a step forward.

The monster inside his lover tilted its head, processing the scene before it. Oskar reached out his arms as he walked forward, the monster before him mimicking his stance. He took another step, keeping his eyes forward, not letting himself look at the broken branch lying to the side as he closed the distance between them. He stepped into reach of the branch and slowed, looking into its face, addressing whatever remained of his husband. 'I'm so sorry my love.'

Oskar dropped to his knees and grabbed the branch from the ground. He raised it behind his head, adjusting his grip on the back stroke so that he held it tight as he swung it forward again, slamming its weight into the middle of its shin.

The blow knocked it off balance and it flailed as it fell, reaching out even as it slipped backwards. It put one leg out to stop itself from falling but its foot caught a stone as it landed, and Oskar hear a crack as it landed awkwardly on the ankle.

Not-Duncan grinned at Oskar as it got back to its feet, but the expression changed as it fell back down, unable to support its own weight on the broken bone.

Oskar couldn't bring himself to kill it, but he could at least slow it down.

It started to get up again. He gave his lover's body one last look then turned back towards the house and ran.

The Fire knew it had failed.

The host was rapidly rejecting it and he could feel the temperature rising in the body. With no chance of spreading now, its focus flipped to the other reason for its existence and turned the host around, feeling the tree behind it.

There was not enough time now, the broken leg would slow it down too much.

It dropped to the ground and pushed slowly through the trees regardless, propelling itself forwards on three limbs, the broken femur dragging behind it.

Branches tore at the flesh as it forced itself through the most direct path back.

It could still feel the tree in the distance but knew it would now fail on both of its objectives.

It dragged itself past Dean and Shreya who had hidden at the sound of its approach, climbing up into the branches, pulling themselves into the thick foliage as it scraped past them, oblivious to their presence, only aware of its destination.

It started to glow as it passed the tree in which they hid.

Its pale skin blistered and popped as it burned from the inside. The hair caught first, bursting into flame, instantly filling the air with an acrid stench as it continued its relentless pursuit through the orchard.

It made no noise as the flames erupted through its crisp skin, quickly consuming it as the rendered body fat fueled the flames.

It stopped moving forward as the muscles burned, no longer able to move the skeleton of the host. Bones dropped to the ground as connective tissue, ligaments and tendons were consumed in the flames until all that remained was a smoldering pile of lumpen ashes.

Dean and Shreya dropped down from the tree, staring through the scorched leaves.

There were no words to be said, not now.

They turned around and walked back down the path towards the villa that lay beyond the trees.

28

Shreya looked around at her three remaining friends huddled around the table in the kitchen. 'We can't stay here; we have to find a way out.'

'I'm sorry but you're going to have to go through it again,' said Jess. 'A fucking tree?'

Dean had been over the story twice since they had gotten back and found Jess and Oskar already back in the house. He did his best to explain it but saying it out loud had made it sound ridiculous.

'I don't know what else you want me to say, Jess, some kind of glowing spore flew from the tree and tried to infect her. Batshit as it sounds that is exactly what I saw. If I hadn't pushed Shreya out of the way she would have swallowed that fucking seed and gone mental like Duncan.' He looked at Oskar who had barely moved since they had made their way back to the safety of the villa. 'I'm sorry mate, you know what I mean though.'

Oskar nodded.

He hadn't cried when they had told him how they had seen Duncan die, how fire tore through him until he was reduced to ashes. He hadn't felt anything. The time for despair and mourning would come later, for now he could only be glad that Duncan was no longer suffering, that for him it was all over.

As soon as he had heard the thing inside Duncan parroting their words, he had known that Duncan's memory was still active, that he was still in there somewhere, trapped, and unable to break free. He couldn't kill it, terrified that the last thing Duncan would have seen was his husband murdering him. Maiming it hadn't been much easier, but it was all he had been able to do.

He shook his head, snapping himself out of his thoughts of Duncan. 'Ben must have been infected first. He vanished twice so we don't know when it happened, but I am guessing it must have been last night. Duncan showed no signs of being anything but himself yesterday so I think he must have been trapped by Ben after we all went to bed. That means sometime after midnight he was infected and by 3am he was trying to infect Jess.'

'If you're right then this thing is really fucking quick,' said Dean. 'Duncan said that he had to give it to you Jess, is that right?'

She nodded.

'Let's assume that Ben was infected in the same way that Shreya almost was. He finds Ben, passes this thing on to him, making him want to pass it on to Jess. It's either reproducing itself or just moving from person to person. Why does it need to spread?'

Shreya stood up, pacing as she thought through it all. 'That's not all it does though, is it?' she asked. Jess and Dean stared back at her blankly, but she could see Oskar catching on. 'At some point after he had passed it along to Duncan, Ben went back to the tree.'

'Maybe he was programmed?' Oskar pondered, looking at Shreya.

She nodded, working through the implication in her own mind. 'Like the ants…'

'Now there are ants?' asked Jess, 'Did you ever see the David Attenborough programme about insects in the jungle?'

'Sorry babes, must have missed that one,' joked Jess, trying to break the tension but failing.

Shreya ignored her, lost in a train of thought. 'Let's take a step back. Everything in nature is a balance, right? Tip the balance and it changes everything around it.'

Given their current situation she found slipping back into teacher mode almost comforting but looking at the three blank faces staring back at her it wasn't going well for them. She had to get them to understand before they would ever believe her theory.

'Okay… I know. In America in the early nineteen hundreds, they decided that the danger posed by the gray wolf to human life and livestock was so bad that they decided to cull them. Great for the humans, bad for everything else as the gray wolf also hunted other animals such as moose, deer, coyotes, beavers, and raccoons. So now populations of those species increased, as did their need for food. So, they ate away at the forests meaning there were fewer places for birds to thrive. Birds who ate the mosquitos and insects that lived in them. And so on and so on. Change in one species impacts everything around them.'

'That makes sense but how is that important here?' asked Jess.

'In the Attenborough programme he talked about a species of ants that were native to a jungle. They are so successful that by sheer size of the colony they are a threat to the balance of the ecosystem, so nature has found a way to restore the equilibrium. There is a parasitic fungus called the cordyceps which releases a spore that get inside the ants and infects them. It takes over their bodies and their brains and makes them climb high into the jungle canopy and then the fungus grows out of their bodies and releases more spores into the air and the cycle repeats.'

'No,' said Oskar, shaking his head, trying erase her words from his mind.

'How do you even know that?' whispered Jess.

'Are you kidding? I must tell that that to every class I teach, it helps them get interested in biology, they all love zombies…'

Jess looked at her in horror. '

'Look, I'm saying that's what is happening but it's as good a possibility as anything,' said Shreya, her voice rising as her emotions broke through her control, the horrors of the last few hours flooding her mind. 'Dean saw some kind of spore try and enter me. Duncan was attacked by Ben who was under the control of something. Ben was sent back to the tree with some fucking tube growing out of his arse, draining him into the ground…'

She clapped her hand over her mouth, trying to stop the words. Jess grabbed her, drawing her to her chest and holding her tight as the sobs wracked her body. 'I'm sorry, I'm sorry, I'm sorry,' whispered Shreya as she gasped for air. Jess rubbed her back, rocking her slightly as her shaking gradually slowed. She could feel the sweat dripping down Shreya's back. The hot and humid room was doing nothing to help their emotional state.

Jess lifted her friend's face up and kissed her on both cheeks. She waved Dean over and he sat down next to Shreya who let herself be passed into his arms.

Jess looked to Oskar and smiled, 'I don't suppose Mr. Attenborough gave any tips on how to stop this fucking mushroom did he?'

'Aren't we missing the silver lining?' asked Dean. 'Ben somehow infected Duncan, but Duncan didn't get the chance to pass it on, did he? It's been more than three hours since he attacked you, Jess; you haven't been infected or we would have seen signs by now. Duncan and Ben are both… gone, doesn't that mean we are safe?'

Shreya sat up and wiped her eyes, beaming at Dean. 'You make an excellent point. Come on, I can't be in here right now.'

She crossed the kitchen and flung open the back door, stepping out into the cooler breeze of the garden. She walked to the edge of the orchard and plucked four plump oranges from the nearest tree, the others joining her, and they sat with their feet in the cool water, discussing their options and peeling fruit.

'If we stay away from the tree then we just have to find a way out of here,' said Jess.

'Easier said than done,' replied Dean. 'We can't go through the gate as Christina will be expecting that. But they might not be looking for us to try and climb the wall though.'

Oskar meticulously cleaned his orange, stripping each segment of the plump, white pith that coated them. His focus allowed his thoughts to roam. He thought about the camera in the bookcase, the website, and the wall around the villa.

'This isn't the first time they have done this,' he said.

No one reacted to his words. Clearly, he wasn't the only one to have come to this conclusion. 'If we take that as true, it also means no one has ever escaped from the island or they wouldn't still be able to do this. People will have tried to climb over the walls, dig their way out, break the walls down. They will know all the tricks and be ready for us at every turn.'

Three dejected faces stared back at him.

'Only if you are right,' said Dean. 'What if you're not? What if we are the first people they have lured here? Or what if this is only the second or third time? We can't assume anything at this stage.'

'Last night,' said Shreya, 'at the bar, he said that they *worshipped the tree and gave gifts to keep balance.'*

'So?'

'*So*, we were talking about the whole species of those trees, but he said, "the tree". One tree.'

Dean knew then that she was right. 'The same tree where we found Ben…'.

29

'Ok then,' said Oskar, 'in that case we need to search the villa. They can clear the house after it is all over but maybe others have been brought here and managed to hide things? Something that might us help get away from here?'

Oskar's plan gave the group a sense of purpose and he could feel the mood change around the pool.

'Ok, let's do this. Check your own room first, look under furniture, behind cupboards, anywhere you could hide something that they might not have thought to check.' Dean paused, remembering their lost friends. 'I'll check Ben's room.'

They rushed off to search their rooms, finally feeling like they were doing something.

There was no one there to see Jess turn around and head out of the front door, pulling it quietly closed behind her.

Finding something in the house was bullshit, she knew that, and she was sure the rest of them did too. There was only one sure fire way to find out what they needed and that wasn't in the villa. Oskar had it right, the set up on the island was way too slick for this to be a first time. Even if they found some sad note from previous victims it wasn't going to do anything to help them now.

It was still impossible for her to process losing Duncan. She had held it together so far for Oskar's sake but her, out of the house and alone for the first time, it hit her.

Duncan was gone.

There were thousands of happy memories of him but the only one she could see was the warped version of her friend standing over her by the pool, dead eyes staring at her as he loomed over her. Even then though he had found the strength to somehow break through and tell her to run, still looking out for her even though must already have known he couldn't control it for long. She heard him telling her to run over and over as she walked. With each plea the despair inside her was replaced by a growing anger.

Christina.

It all came down to that bitch. She was the mayor of the island, all of this was controlled by her, it had to be. The reason behind her actions didn't matter to Jess. They could try and work out what was going on, but simple truth was that Christina had locked them in this place and didn't expect them to be getting out. There was clearly something fucked up going on inside the walls, but Jess was not going to let it take any more of her friends. She let the hatred and anger fill her body until she was shaking with rage, the energy pulsing out of her as she made her way to the gates.

She let out a grim laugh as she saw Christina standing at the gates, waiting for her arrival.

Of course, she knew.

The house couldn't be seen from the gates but still she was stood there, her face hidden in the shadows as the sun rose behind her. They still had eyes and ears on them somewhere in the house.

'You killed them,' she growled, marching right up to the gate. Jess punched her arm through the bars to grab Christina, but her fingers swiped through the air, she had positioned herself just out of reach.

'I didn't kill them, they were given to the island,' replied Christina, unmoved by Jess's accusation. 'None of this is personal, I hope you understand that at least. I am simply doing my duty for my people.' Her hands rested in front of her, fingertips pressed together, thumbs touching to create the shape made famous by Angela Merkel.

'How many have died here?' Jess demanded.

'You ask an impossible question. The sacrifice is older than both of us, generations people have given their lives in this place. It is had been the noble duty of my family for hundreds of years.

'Sacrifice implies we had a choice,' snarled Jess. 'If it's so fucking noble, why don't you give yourself up? I'll be the mayor and you can be the sacrifice.'

'You must excuse me, but I cannot stay and talk, I am needed back in town. I'm sure you understand.'

The mayor turned from the gates and walked towards the red Jeep parked at the side of the road.

'Get back here you bitch!' yelled Jess.

Christina opened the door and turned back to the gate.

'I don't enjoy this, but it is necessary to keep my island and my people safe. You judge me, I know that but sometimes it is necessary to put the needs of the many over our own.'

'Cut the morality crap. I don't give a shit about why you are doing this, but I *am* going to stop you.'

'Please don't try and escape.' Christina raised her fingers to her mouth and gave out three sharp whistles.

Jess turned and looked along the wall, hearing scraping noises on the outside. Fifty feet along from the gate Jess saw a head appear from behind the wall; Mateo, or was it Mathias, stared at her, brandishing a long spear.

Crude but effective.

There was a gap along the wall and then another head appeared.

Another gap, another head popping into position.

On both sides of the gate people were climbing up behind the wall, standing on some kind of lip running along it, high enough to reach over the top and stab at anyone trying to get over.

'We take this very seriously; you can see that this isn't a game to us. You are surrounded, you are not going anywhere.'

She climbed in the Jeep and started the engine. Before driving off she rolled down the window and shouted back at Jess.

'When we arrived here on that first day, I told you this place was called the orchard of the gods. That was a lie. La Arboreta del Dios means the *grove of the God*. We will all do everything we can to make sure you never leave this place; we will not fail the Heart Tree.'

'You fucking cunt.' Muttered Jess.

She turned away, unwilling to give Christina the satisfaction of watching her drive away.

It had been a mistake to come to the gate. She hadn't learned anything that could help them, she just felt defeated.

The villa came into sight, and she saw the others come running out of the house, calling her name. They spotted her and ran, huddling around her and walking her back inside.

'We thought you had gone to the tree,' said Shreya, visibly shaken. 'Dean was just about to go after you into the woods… Where did you go?'.

Jess couldn't answer her.

If she spoke now, she would lose it, the tears would come, and she was afraid she would never be able to stop them.

30

For an hour they searched the house, feeling along shelves, behind the pictures on the wall, looking for anything out of place. Christina had known Jess was coming so it was a safe bet that they were still being watched somehow but their combined surveillance knowledge taken from the James Bond back catalogue and the Bourne films revealed nothing. If there were hidden cameras or microphones, then they were well placed as their search turned up nothing. They gathered back together in the kitchen, empty handed.

'Does it matter if they can see us?' asked Shreya. 'Maybe there aren't any bugs hidden around the place, maybe they are watching the outside of the house? If they have done this to others before us, then it's not surprising that they seem to know what we are doing before we do it. We are just repeating a familiar pattern to them.'

Oskar nodded. 'You're right. We need to be different.'

He went to Ben's bedroom and started to empty it of its contents. Ben's suitcase, still packed, came first, then the lamps, his bedside tables, and his mattress, all were stacked up in a pile in the lounge. By the time he got to the bed Dean had joined him and they worked it out of the narrow doorframe together. He stripped the walls of their pictures and mirrors, until the room was just an empty shell.

'I need some tools or some masking tape,' he said. 'And bedsheets.'

Jess grabbed the sheet from her bed as Shreya ran outside, returning moments later with a small box boasting a paltry selection of tools. He grabbed the hammer and a small bag of nails.

Within a few minutes he had tacked the sheets over the walls and windows, covering them completely.

Dean ripped the light fixture from the ceiling, leaving only the exposed bare wires hanging down.

It was stuffy and dark in the room, but at least they were sure that no one could see or hear them.

'Well done MacGyver,' said Jess, dragging two duvets into the room for them to sit on, 'I'm assuming they wouldn't hide anything in these? I thought we might also need this,' she said, holding up the bottle of bourbon she had spotted in Ben's suitcase.

Shreya grabbed the bottle from her and pulled the stopper out, marveling at the racing horse perched on the top. 'I hate bourbon, but this looks expensive and strong.' She took a swig and passed the bottle to Dean.

'Ben always brings a bottle of bourbon and stashes it in his room, I think he likes to top up his levels on the quiet. Liked to…,' said Dean.

Oskar took a sip and passed it around to Jess, lost in his own thoughts.

'To Ben and his secret, expensive tastes,' she said and put the bottle on the floor.

They settled into the bedding, each lost in their own thoughts. The sudden stillness of the room let the demons crawl into the corners of their minds, the dread building up as they relived the previous hours and contemplated their short futures.

'No!' said Dean, sitting up, 'Fuck this. Fuck this island and fuck Christina! We WILL get off this island, we just need to work out how.'

Oskar sat up, happy to be dragged away from his thoughts of Duncan. 'Ok, so what do we know then. We can't go over the wall as they will be watching and waiting.'

'Same for going under the wall,' said Shreya, 'even if we could somehow dig under, they would be waiting.'

'If we still had the car, we could crash through the gates, but they clearly know that trick,' said Jess, 'It certainly explains why they got us drunk in town and ever-so-kindly offered to drive us back.'

'Well, if we can't get out could we get them to come in here, then?' asked Dean. 'Maybe we could draw them in somehow, escape out of the gates whilst they are distracted?'

'Not bad at all,' said Shreya.

Oskar nodded in agreement. 'That's good, but how do we get them in? What would make them risk breaking the perimeter? If they are all around the wall, then there must be at least a hundred people out there.'

Jess was trying to contribute, think of clever plans to help but she couldn't concentrate. Her head was buzzing. She kept thinking of Duncan attacking her. The shock of seeing him looming over her, naked and hard.

The vibration in her head was building.

The others were all clinging on to hope but she couldn't see how they were going to get out of the compound, Christina seemed had thought of everything before they had. Her thoughts turned to the tree where Dean and Shreya had found Ben's body. Everything was linked to it. *La Arboleda del Dios.* The tree was the god that Christina had talked about. It had somehow infected Ben and Duncan, nearly taken Shreya earlier that day and clearly Christina expected it to take the rest of them soon.

They had to be different, that is what Oskar had said and he had been right. Fighting Christina would never work from behind the gate, and they couldn't get out of the gate without beating her. They had to be different…

A plan was emerging in her mind; she already knew there was no way that anyone else would agree to it.

This was something she was going to have to do alone, she couldn't risk getting the others involved in any way. If she was making a mistake, then it would only be her that suffered because of it.

Oskar and Shreya were deep in tactical conversation, so no one questioned her when she made her excuses and went to the bathroom, locking the door behind her. She dropped the toilet seat down and turned the tap on to a slow trickle. With the water running she grasped the edge of the window frames and pulled herself up, hiked her legs over the edge and dropped to the flower bed below.

The buzzing was louder outside but she pushed it away, letting her anger at Christina fill her mind instead as she stepped into the trees.

Out in the open air she heard the hum return once more, softer this time, guiding her to the Heart Tree. As she stepped into the tree line her confidence increased. There was no more fear, just a new sense of purpose. She focused once more on her hatred for Christina as she made her way through the gaps in the branch. The path she was following meandered through the trees, leading her deeper into the shaded wood. She forced herself to start straight ahead as she passed a section of scorched branches to her right, the acrid smell of smoke still hanging in the air.

There was no need to look, it wouldn't bring him back.

She sensed the tree before she saw it.

Then the trees ahead thinned out and she was in front of it. It was suddenly strange to her that they had feared something so beautiful; so pure and ancient. The humming that had led her from the house faded away now that she was in front of the Heart Tree. Shreya had described it, but her words could never do it justice. Its trunk looked like it had been thrust from the earth, an explosion of sinews shaping themselves into a living, breathing organ. The scaly bark had split, like the tree had swollen, cracking its armor the flesh engorged below it. Thin trails of red blood seeped from the cracks in its skin, oozing down the trunk into shiny puddles that pooled where the roots met the soil.

Jess stepped forward and placed her hands against the bark, showing no fear as she spread her fingers over the umber husk. A rivulet of the viscous, crimson liquid ran over her index finger, clinging to it as she pulled her hand away and sucked at the sanguine nectar. It was at once bitter yet sweet, bursting with rich minerals.

It tasted of life.

She had made the decision; she was sure of that now. Her eyes never left the Heart Tree as she stepped backwards and waited.

The glow started slowly, barely perceptible in the bright morning sunlight. She wouldn't have spotted it had it not been for the deep shadow cast by the canopy of the tree. They were all over the tree, a vast string of pulsing fairly lights that reached from limb to limb.

Please let me be right she thought.

One of the glowing fungi flared brightly and she saw a single luminescent spore begin to drift towards her.

31

It was Shreya that had finally spotted that Jess was either doing an incredibly long piss or something wasn't right. When Dean had kicked open the bathroom door and seen the open window, his mind immediately torn between worry for Jess and anger that she had, once again, gone off on her own and put them all at risk. If they couldn't stick together and work as a team there was no hope of them getting out of this alive, why couldn't she see that?

He had wasted valuable time running to check the gate but as soon as he saw the road was clear his heart sank; he knew there was only one other place she might have gone.

He ran into the trees, yelling to the others, hoping they could hear him shouting out his destination as he crashed through the branches. This time there was no attempt at caution, he covered his face with his arm and plowed through, squinting to protect his eyes from the branches that whipped at him as he ran.

Jess was already kneeling in front of the tree when he got there, her mouth wide open like Shreya's had been hours before. In the daylight he wasn't sure if he could see a spore or not but there was no time to second guess, the priority was to get her out of there and back to the villa.

She didn't respond when he called her name but apart from being barely conscious, she didn't look to be injured. Just because he hadn't seen a spore it didn't mean she hadn't already been infected, if she had then they would have to deal with that later.

Behind him he heard Shreya breaking through into the clearing behind him. Between them they half dragged, half carried her back to the safety of the villa, manhandling her in their urgency to get her as far away from tree as possible.

Once they had her back inside and settled on a duvet, safe once again the sheet lined room, she began to come around. Her mouth moved as she was tried to tell them something but what came out was a jumble of words that didn't make any sense. Over and over, she muttered that she had the pictures, growing increasingly frustrated by their confused looks on their faces. The more she tried to explain the more her words deserted her, until she finally gave up and sank back into the pillows, her lips still moving as she fell into a deep sleep.

The three friends stepped out of the room and gathered outside the door, wanting to be out of earshot but not trusting her to be left alone again.

'What just happened?' whispered Shreya.

'Fuck knows,' said Dean, 'She either decided to pay a visit to the tree or she was drawn to it. Either way we've got to assume she has been infected.'

'What do we do?'

'Nothing,' said Oskar, 'we secure her here and keep an eye on her. When she wakes up, we will know if she is different.' He grabbed a sheet from the bedroom next door and took it to the kitchen.

'Then what?' asked Shreya, watching as he used a pair of scissors to it into several long, thin strips.

'I honestly don't know. For now, we just tie her up while she is out and then we decide what to do when we know more.'

Jess murmured softly as they bound her hands and feet together but never woke up. Oskar made sure the strips were tight enough to keep her in place without hurting her then sat back and watched as she fitfully slept.

At first the rapid stream of images was overwhelming. A nauseating deluge of moments in time that joined together into a jarring time lapse of the island's past. Jess saw the island morph from a barren volcano to a rich microcosm, vital and thriving, each organism playing its part in the life cycle of the island in the never-ending change of the seasons. Mighty storms battered the island in stop motion displays, rogue waves covered the land but each time it recovered, new life replacing the old, just as it always had. The story changed as people arrived on the island in great boats, settlers clad in old-fashioned garments sent to claim foreign lands in the name of other kingdoms. With each image the forest shrinks, great sections of the forest were cleared, replaced by strange crops and shelters built from the timber they harvested. The rudimentary shelters grow into houses as more people settle, a church appears then a school, more sections of the original vanishing as they carve their way deeper and deeper into the island.

In her deep state of sleep the images flowed, one after another, layer upon layer of the island's history building until her mind could take no more.

Jess woke with a start, her eyes adjusting slowly to the dim light in the room, the sun having long since disappeared behind the hill.

'Hello, sleeping beauty,' said Oskar from the floor next to her.

She went to sit up but found herself held back by the strips of material that bound her.

'I'm sorry,' said Oskar, 'but we had to be sure you weren't infected.'

'How long have I been out? What happened?' She remembered being at the tree but then nothing until she came around in the shrouded room.

'All day. Dean found and we managed to get you back to the villa, but you were out of it. You've been asleep ever since.'

She had been having a vivid dream, snatches were still there but the more she tried to remember, the quicker the memories faded.

'Well, hopefully we can all agree that I haven't been infected?' she asked, holding up her tethered wrists.

Dean and Shreya traipsed back into the room, watching her intently, looking for any signs that she was anything other than Jess.

'Boo!'

They jumped but soon were smiling as they saw the glint in her eyes.

'It's fine, I get it. It didn't infect me, and I don't think it wanted to. I know how that sounds but I also know it is true. I can't remember what happened while I was asleep, but it showed me everything, why all of this is happening, and I think it showed me how we can stop all of this. Something… I just can't remember what we are supposed to do.'

'A few days ago, I would have had you sectioned for saying the trees were talking to you,' said Shreya 'but given our current predicament nothing can surprise me now.

They cut the ribbons from her wrists and ankles and filled her in on what she had missed - thankfully that seemed to be nothing. They had eaten more oranges and brainstormed ways to get off the island but all in all they seemed to be no further on than they had been hours before.

Shreya went to the kitchen and brought back some tea lights and dropped them into jars, lighting them with the long matches Duncan had bought days before. Shadows danced around the room as the candles caught, burning brightly then dipping low until the wax melted, feeding the thin wicks with fuel.

Dean went over some of the possible plans they had come up with, but Jess didn't hear him. She stared into the jars on the floor, afraid to look away as she parts of the dream began to drift back to her. The tiny flames crackled behind the glass and piece by piece she remembered. The only problem was going to be persuading the others but based on what seemed to have come up with so far hoped that wouldn't be too difficult.

'I know what we have to do,' she said, the plan now taking shape in her mind.

They would agree to her plan, she was sure of that, the only thing she had to be careful of was that she didn't tell them the truth.

32

Outside the wall Christina paced, walking between the monitors and the gates, straining to get any sign of the members of 4. They had followed the same pattern as the previous three groups until now:

> Stage one - panic as they work it out
> Stage two - determination to escape
> Stage three - failure to escape
> Stage four - resignation
> Stage five - submission

But with 4 something had changed. They were the first to have found one of the cameras and since that discovery they had found a way to go silent, somehow managing to evade their cameras and microphones. When this was all over, she was going to have to work out how to avoid this happening again. Build this into the scenario plans before Batch 5 arrived in the new year. It must have been moving the can that had blocked the camera in the living area. It had been a risk, but they couldn't afford to lose their eye in the house.

Each group had forced them to evolve and develop their plans so that they made it as seamless as possible. This was just another learning point; it was nothing to worry about.

And yet she was worried.

There was a moment of relief when 4-J had reappeared in one of the garden cameras, sneaking out of the house and then heading inevitably into the trees. It had been a good sign of things progressing in the compound, she had even allowed herself a moment of excitement, hoping it might even mean they could skip the whole escape scenario if the infection could be spread quickly.

She was blind to 4-J once she entered the trees, but her path seemed set. They had never managed to get cameras into the trees, every time they tried the forest had rejected them; stray branches knocking them from the trees, vines growing through the lens… bees had once built a hive around one unit.

It had been made clear that they had no place in the woods.

There had been enough gossip in town about this group, whispers of things going wrong tended to circulate quickly. A quick email update informing the inhabitants that 4 were on track should help cut the noise, she could hint that there was a chance this batch could end early. God knows they could all do with the boost of an early completion. Helé had been particularly affected by her unexpected encounter in the store. Ultimately it had been her own fault but looking 4-S and 4-J in the eye had left her shaken. She had already vowed to keep the shop shut for the duration of any future batches.

Yes, an early completion would bring the Thanksgiving Festival forward which would do them all the world of good. Three groups had taken its toll on them all this year, taken its toll on her as well.

She went to hit send but stopped as a blur in one of the monitors caught her eye, 4-D1 was out of the house and approaching the gate. The screens were old and too small to make out any detail but, even so, it was clear that he was agitated and looking for his missing friend. The slightly blurred figure on the screen stopped as the gates came into view, then turned and ran into the trees.

She willed herself to send the email but didn't, better to be sure before she raised their hopes.

Christina hadn't known she was holding her breath until her lungs contacted, forcing stale air from her lungs.

The relief of oxygen back into her bloodstream was cut short as she spotted more movement at the rear of the property, 4-S and 4-O running into the forest, chasing 4-D1. Christina guessed he had called to them but couldn't be sure. Microphones needed to go into the model revision once this lot was complete.

Her eyes didn't leave the screen for the next five minutes. She stared until her eyes burned, not wanting to miss a thing but nothing was moving out there.

Fuck.

She slid back the window and shouted up to Mateo who held his post at the top of the wall. 'Perimeter visual?' He scanned the grounds from his vantage point and shook his head.

'Negative. Visual right?'

The call went out around the wall, each look-out scanning their zone and reporting. The cry came all the way around the wall until it reached Mathias at the left of the gate.

No one had a visual on any one of 4.

From the intelligence they had managed to gather so far, the batches had all reacted in a relatively similar manner, but the timescales had varied so lulls in activity were not uncommon. This group had only been on the island a matter of days and already two had offered which was a good start, if the spread continued as it had, it would be their most streamlined to date. She knew she shouldn't be concerned at this early stage but this blindness inside the house was troubling.

Too many mistakes this time.Maybe there was some complacency creeping in already, three successful groups creating a false sense of security. She would hold more practice drills once this was over, build in some new protocols, they needed to be on the ball if they were going to keep this going.

It wasn't the lack of visuals that was really troubling her though, something felt different this time.

Christina was born in the shadow of the forest; her father taught her to fear and respect it before she could even walk. He was the mayor of the island as she was growing up, even as a child she felt the weight of his burden. In private he taught her about her heritage, explained how the burden of caring for the island had belonged to her family since anyone could remember. She found the lessons dull and boring, wishing instead that she was out having fun with her brother. She resented him for the life he had whilst she was cooped up, learning about ancient history and governance.

Her father made her skulk outside his office door when the villagers came, listening to him deflect their pleas for clemency, begging for the lives of their children. He never wavered, always sticking to the rules that had been set out generations before, a tithe of the first-born child per family, no exceptions.

Learning the theory was all well and good but it wasn't until she was fifteen that the reality of the rules hit her.

Her father had told her that it was Marco's time, as the eldest child of the family he had a sworn duty to the island when he came of age. She had helped him dress for his big moment, taking pride in the ceremony of tying his tie for him, making him look his best on such an important day.

He cried when he hugged her goodbye, hating to leave her alone, begging her to be strong for her father.

When the time came her father had walked him to the villa, the men of the village following behind the two of them. Of course, looking back she knew they weren't there to support Marco; they were there to stop him running from his fate.

Her father did his duty to the island but never fully recovered from the loss of his son.

But from that day forward no one ever came to him asking for their family to be granted exemption.

Despite her father's tutelage, she had never truly grasped the fact that he wouldn't be coming home. Two days later she had gone with her father to gather his remains and the reality had hit her - he was gone. Nothing remained of the brother she loved but his bones, stripped clean by its savage hunger. She cried as they harvested the dull ivory from the orchard floor and laid them in the ceremonial basket.

Her father had bled the tree, as was their custom, then daubed her brother's skull with its ruby essence until it gleamed in the sunlight. She bore it to the cave on a matt of thinly woven reeds, eyes never leaving it, staring at the excess sap as it slowly dripped through the gaps in the mesh, leaving a trail of red pearls to mark her way home.

It wasn't just her father that broke from the loss of Marco, something snapped in Christina too. Suddenly she found herself stifled by island life, everything she did and everyone she saw was a constant reminder of his loss and the pointlessness of their small existence. It crushed her until she could bare it no more. One night she slipped away from home and stowed away in the boat that ferried the locals to the big island once a week.

Despite being fifteen, alone and broke she managed to survive on the mainland. She was smart and soon learned how trusting the tourists were. They had no reason to distrust the pretty, young girl selling tickets by the boat tour sign, lost in their holiday mode they simply handed over their cash for the next departure and didn't even see her disappear into the crowds. By night she hid in the music and lights of Playa del Ingles, the constant throng of tourists that distracting her from thoughts of home.

Who knows, if she hadn't become pregnant, she may even have stayed there - instead she found herself making the return journey six months later, her belly already pushing out of her skirt.

Back at home she found herself once again obsessing over Heart Tree.

She spent hours walking around the walls that bound it, pressing her hands to hot bricks as they baked in the sunlight. It called to her in those moments, a tiny hum probing away in the back of her mind, seeking out the life inside her. She had known the ultimate price of returning to the island but there had been no other option for her.

The birth of a child should have been the happiest day of a mother's life, but when it finally happened for Christina, she had sobbed for hours, unable to look at the crib at her side. The constant wailing made her nipples ache, the pain growing as she failed in her duty to feed, denying the nourishment required. It was too much for her to bear. She had steeled herself to her duty, knowing her first born was never hers, the need of the many coming before her own maternal instinct. But now her faith had been tested in the cruelest manner, demanding a choice of her that she never could make. She would not make.

Her maternal instinct overwhelmed her fear, and she held out her hands to the midwife, she was ready. The first, sharp pain of a tiny mouth latching on to her left breast hungrily sucking down the colostrum that it had been craving. Then a gasp as she the second baby clamped onto the right, not willing to share all the precious milk with its twin.

She decided in that moment that she would devote herself to finding a new way to satiate the hunger of the island. She decided to risk the future of the island, whatever the cost.

She would never choose between her boys.

The solution finally came to her by accident eight years ago, not long after the twins' seventeenth birthday. Tómas had been out fishing and spotted a yacht adrift, two people waving from the deck, desperately trying to get his attention. When he reached them, it was clear that their boat was dead in the water, so he took them onboard, hitched their boat to his and slowly towed them back to shore, radioing Christina on the way back. Their gratitude from the couple began to diminish as the spectre of their impending doom wore away and by the time they had docked the pair were already becoming demanding - greeting Christina with a list of needs and little in the way of humility.

Perhaps if they had been more gracious her passing thought might never have turned into action.

An opportunity had fallen into their laps, and she wasn't going to waste it. Convincing others to help hadn't been as hard as she thought, looking at the island register two couples had children coming of age in the next month and they had been quick to offer their support to secure the lives of their first born. Twenty-four hours later Tómas had dragged the empty yacht back out to sea and set it adrift where he knew the current was strongest. A week later their boat was spotted off the coast of Africa and the couple were reported missing, presumed dead. It had all being shockingly easy.

Once word got around that two children had been saved parents began to show up at her door, begging her to find alternative offerings to take the place of their own children. Her father would have turned them away, but Christina couldn't, not with her boys rising closer to the top of the list.

Her own time living on the main island had taught her how anonymous it could be and for a while plucking stray tourists had worked. No one linked a few disappearances; in the end they were chalked up to drunken misadventure or accidental contact with some of the cartels that used the island to move their drugs from Africa to the Spanish mainland. It had worked to a point, but a few mistakes had made her nervous enough to start looking for alternatives ways to find people, something more controllable.

Gustavo Fuentes, a student of Computer Science at the University of Palma and former inhabitant of the island, had finally convinced her that advertising a villa was the answer they were looking for. He was able to show her that they could attract a sizeable group to the island without leaving a trail. They would place an ad online for a fictitious villa on a different island and he would hide all traces of their involvement. He had tried to explain how he hid his IP address, used VPNs and a host of other methods of cover his tracks but he lost her early in the discussion.

It was agreed that communication with potential guests was her responsibility. Gustavo created a Gmail account to which they both had access and she wrote the emails and saved them in the draft folder, he then copied and pasted them onto a different email address on a computer that he had made effectively untraceable.

Nothing would ever lead back to the island.

Over the years the link to the woods had vanished but the day she had delivered Batch 1 to the villa she felt the humming of the trees return to her. They had held a great feast in the square in celebration, thankful to the strangers that had given themselves in place of their children. The celebration had felt forced, the smiles on their faces too wide but still they rejoiced, pushing the murders to the furthest reaches of their minds, dancing away their guilt.

It was murder, she knew that, but she watched her sons grow and felt no guilt. Better a stranger than her own flesh and blood.

But when 4-D1 had first responded to her ad Christina had considered telling him that the villa was unavailable at the time; a group from the UK felt like too big a risk.

The Canaries relied heavily on tourism from the Britain and there were strong diplomatic ties between the two islands for obvious reasons. If a group of their citizens vanished you could bet it would generate a shit storm and that was something she wanted to avoid - God knows the British press loved a holiday disaster, plastering them on the front pages with carefully worded headlines designed to shock and sell.

She had gotten as far as contacting her man on Gran Canaria to terminate the enquiry, but he had persuaded her that they should go ahead and, if Gustavo said it could be done, that was good enough for her.

Besides, they were already too far along the path with the Batches to back away now, no-one on the island wanted to go back to the old ways now. All that had really mattered was that she trusted him enough to agree to go head.

Gustavo was the first child saved from his fate by this sacrifice of strangers; more than anyone he understood the consequences of getting it wrong.

But Batch 4 wasn't going to plan at all.

Despite her reassurances, things were very different this time. Ever since 4-J had gone into the woods and been brought back she could feel that things were changing. Somewhere in the house they were plotting to get out and she had no fucking idea what they were planning.

Christina swore as she saw the four surviving members of 4 stumble from the woods and back into the villa.

Nothing further happened on screen and by midafternoon Christina admitted to herself that 4-J most likely hadn't been infected. If she had there would have been some evidence of that by now. There were no screams, no panic, no movement, nothing but a still calm from inside the walls.

She paced until the sun disappeared behind the hills and darkness fell around her.

She poured herself another cup of coffee and stared at the dark screens, willing the four remaining offerings to die. Just. Fucking. Die.

Moments later her worst fears were confirmed.

For the first time in eight years, the humming in the back of her mind stopped.

She had been cut off from the island.

33

Oskar listened as Jess outlined the plan to them, trying to forget that it had come to her in a dream sent to her by a tree as she slept.

Despite his scepticism he had to admit it wasn't half bad and was certainly better than anything else they had brainstormed whilst she slept.

'I don't like it,' said Dean. 'If she's wrong then it could basically be suicide. What guarantee do we have that we won't be offering ourselves up for the taking?'

'We don't. But I know that, whatever it is, it has had enough and wants to take back control. Taking the four of us isn't going to do that. It wants as many as it can get, it wants control of them all.'

'Trees don't think Jess, they just…are!'

Shreya perked up at Dean's words, casting her mind back to a lecture she went to a year or two before. 'Actually, that's not true. There have been loads of tests done to show that trees and plants communicate it lots of different ways. Some trees in Africa release chemical warnings to their neighbours when giraffes start to graze on them, allowing them to produce a toxin in their leaves to stop the giraffes eating them. There was also something about whole forests communicating via root systems and vast fungal networks that run through acres of woodland at a time.'

'I don't know how to describe it, but I felt it *all.* It was like I was part of something huge, bigger than I could ever have dreamed of.'

Since she had woken up Jess had taken on a calm, considered approach that was new a little unnerving to all of them, it was almost more disconcerting than their actual predicament.

Oskar was already convinced. One way or another this was going to be their only option, they had spent the whole day going around in circles, this was different.

'I'm in,' he said.

Jess nodded at him and looked over to Dean and Shreya.

Dean shook his head but stopped when Shreya spoke. 'I don't really remember being at the tree before, but I've seen what it can do, we all have. If we do this, we can assume it won't treat us any differently than anyone on the island, so we need to protect ourselves and create a safe place.'

'Of course,' said Jess. 'We need to get ourselves prepared before we go, and we need to do it at night. If they have cameras outside, I want to minimise the chances of us being seen. What time are we on now?'

Dean sighed and checked his watch. 'Nine o'clock. Okay, I'm in too. Not like we have much to lose at this point and I'm fucked if I can think of anything else. What do we need to do?'

Jess went over the plan again, trying to convey everything she had seen and heard. Once they set the wheels in motion, they would have to move quickly so they spent the next few hours getting themselves and the villa as ready as they could.

It was agreed that the bathroom would be their best option as a safety bunker and Oskar and Jess set to work prepping it. They secured it in any way they could, taping off the window, covering gaps and making it as airtight as possible. The sink and the bath were plugged and filled with water; the overflow drains stuffed with wet tissue. They didn't know how long they would have to hide out, but it would be at least a day, maybe two, so the water would be both a defence and a necessity.

Dean and Shreya gathered armfuls of oranges from the trees, each keeping watch over the other in case they showed any signs of veering into the woods. Neither did. They washed them in the kitchen sink and then dropped the clean fruit into the bath. They gathered anything resembling a weapon and armed themselves. Anything that could be used against them was stacked in the shower, safer in their hands than in anyone else's that might find them.

Oskar and Jess set about securing the rest of the villa. They nailed the bedroom doors shut, blocked the back door with the sofa and used the rest of the tape to secure the whatever drafts they could find. They raided the barbecue room, grabbing lighter fluid, matches and charcoal, throwing all the remaining tools, plates, and crockery into the pool, safely out of reach.

By midnight they had protected the house as best they could and turned the bathroom into a bunker of sorts. It wasn't perfect but it would have to do.

They gathered by the front door, two suitcases standing between them, full to bursting with cans of hairspray and insect repellant, charcoal, lighter fluid and matches from the barbecue room, papers, magazines, and the splintered remains of the dining room chairs.

Once they started there would be no going back. No one seemed ready to open the door.

Dean took Shreya by the hand and pulled her into him. 'I love you. This is not at all how I planned to say those words to you, but I can't to go out there without having told you that.'

She wiped away the tear that ran down her cheek. 'I know you do, and I love you too.'

She turned and looked at each of them. 'We are going to get out of this mess, you hear me? All of us. We will not lose anyone else to this hell hole.'

Jess stepped forward, grabbed the handle of one of the cases and pulled it to the door.

'We do this now, for Duncan and for Ben.'

She blew out her candle and opened the door into the dark.

They followed her out of the house, following the sound of her case rolling over the stones until their eyes adjusted to the moonlight.

Their progress through the trees was slow, the cases caught on the uneven ground, unseen branches clawing at them, roots tripped them as they pushed forward in the absolute darkness that surrounded them. Once they were deep enough into the woods, they decided they would be safe enough to relight a candle to help them on their way.

No one talked as they traipsed through the trees. Planning had been one thing but as the reality of the hours and days ahead sank in so did the doubt and the fear. Jess was the only one who walked with confidence, her certainty that they were doing the right thing increasing the closer they got to the tree.

After the initial struggle through the trees the journey seemed to become easier. There were no more roots tripping them up and the gaps between the trees seemed somehow wider. Step by step their control increased, and their confidence grew as they were seemingly allowed safe passage into the heart of the woods.

Oskar was the only one stepping into the clearing for the first time and the last of them to set eyes on the tree. It was truly majestic. He knew that the roots of trees reached well beyond their crown so, given the staggering breadth of this specimen, its roots were already winding below their feet.

They had come this far and been granted passage, he had to take that as a good omen.

He looked around and stopped at the sight of a scarecrow under the tree.

No, not a scarecrow.

The gold Casio watch hanging around one of the spindly arms was the only evidence that the decrepit remains had once been Ben.

For the first time he found himself glad that Duncan was dead.

Better to have burned before he could get back to the tree to be used as mulch, his life sucked out of him ounce by ounce. He just prayed that Duncan hadn't been able to feel it, that any trace of him has been destroyed long before the flames tore through his body.

He contained the rage that built up inside him, binding it tightly up inside him out of fear that he would lose control and let the others down. He felt a strange respect for the ancient power he felt here, but it paled in comparison to his love for Duncan. He was looking forward to what came next, even if he knew it would only help the island, it would be action.

They unpacked the cases, quickly sorting them into piles of fuel and ignitors.

With the cases empty it was quickly apparent that they had seriously underestimated what they would need. Back at the villa the two cases had felt excessive but now Jess saw how insignificant it was. They could have brought a case each and still not have had enough.

'Scour the tree line for more branches, only grab dry wood from the floor, branches that haven't fallen will be too green. Oskar, you're with me, Shreya you go with Dean. Stay close and yell if you see any signs of light.' The other three looked at her, shaken by her warning. 'You won't, I know it, but it doesn't hurt to be vigilant.'

The two groups splintered off to hunt for kindling but soon regrouped. There was scant wood to be found around the clearing; here the trees brimmed with life leaving the ground clear of dead wood. Ignoring Jess' warnings, Dean tried tugging at some of the lower branches, hoping to find something that might give but nothing shifted.

They debated their limited options. The outskirts of the compound were lined with weak, dying trees but scouring the woods in the dark would take them hours. There was little left at the house that they could bring over either, what was left too cumbersome to lug through the trees.

Dean was suggesting they return to the villa to try and break up the dining room table when the first cracking sound split the night.

He spun to around, trying to pinpoint where the sound had come from, fearing the worst.

At the edge of the clearing a thick branch was sagging from the trunk of one of the healthy firs, swinging under its own weight, losing its battle with gravity. Its healthy green needles were now shriveled and dried, barely clinging to the branch.

A moment later they heard a small split and it fell to the ground.

Oskar ran over to it, dragging it away from the tree and back to the group. Jess felt along the branch, crushing the dead needles that clung to it, digging her nail under the bark and smiling as it crumbled away. She felt the jagged points where it had split from the tree.

The wood was completely dry.

'It's helping us,' marvelled Shreya.

Another crack to the west of them cut her off.

Dean ran to the edge and returned seconds later dragging a second huge branch. The trees around them exploded with the sound of splintering wood, the noise deafening in the still of the night. By the time the noise had died away the ground around them was littered with kindling, great boughs sacrificed by the woods, the survival of the whole greater than the needs of the individual.

They quietly reaped the limbs that had been offered to them, in awe of the true power of the island. Stacked at the base of the trunk, their desiccated branches reached up into boughs of the mighty tree above. Dean wrapped tea lights into balls of paper and stuffed them into gaps in the branches while Shreya sprayed lighter fluid on the dry wood surrounding the base of the tree.

Oskar hung the cases by the handles at the top of the pyre, not wanting to waste anything that could burn.

They exhausted all their supplies and moved back, admiring the stack they had built around the trunk.

Dean took out two cans of hairspray from his pocket and gave one to Oskar. 'Are we ready?'

They all nodded.

He moved to the back of the tree with Oskar and handed him a lighter. 'If this catches before we get back, you lot run, got it? Straight back to the villa and into the bathroom. Ready?'

He held his lighter in front of the can and sprayed. Plumes of flames shot out from the tiny nozzle, the dried needles catching immediately as the flames hit them. Oskar followed suit and they circled the tree, spraying short, controlled bursts, targeting the fuel-soaked balls. They moved quickly around the tree in opposite directions, setting sections ablaze as they went.

Reunited at the front of the tree they watched the fuel-soaked branches quickly catch, the fire spreading through the small branches and spreading upwards towards the trunk.

As the heat rose, they saw they fungus on the tree begin to glow, tiny spots of white light appearing as the heat rose, catching spores as they were released, carrying them high into the night air.

'Run!' yelled Dean.

34

Christina had somehow managed to fall asleep.

She had been watching the screens, her head propped up in her hands, until her eyes closed as her exhaustion kicked in. Something had woken her, there had been a cracking sound in her dream. She wiped the thin trail of drool from the corner of her mouth and used her sleeve to blot the tiny puddle on the tabletop.

CRACK!

The sound hadn't been in her dream.

She leapt out of the van. The sound was already dying off, but it had come from inside the compound.

'Report!' she yelled.

'There was one crack, then another, and then it sounded almost like gunfire. I don't know what it was, it all happened so quickly,' said Mateo.

Mathias nodded in agreement, backing up his twin. 'It all came from the direction of the Heart Tree, Mama.'

Christina climbed the ladder and took a stand next to him.

Beyond the wall silence had once again fallen. There was nothing to see in the darkness, just the faint silhouette of the tree line.

She dropped back down to the ground and set off running clockwise around the wall, trying to get closer to the heart of the woods. That was where the noise had come from.

The grounds of the villa were vast, deliberately so to ensure the containment of the spores. She ran past fifteen sentries, all standing to attention at their posts, staring into the dark. She called out for updates as she ran but nothing changed, no one had seen or heard anything different from the twins.

It took her five minutes to run a quarter of the wall's circumference, bringing her to the marker for the spot closest to the Heart Tree. The sentry at this point had nothing new to share so she called him down, taking his post on the wall. She stared into the dark, straining to see anything unusual in the silent woods.

Darkness.

There was nothing but darkness in the trees before her, the gentle rustle of leaves on the breeze. Then a sudden cry, the word unclear but the urgency palpable.

She begged for this to be another infection, someone shouting in fear, trying to escape.

Silence reigned again but now she noticed that the sky above the woods was brightening, a dull orange glow flickering in the canopy of the trees, barely noticeable. The first faint wafts of smoke drifted from the woods but by then she already knew what they had done.

'Puta Madre!' she cried, cursing 4.

Broken glass sliced into her palms as she gripped the top of the wall, but she felt nothing as she strained into the dark surrounding the villa.

Inside her skull the humming kicked in, vibrating louder and harder than she had ever felt it. She clamped her hands against her ears, trying to block it out but it rang ever louder, jubilant in her ears. She dropped to her knees and closed her eyes, pressing her forehead against the cooling brick wall. The buzzing calmed slowly, gradually dimming away entirely. The silence was blissful and for a moment she forgot about the fire. Shouts all around her brought her back and she jumped up from her knees, once more scanning the tree line.

Tiny, bright orbs floated on the night sky, born high by the heat of the flames they drifted along, lighting up the trees and the surrounding walls. The shouts of the guards had stopped, they stared instead at the orbs, coasting on the breeze. Hundreds of them, flying in different directions, some rising high above the trees, others coasting low, hovering above the canopy as they sailed towards the wall.

'Don't look at them! Abandon your posts and head for town, now!' she screamed.

No one heard her.

They were lost to the spores that homed in on them, their mouths slowly opening as the distance between them closed. She jumped down, landing heavily on her ankle. Ignoring the pain cursing from her already swelling ankle she ran back around the wall, ran back to her boys. Around the wall every face was turned upwards in wonder, ready to take a spore.

She picked up her pace, keeping tight to the curved wall. She had covered most of the distance when she saw the first one cross over the wall and into the mouth of Joseph Martin, the butcher's eldest son. He took it happily, swallowing it down. She pushed herself harder than she had ever run, she didn't have much more to give but pushed on regardless.

As she rounded the final section she saw Mateo, still standing at his post, his mouth open, eyes staring ahead at the glowing ball that floated towards him.

'No!' she yelled.

Two meters was all that separated them, but he couldn't see or hear her; his world now reduced to the bright light that entranced him.

Christina leapt across the final distance and swiped at his ankle, hoping to knock him off balance before it was too late.

Her heart surged as she felt her hand grasp him. She shoved his leg with all her might, and he staggered backwards, automatically waving his arms to try to regain his balance. He nearly caught himself, but his body had passed the tipping point and he fell backwards from his post at the wall.

But she had seen it. One second was all it had taken. As he fought to balance the spore flew forwards and closed his mouth around it as he fell.

Christina screamed as he hit the ground.

He lay there unmoving and for a second, she hoped the fall had killed him; saved him from turning; saved him from what now lay ahead for him.

At the other side of the gates the primal pain of his mother's scream broke Mathias from the hold of the spore that floated towards him.

He ducked away from it as it sailed past him. He grabbed his bottle of water from top of the wall and filled his mouth, spraying a fine mist at the spore that had changed direction, heading back towards him, flying at him against the gentle wind of the night.

The spray hit the spore and it hissed as it burned.

He looked up and saw his brother lying motionless at his mother's feet. 'Mama?'

She sobbed as he jumped down and ran over to them. 'He swallowed one, I saw it happen. Even if he seems alive, we have lost him.' Mathias turned his brother over, frantically feeling for a pulse. He hammered on his chest, willing him back to breathe as his mother watched. She shook her head, tears pouring down her face. 'It's too late, he is gone! Get back to the town before it is too late. Back to town and hide, too many have turned already, it is not safe here now.'

'No! I have to try.' He pounded against his chest, mimicking the chest compressions he had seen in movies. He pushed down repeatedly on his chest, pushing his palms against his twin's ribcage. Christina screamed again as he bent forwards and pinched his brother's nose, locking his mouth against his brothers and forcing his breath into his lungs. Mathias's eyes widened as the air was forced immediately back into his own mouth, choking him in surprise.

It had only taken seconds for the spore to take control of Mathias and it wasted no time in taking the first opportunity it had to spread, passing into the lungs of the nearly identical host.

Christina staggered backwards, staring at her boys, both lost to her in a matter of moments. She had done everything in her powers to protect her boys but now they had been taken from her. She had been greedy and paid the ultimate price.

Mathias sat back on his heels and watched his brother get to his feet. There were no final words for the boys who had been inseparable for twenty-two years. Mateo simply turned away from his twin and, without a look back, climbed the ladder and jumped over the wall into the grounds of the villa.

There were no thoughts in the mind of what had been Mateo moments before, the only instinct now was to get back to the Heart Tree.

When her other boy turned his head, towards her, Christina could see that he was already gone.

Her only hope now was to get to the van and head to town, there was no hope of survival if she stayed here. Sixty people guarded the perimeter wall, and it was safe to assume that nearly all would have been infected by now. Spores floated around her, but she kept her eyes down and clamped her hand over her nose and mouth.

Mathias stared at her, no trace of love in his eyes, just a pale imitation trying to trick her.

The keys were in the van; the engine was still running to keep power to the screens in the makeshift operations base. It was only fifty feet away, if she could slam the door she should be able to make it. She prayed the windows were closed as she didn't have time to wind them up.

Mathias watched her body, sensing the change in her movements.

'No Mama,' he said, taking a slow step towards her, raising his arms in a hollow embrace.

'I love you my baby, Mama loves you.'

She jumped to her feet but had forgotten her injured ankle.

It buckled beneath her, sending her sprawling forward. She tried to break her fall but tumbled to the ground. Before she could push herself up Mathias had closed the gap between them and jumped on her, straddling her back, pushing her face down into the dirt.

'I love you too Mama.'

He leant down, his mouth brushing against her ear.

She bucked underneath him; the shove lifted him off her, but she wasn't strong enough to shake him off her back. He landed heavily back on top of her, winding her as the full force of his weight crushed her lungs. She tried to breathe but still he pushed down on her, grinding her face into the dirt. She couldn't breathe and her arms were trapped to her sides. She rocked desperately, trying to dislodge him enough to get some air.

As she flailed her hand rubbed against the knife on her belt.

She was close to passing out, her lungs burning as they fought for oxygen, but she knew she still had one more chance. She curled her fingers around the handle of the knife, slipping it from the holster until she had a firm grip. Angling the blade upwards she thrust it with everything she had left.

It cut through the air before connecting with his torso, the knife slicing through flesh and muscle. His leg gave way under him, and he slipped sideways on her back, hanging side saddle from his mother. She gulped in fresh air at the sudden relief of pressure, pushing upwards as she did. He fell back enough for her to get out from underneath him and back on feet. Despite the injury he jumped up to grab her but immediately fell to the side, the wound in his left leaving him physically unable to bear his own weight.

Christina backed her way to the car, unable to look away from her boy, still brandishing the knife at him. Her hip connected with the rear of the car at the same time as she heard footsteps approaching from behind. She scrambled backwards, running her left hand along the van, feeling for the handle, too afraid to look behind her.

Her hand hit the cold handle and she spun, opening it and leaping into the safety of the van. A hand reached through the window as she slammed the door shut. Fingers grabbed at her hair, but she had already slid the car into gear and floored her foot on the accelerator.

The car jumped forward, knocking down a dark-haired man before she had even seen him lurch into view. She turned the wheel and drove the car forward, rolling over his legs and down the road towards the village.

35

The heat rose behind them as they ran through the trees, retracing their route and alert for any sign of light around them. It was the same path as before but their easy passage they had received earlier was now gone. The trees seemed closer together, branches clawing at their faces and snagging on their clothing, slowing them down as they tried to push through.

Dean pushed forward, carving out a path for them but soon came to a halt at a fallen tree. 'We need another path through. Spread out and yell when you find a gap'.

They moved along the trees, probing in the dark for a break in the branches.

'Here!' shouted Jess, her voice coming from somewhere to his right.

He followed it, checking Shreya and Oskar were behind him. They set off once again, starting to gather pace this time. He looked back through the trees and could see soft green light starting to illuminate the treetops behind them. The glowing blobs were still a way behind them but seemed to be following their progress.

From somewhere ahead he heard the crack of wood snapping, followed seconds later by the long creak of a tree slowly falling, its leaves tearing from branches as it collapsed against its neighbour. They walked forward and found their route blocked once more.

Any detente they had apparently forged with the woods had clearly been terminated, their part now complete.

The sky above them started to glow, lit by three bright orbs swirling overhead, waiting for a clear spot to descend.

'Don't look up!' shouted Jess.

Oskar was already staring up, mouth open as he watched them in wonder.

'I'm sorry Oskar,' she said as she slapped him hard across the face, snapping him out of his trance. He looked at her with a dazed expression. 'Come on, we've got to get away. Keep your eyes down, let's use the light to find a way out of here.'

The four ducked left, pushing through the trees, determined to get back to the relative safety of the villa. Dean barged his way through more densely packed trees, until he emerged in a tiny clearing. The light around them grew brighter as they huddled together, taking a moment to catch their breaths. Dean looked at the shadows on the trees around them, careful to avoid looking up, they were elongating rapidly which had to mean that the spores were moving quickly. 'Back into the trees!'

He dragged Shreya behind him, ignoring the pain as branch after branch tore into his face. He prayed Jess and Oskar were still with them but couldn't look back, he had to keep moving them forward into the cover of the trees.

'Wait!' cried Jess from behind them, pointing through the trees, 'I think can see the house ahead!'

He peered through the gloom, heart surging as he spotted the outline of the roof. Somehow, they had ended up at the side of it in their struggle to find a path through. The had planned to emerge directly opposite the back door, allowing them to clear the open patio quickly and get themselves to the safety of the bathroom. From here though they had a much longer run to safety: across the open patio, past the barbecue room, around the pool and on to the back door.

It was risky but they had no other choice.

The light from above them dimmed as the spores moved away, illuminating the house as they drifted along towards the villa, their dull glow almost daring them to make a run for it.

'Shit,' said Dean, 'it's too far. It's almost like they know what we are trying to do.'

'What if we go around the front? Cut through the woods and aim for the front door?' asked Oskar.

'You see how we have been blocked so far, there's no way we will be able to get around the front,' he replied.

Shreya grabbed Dean's hand and pointed, 'The spores will try to get to us as we run for the villa.' She stopped, working through a plan in her head. 'So, we let them.'

'Are you crazy?' he cried, 'we haven't come this far to just give up.'

'What is the one thing we have seen that can stop them?' she asked.

'Water.'

'Exactly. We let them get close to us as we cross to the door, but instead of running around it, charge straight ahead, bomb into the pool, make the biggest splash we can and take them out.'

The pool was a few hundred yards away, if they kept their heads down Jess was sure they could make it.

'Let's do it,' she said. 'What do we do if we don't hit them when we jump in?'

'Stay underwater,' replied Dean. 'Hold your breath as long as you can if it goes dark, we know got them, if not then kick with your feet, get water flying everywhere.' They had seen the apparent consciousness of the spores, seeming to follow them through the trees, looking for their best opportunity to attack. Dean just hoped they were reacting to visual cues rather than some kind of telepathy, if that was the case they were truly screwed. 'Take a big breath as you jump in. Everyone ready?'

A thin line of trees stood between the group and the pool. They each took a clear spot and lined up, ready to plunge out into the open air.

'Go!' shouted Dean.

Oskar was first out, quickly followed by Dean and Shreya. Jess lurched forward but was yanked backwards as her branch snagged the back of her hoodie, choking her as she fell backwards. She reached behind her, frantically working her fingers into the hood, trying to set herself free. Her fingers found the hooked limb and snapped it, jumping to her feet as she released herself. The others were close to the edge of the pool, but she was too far behind now to risk following them.

They were almost there but the spores were fast, closing the distance in seconds as they soared towards them. Jess watched as the spores moved to the side of the pool, anticipating the shortest route the door for the runners. The misdirection bought the others a vital moment, by the time the spores noted that they weren't changing direction, the group were airborne. They leapt at the same time, tucking their legs up and shaping themselves into tight balls. They hit the water arse first, sending jets of water into the night air, droplets spraying high and wide as they sank below the surface. Jess saw two bright flares as the spores were hit by drops of saltwater followed by an angry fizz. Steam rose from the pool in plumes as the inert spores sank into the darkness. The remaining spore zipped over the water briefly then returned to its lone sentry above the door to the villa.

Jess crept as close to the edge of the trees as she dared, watching the water settle into pool. There wasn't enough light for her to see any shapes in the water, the remaining spore casting a meagre glow which barely reached the edge of the pool. The others might mistake the gloom for success, Jess worried they would take the chance to get out and flee into the villa. There was no movement on the surface, so she stripped off her hoodie and wrapped it around her face, tying the arms tightly over her mouth. Now ready she watched the water intently, ready to break cover as soon as she saw anyone move.

Ten seconds ticked by without anything breaking the surface. Twenty. She was starting to worry that something had gone wrong when she saw the top of a head rise out of the water. The spore immediately moved towards the pool, dropping low to the ground, moving slowly this time, gliding stealthily above the stone flags. She heard a deep breath and then saw two more domes break the surface, oblivious to the creeping light beyond the wall of the pool.

It began to pick up speed.

Jess broke from the trees as quietly as she could, silently covering the ground at pace. The spore reached the pool, rising over the water. Shreya and Oskar ducked below the surface at the sight of the light, but Dean kept his head above the water, caught in its sights.

She wasn't going to make it.

She pumped her legs faster but there was still twenty feet to the water and the spore was moving quickly forward towards Dean's open mouth.

She had to risk it.

With 10 feet to go she pushed off from the ground, hoping that she had enough momentum to carry herself over the remaining distance and into the pool. She clawed through the air, drawing her legs up and tucking herself tight as she started to drop. She felt her bum hit the water just as the edge of the pool scraped up her back, ripping her t-shirt and drawing blood. Water sprayed forward and she saw a bright flash as the back of her head connected with the edge of the pool.

Then she felt nothing.

36

The town was deserted when Christina pulled up to the square.

The sky above was still dark but to her right she could see a faint glow in the sky, a fake dawn rising in the north. She leapt up the stairs to the doors of the town hall, fumbling with her keys in her haste to get inside. People had to be warned but she couldn't risk sounding the town alarm, that would just bring people out into the streets where they would be easy targets when the spores arrived.

The office was simple but effective. A large wooden desk, framed by portraits of her father and brother, dominated the room. The portraits were initially raised as a reminder to those who had come seeking her leniency after her father passed away but were now simply a reminder of her family, lost to the spores.

A small collection of silver photo frames sat on her desk, pictures of her twins beaming out at her. She turned them down one by one, treasuring the memories but unable to cope with the pain of seeing them now. There was no time for distraction.

Her fingers punched out Anita's number on the old melamine phone as she shook the mouse on the table and the computer hummed to life. Anita answered after two rings, her groggy voice sharpening as she heard the tone in Christina's voice.

'Anita, the worst has happened.' She paused momentarily, trying to find the right words, strike an authoritative tone when all she wanted to do was cry. 'Don't leave the house, try and secure your bedroom, block off the windows, wet towels and put them at the bottom of your door. Do you hear me?'

'Of course.'

Christina could hear the fear in her voice. She brought up the emergency contact plan and forwarded it to Anita.

'When you are safe, I need you to open your email and start the calls on the emergency cascade. We need to warn people now. Repeat my instructions to them and have them cascade it as planned. We need everyone to hear this message as soon as we can.'

'Of course, nińa but tell me, what has happened?' she asked, her voice trembling, fearing the words she knew would come out of Christina's mouth.

'The spores are coming.'

She printed off the list and for the next ten minutes she made her way through it, repeating the message to scared islanders until she was sure that phones were ringing all over town. The news was being passed on, but she knew that also meant that the fear would be spreading. There was still no noise out in the streets, she just prayed everyone would get the message and stay inside. It was the best she could hope for now.

The square grew brighter as she called until it looked almost like daylight. In her panic to warn everyone else she hadn't considered her own situation. The spores were coming and she wasn't ready. Everyone on the island knew the bathroom was the safest space to hide should this very moment arise; around the island she knew others would be blocking of any entrance routes and filling the bath and sink in case they needed to submerge themselves.

They all knew water was the only way to stop them.

Christina grabbed a towel from the office's bathroom, soaking in the sink as she plugged the bath and began to fill it.

She stretched the sodden towel out along the gap between the office door and the floor, but it barely covered one of the doors. It was never going to keep them out.

She ran back into the office and grabbed the curtain from the window, yanking it from the rail. The thick curtains pulled the wooden pole out of the wall with them, the loose pole swinging as she bundled up the heavy curtains and dropped them into the slowly filling bath.

From her office she heard a soft thud as something hit the floor.

The one remaining screw still holding the pole to the wall had given, pulled out by the weight of hard wood swinging from it. Through the door she saw it rocking on its end, briefly swaying before gravity pulled it inevitably downwards, falling back towards the window.

In that moment everything stopped.

Christina prayed for a miracle, but no higher powers were looking out for her tonight.

The pole struck the middle of the large old pane, crashing through it, sending shards of glass cascading into the square below.

Light shone through the broken glass as the first of the glowing snowflakes drifted over the rooftops and down into the square. She watched their unnatural movement, tapping at windows, looking for ways in. There was no time to run now or gather supplies, this would be where she hid.

She slammed the bathroom door closed and stuffed the wet curtain into the gaps, making it as airtight as she could.

How had it come to this? Her beloved boys were gone, and she hoped she would never have to see them again. Mateo was already called to the tree, but she couldn't bear to see

Mathias again. She had no idea how many were infected and by morning that figure would likely be doubled or tripled as the threat spread. Somehow her idea to save her boys had ended up bringing about the end of their community, she had killed them all through her selfish need to preserve her own family. Maybe her father had been stronger than her. He had respected it more than her, had given up his son to pay the cost of living here and made sure everyone else towed the line. She had been foolish to think she could ever work in harmony with something so ancient, so evil. She had failed them all by bringing strangers to the island instead of doing their own duty. But it had worked so well for so long! They had brought people to it, and it had let them live their lives. Everything had been good before 4 arrived. Something had changed this time and out-thought her.

How had they been able to set fire to the Heart Tree? She had no doubt that the flames had fed the spores, giving it strength, it would never have had on its own. Perhaps the fire would destroy the damned thing, maybe something good could still come out of this. They could rebuild, start again, no more fear, no more sacrifices.

And yet she knew that wasn't true. The Heart Tree had allowed itself to be set alight, it knew the price and hadn't feared it, allowing them to set it ablaze.

That could only mean it would survive.

A gentle noise interrupted her thoughts, the sound of a moth flickering against a light bulb. A spore softly fluttering at the locked door, probing for a way in. She had no weapons, nothing to defend herself, if it got through a gap her worries would be over one way or another. The idea of ending it all was almost tempting, just give in now and make it all stop. Religion had never been good to Christina, so she had no delusions of an afterlife. Her boys were gone and there would be no reunion in a tunnel of light. No, for her the attraction was more prosaic; simply avoiding spending the rest of her life without them.

She was lost in her thoughts, staring vacantly at the jar of tea lights that she kept by the bath. Those moments when she could just hide away from the world and soak in the tub seemed so far away now. There was no music softly playing or flickering candlelight to soothe her mind today.

Christina made herself get up and stared at her reflection in the mirror, barely knowing the woman staring back at her. The strength that the islanders had relied open for so long had taken its toll, but the last twenty-four hours had turned her into someone she didn't know.

No.

Despite everything she was still the mayor, and she was not going to go down without a fight. This was not the time to give up. The memories of her candlelit baths had shown her another way out.

Christina grabbed the box of matches from behind the jar of candles and climbed on the edge of the bath, reaching up as high as she could. The match sparked on the first strike, filling the air with its unmistakable scent. She lifted it to the metal rose in the ceiling and waited.

As an official building her offices had been fitted with security systems to protect them should anything go wrong. A shrill beep rang through the building, the sound deafening her in the tiny, tiled room. Seconds later water burst from the sprinkler system, spraying water into the far corners of the office.

The bumping outside the door stopped and Christina smiled for the first time in hours.

The Heart Tree may have found new allies in 4 but she could still beat them all. She still had a village to protect, and she would avenge her boys.

She wasn't going to hide in the bathroom as it all went to shit around her.

37

Time stood still as Oskar waited, lungs burning as he forced himself to stay underwater, eyes straining through the salt water, looking for any sign of light above.

He couldn't hold his breath much longer. There was no sign of Jess, but she had to be down here. The sound of her head cracking against the concrete had carried clearly through the water. He knew she was somewhere, doubtless unconscious from the sound he heard.

In the dark he turned around once more, frantically feeling for her in the depths of the pool. His night vision was still returning after the brightness of the spores but through the murky water he spotted her floating and unconscious. Her hair drifted around her still face, eyes shut, blood clouding around the back of her head. He grabbed her by the arm and pulled her to the surface, calling for the others between gulps of air. Between them they managed to haul her lifeless body from the pool and into the safety of the villa.

In the safety of the bathroom Oskar put his palm flat on her chest and began pressing down repeatedly, short sharp compressions as he begged her to breathe. They couldn't have come this far without her, and he wasn't going to let her down now. He kept the compressions going, counting down from twenty, pausing long enough to allow Shreya to force air into Jess's lungs before restarting the countdown.

He jumped at her cough, warm water spraying them as she cleared her lungs.

Shreya and Oskar fussed over her, treating her wounds with the sparse supplies they had to hand. Dean slipped out of the bathroom to secure the rest of the house, wiping tears away from his eyes as he checked everything was locked. Jess had nearly lost her life to save his, he hoped he would have her courage if it ever came to it. He dragged furniture against the doors, wedging them shut as best he could and returned to the bathroom. He locked the door behind him and pushed a wet towel into the crack at the bottom of the door.

All they could do now was wait out the coming storm.

Jess had been quiet and withdrawn since they had dragged her from the pool. She lay in the corner, wrapped in a duvet, staring at the wall. No one had been able to draw her into conversation, so they simply kept an eye on her, looking out for signs of concussion or anything more sinister.

The minutes dragged by. There was nothing to be said now, they had done all they could for the time being and none had the energy to think beyond the room. Oskar now wished they had thought to bring spare clothes into the bathroom. His shorts were damp, clinging to him when he changed his position, fabric digging into his thighs.

He grabbed an orange from the bath and took his time to peel it, taking the skin off in one long, thin coil of peel. It spiraled downwards as he dug his nails into it bit by bit, the scent of the oil in the skin filling the still air of the small room. He had nearly unraveled it all but at the last moment it split, and the weighty orange ribbon dropped to the tiled floor. He hadn't been aware of them watching but when they all groaned in disappointment he smiled.

It was going to be a long night.

For the first hour the window to the garden had glowed, softly lit by spores as they drifted through the air, seeking out human hosts. Gradually though the sky dimmed as they spread further afield, leaving them once more in the dark as the seemingly endless night dragged on. It was quiet outside of the bathroom but occasionally they would start at the sound of a scream cutting through the silence, before settling back as the silence returned.

They took turns sleeping, trying to get as much rest as they could while they had the chance. Oskar drifted in and out of sleep, his mind wandering between dreams and thoughts. He felt Duncan's hand slip into his as they walked in the woods near their house, comfortable in the shade of the trees. They talked for hours and laughed about stupid things they had done in the past, reliving memories and holidays, New Year's Eves in cities around the world, tiny tokens of love they had made for each other and kept, forever cherished. Finally, Duncan let go of his hand and walked away through the trees.

Oskar woke with tears running down his face. It was as close to goodbye as he was going to get, he tried to hold onto the feeling as long as he could. Jess wrapped her arm around him, pulling him in and spooning. They cried silently, clinging onto each other as the day started to dawn outside the bathroom window. By the time the sun rose above the hills they were all awake again, eating the breakfast of cheese and oranges that Oskar had pulled together.

'God I would kill for one of your coffees right now Oskar,' said Shreya. He smiled at her and wished they could be having a normal morning on holiday, laughing about the night before over lattes and bacon. They lapsed into silence again, each lost in their own thoughts as they ate more orange segments.

The daylight had brought Jess back into the fold, the fug of the previous night slipping away with the darkness.

'It's been four hours since we set the fire," said Jess, 'but it seems too quiet out there. Do you think the spores will all have either taken or died out?'

'If I had to guess I'd say the spores themselves have a relatively short life,' said Oskar, "but so far that is the one thing we haven't seen. We've stopped them but never seen them die out naturally.'

'So how long do you think we need to hide in here?' whispered Shreya. She was sure no one could hear them but was still reluctant to risk any noise that might give them away.

'I don't know,' said Oskar. 'Twelve hours? Twenty-four to be safe? We think it was around six hours between Duncan being infected and… passing.' He paused, choking the crack in his voice. 'Anyone around the wall will have been infected quickly and will need to spread, if they can't get in here that would mean them heading into town. They seemed to be programmed to return to the source so they will probably cut off at a certain point and come back here. They only have two functions; to spread and to feed, they won't risk failing on both fronts.'

'And what happens if they can get in here?' she asked.

'Then we fight our way out and we get out of here. If they get in, then there is a way out. They will either come through the gate or over the wall. Either way the wall won't be guarded anymore, and we can climb over and make our way back towards the town.'

Something had been troubling Dean since they started to plan. He hadn't wanted to vocalise it before but now he couldn't keep it to himself any longer. 'We know they have help on the main islands, Christina told you that, right?'

Jess nodded.

'I'm guessing they know about the power this place has and can't risk it spreading to the other islands,' he continued, 'that must be why they hide what is going on here. Let's assume we get out of here and make it to a bigger island, what then? We have no passports; we can't use our own tickets as they will know who we are. How do we get away?'

'We contact our families, we call them, and they can help us to get out,' said Jess.

'Telling them what? We're on the run from a dangerous tree, don't tell the authorities because they are all in on it? We'll sound crazy. Even if they believe us, it risks being found before we can get off the island.'

Shreya sat in the dark, her fingers rolling over the mesh of the necklace she still wore from the other night, memories of the old lady running through her mind.

'We need to get to the shop,' she said simply.

'What shop?' asked Dean.

'The place I got this necklace,' she replied, reaching behind her neck to undo the clasp, suddenly desperate to take it off. At the time she hadn't thought anything of but thinking back now, the old lady in the shop had seemed to know who they were, her only surprise had been to see them standing there when she hadn't been expecting them. She had been quick to spot that the receiver of the old phone hadn't been sitting in the cradle properly.

There had been no warning call for her, the same call that had likely cleared the square.

No one wanted to hang around to watch the doomed tourists arrive, their very absence betraying their complicit shame.

As she pictured the shop again all Shreya could think of were the tables tucked away in a corner, adorned with bikinis, sunscreen, and hairdryers. They were the remains of previous groups of holiday makers that had never left the island. The necklace had been brought here by someone like her, someone that had long since died and rotted in this godforsaken place.

'They take everything from the villa to that fucking shop and sell it on,' she said.

Jess knew Shreya was right. They weren't the first group on the island, they knew that now, but the sheer volume of clothes and belongings they had seen put it all into perspective for her. Dozens of people, maybe hundreds, had died in this place and they would keep dying unless they ended it now.

'Why there?' she asked Shreya.

'If they take all their possessions there maybe they take everything there.'

'The passports,' said Dean.

'Exactly. We break into the shop, find the stack, and hope we can find four that look enough like us to be able to use them then get home.'

'What do we do if they haven't kept them?' asked Jess.

'If you have a better plan, I'm all ears…'

No one had anything.

'The thing I don't get is why it would decide to kill all the humans on the island now?' said Dean. 'If it needs to feed on people, what is it going to do when it has had them all? It's not like it can store them all for when it's hungry. Can it?'

'Shit. You're right,' said Oskar. 'This thing isn't going to kill everyone. That isn't in its interest. All it will do is take enough to bring the balance back to the island, reduce the impact that people are having.'

'And this is bad because…?' asked Dean.

Shreya swore under her breath.

'Because it means that we won't have a clear run out of here at all. There will still be people in the village, people around the shop, near the boats…' She thought through the implications it would have and didn't like where it took her.

'What if we are wrong to hide out until things die down? Maybe we should use the chaos in town as a distraction to slip away.'

As dull as it was to sit around in the bathroom there still wasn't one of them that liked the idea of leaving its comfort and security to venture back out into the island.

Oskar stayed silent, mulling over a further problem.

If there were going to be survivors on the island then this wasn't going to stop, they would also need to make it impossible for them to tempt in any visitors in the future.

38

Christina waited in the bathroom until she saw daylight light creep around the edges of the door frame.

Outside the door to her office was quiet, the water had long since stopped spraying, but she could still hear the occasional drip but nothing more. She opened the door cautiously, ready to slam it shut should anyone be outside but straight away she saw that her office was clear.

The breaking of the window had inadvertently helped her. From the outside her office would look like it had already been attacked, the smashed window and curtain pole jutting through the glass putting off any would-be attackers. She edged to the opening and looked cautiously down into the square, trying to stay out of sight.

Across the way a door opened clumsily, yanked open by hands that seemed unaccustomed to gripping, like a child picking up sticks with a grabbing hand for the first time. Marco Sanchez stepped through the door of his house and walked awkwardly down the three steps. Ordinarily he would have leapt down the stairs, Marco was always rushing to get somewhere, never walking when he could run. But she saw now that the Marco she knew was gone. This one ambled slowly but with clear purpose, crossing the square before heading down the road towards the villa.

She watched him until he disappeared out of sight.

For more than an hour she stood watch, counting the numbers of people she saw that were infected. She saw twelve more follow Marco's route to the villa, three of whom she knew had been stationed around the wall at the villa. They had been forced to come back here to spread which had to mean there was likely no one left uninfected around the wall.

If 4 were still alive they would be uncontained by now.

She hoped they were all dead but based on their actions so far though she feared they would be safe and hidden away, already plotting their next move.

Christina ran the maths in her head, trying to work out the worst-case scenario. Fifty-six men stationed around the wall, if even half of those came back to the town the rate of infection would be a disaster.

The island population was small, just over a thousand people, mostly congregated around the town. It wouldn't take long for the infection to spread. She clung on to hope though, it was entirely possible that they had failed to spread. It was five hours since the spores were set alight and just under an hour's walk to the villa they could well be returning before the spores inside them perished.

She had seen the results of previous batches trying to save their members by tying them up, hoping that they would find a way to save them. They always burned fast and bright, reduced to little more than ash in minutes. If she was right, the men had failed, then that gave her hope for the rest of the island - this was still a situation that could be salvaged. If there was any hope of stopping 4 escaping and then she needed to get an idea of the spread of the infection before she could pull together a strategy to salvage the situation and exact her revenge for the death of her boys.

The sprinklers had knocked out the power in the office, so she was relieved to hear the familiar hum when she put the phone to her ear. There was something to be said for an old-fashioned phone line.

Anita answered on the first ring. She hadn't dared unplug it in case Christina called but had kept it close to her, scared the noise would attract unwanted attention. They hadn't had vibrate mode when her old melamine dial-up phone was made.

'Hello?' she whispered, her mouth pressed to the phone, trying to make as little noise as she could.

'It's me. Are you both safe?' asked Christina.

'Yes. Someone tried to get through the front door, but Tomás had nailed it shut and they gave up. What is going on out there?'

'I don't know how far the infection has spread but I have seen signs that it might not be as bad as I feared. Can you see anyone in your street?'

'Let me check.' There was a soft clunk as Anita placed the receiver down, followed by silence as she cautiously made her was to the window, avoiding the creaky boards of the house she knew so well. Minutes later she returned. 'Felipe Marin is outside, trying to get into people's houses.'

'Felipe? Jacobo was one of the sentries on duty last night, he must have come back and infected his father. Is the rest of the square empty?'

'Yes, I can see a few people watching from their windows, but no one has gone outside yet.'

'Ok, we need to ring around again. Call everyone and tell them to overpower any infected they see, tie them by the arms and legs and leave them in the middle of the street. It is too late for anyone infected, make sure you tell everyone that. They cannot be saved. Our only hope is to stop them where they are and leave outside them to burn. Got it?'

'Of course. I will call right away.'

'We must get everyone to safety. Tell everyone who can to head to Iglesia de Santa Maria, bring food, water and any kind of weapons they have. And tell them to be on the lookout for anyone from 4. If anyone sees them, I want to know about it.'

She hung up the phone and grabbed the same, sodden list as before. She dialled a handful of others and repeated the conversation, calling them to action. The town once again rang with the sound of phone calls, the plan whispered from house to house.

This time it wasn't the sound of panic, it was the sound of control being taken back.

Her stomach protested loudly; she hadn't eaten for hours. There hadn't been time to grab supplies when the window broke earlier, and she couldn't remember the last time she had put anything in her. Fortunately, her office had a small fridge, big enough for chilled beers and wines to placate the most agitated of visitors and some food for herself. There had been no power for hours, but the plate was still cold to the touch as grabbed it from the top shelf and took it to her desk, tearing off the cellophane in her hunger. The food was good, and she tucked into the spiced potatoes with gusto. It wasn't until she had wolfed down half the plate that she stopped.

She sat back and looked at the plate of food. Mateo had brought it to her last night when she had come back from the villa for a rest. He had told her that she needed to eat and had brought her a mixture of her favourite foods from the restaurant.

Tears welled in her eyes as she looked down. This would be the last plate of food her baby would ever make for her. She put down the fork and pushed the plate away. How could she eat when her boys were gone? None of this was important now, she couldn't be expected to carry on in a world without them. She could still taste the mojo that covered the potatoes. Mateo had brought it over, but it would have been Mathias that cooked it for her earlier in the day.

Christina picked up her fork again and ate, savouring every bite. He had made this for her with love, crafting the food he knew she adored not knowing it would be the last he would prepare for her.

Energy flowed back through her as she scraped up every drop of sauce from the plate, her purpose returned by the love of her boys.

39

The sun burned down directly onto the mottled glass of the bathroom window, quickly heating the small, draft-free room until it became hard for them to stay. The temperature rose steadily as the day wore on, even with shutters the heat seeping through the windows was relentless and by early afternoon they agreed to try and escape the compound while they could. If they were right and the infection had been more limited than they expected, then it wouldn't be long before someone worked out that they had been left unguarded.

They gathered up their bags, filling them with the remaining fruit and supplies. They saved their bottled water and packed it away, drinking from the bath instead.

'If we are going to be leaving soon, can I please have a moment alone in here?' asked Jess, pointing at the toilet. She had been trying to deny her body for over an hour and was rapidly losing the battle. She shoved them out and locked the door behind them, wasting no time to make use of the facilities now she was alone.

The relief felt so good that she didn't even care about the noise or the muffled laughter from the kitchen. It just felt so good. Clearly a citrus based diet was not going to be a long-term solution.

When she was done, she flushed and washed her hands in the sink, drying them on her shorts. It took her a moment to spot the shadow in the window, by the time she processed what she was seeing it was too late. A stone came through the window first, shattering the glass and spraying her with shards, then a thick hand reached through, swiping at her, and clutching at her hair before she could jump out of the way. The hand yanked her forward, dragging her by the hair towards the broken glass in the window frame.

Behind her the toilet door rattled as Shreya and Dean tried to get in, alerted by the scream that was coming from her. When had she started screaming?

Jess spotted a pair of scissors by the sink, part of the pathetic arsenal of weapons they had foraged from around the house. She grabbed them and started to cut through her taut hair, pulling back despite the pain to her scalp. Her hair was thick, and she struggled to cut through the dense rope tethering her to her assailant. She had barely managed to hack halfway through when she fell backwards, her shoulder hitting the bathroom door.

Stunned, she reached around and found the door handle to unlock it.

Shreya and Dean pushed the door open and dragged her back out into the hallway. Through the broken window she saw Oskar's face appear.

'Are you ok?' he asked. She nodded and he vanished from sight, dragging something behind him.

They rushed to the back door which was still open. Oskar had pulled the table away and run outside when he heard Jess scream. He was making his way back to door, dragging someone by the heels behind him.

'Get belts or cords and help me tie it up.' He said as he dragged the squirming figure through the door.

They managed to tie a sheet around its arms, pinning them to its chest. With the arms tied down they were able to repeat the tactic on the legs, fully immobilising it. Confident that it wasn't going anywhere they stood up and stared at

Oskar. 'Are you going to tell me why the fuck we just caught one of them?' demanded Dean.

Oskar stood back and smiled. 'Abso-fucking-lutely.' He walked around the room grabbing cushions and soft furnishings, piling them around the bound form on the floor. 'We are going to burn this place to the ground.'

He grabbed the wooden chopping board from the kitchen and the knife block, adding them to the growing pile of flammable materials on the floor. 'When this thing burns up it is going to take the house with it, raze it to the ground until it is nothing but a pile of rubble. No one is ever going to be tricked into staying here again. With any luck the wind will catch the fire and spread it to the trees, let it all fucking burn.'

Jess hugged him, whispering thanks in his ear before joining in the hunt for materials for their bonfire.

They had no way to know how long it would be before the body on the floor would burst into flame, so they wasted no time in getting their things together once they had amassed their pyre.

They stood by the front door, ready to go but were unable to turn away from the figure in the living room. It was tempting to wait to see it burn but knew they would have to be quick once the flames started. The fire and smoke would likely become a beacon, alerting the town to the fact that they were still alive.

The plan was to head straight for the gates. They were gambling on the fact that people would have more pressing things to do than guard it whilst everything was going to shit around them. From there it would be a case of clambering over the rails and heading straight into town, sticking to the shadows where they could.

They hesitated for a few minutes, torn between their desire to leave and their fear of being outside.

Finally, Dean's nerves got the better of him. 'We can't wait forever, we have to get moving,' he said. 'If we are going to try and get back to town without going on the road then we need to do it in daylight, we won't…'

His words were cut off as the bonfire in the living room roared into life behind them. Flames rose to the ceiling in seconds as the pile around it caught, the heat of the pyre forcing them from the house.

Oskar slammed the door behind them as they ran to the relative safety of the tree line, watching from the shade as the ceiling timbers caught, sending black smoke billowing into the bright sky.

'Come on!' said Dean, 'we've got to go. Now!'

They pushed through the trees as the glass windows popped behind them, the flames now consuming every part of the villa. The whole thing would be nothing more than a pile of rubble in minutes.

Oskar set off on the path to the gates but stopped when Jess yelled.

'No!'

'What's wrong?' he asked.

She paused, eyes scanning through trees to where she knew the gates lay. 'We have to go around the side, the gates aren't safe.'

'How do you know?'

There was no way to explain that she could sense two infected people walking towards the gates and a third already scaling them, on her way back to the Heart Tree. If she told them it would lead to more questions, the demand for answers that she couldn't give without telling them the truth. There was no way she could do that.

'If there is anyone left guarding the gates then it is much more likely that they would be on the gate, right? Otherwise, they are just picking a random spot on the wall,' she ad-libbed.

Shreya pondered it for a beat and nodded. 'She's right. They will most likely have all fled or been taken but we don't know that for certain, might as well be cautious.'

With no objections they cut off the path and headed for a gap in the trees, easily wide enough for them to see the white of the wall ahead in the distance. Dean ran in front with Oskar bringing up the rear, Shreya and Jess watching the trees as they ran, scanning for any signs of life. They crossed the distance in a matter of minutes, reaching the wall as they heard the roof collapsing back at the villa, the weight of the terracotta tiles too much for the burnt timbers to bear.

Oskar scanned the wall for any signs of guards but could see no one.

The thought of scaling the wall had been daunting when they also had to get past the local militia but now, without the threat of being stabbed by spears, it proved to be relatively simple. After a couple of failed attempts, Dean and Oskar were able to hoist Jess up to the top and support her weight while she broke off the shards of glass that had been cemented into the top of the wall. She had taken her time but still managed to cut herself as she flipped her legs over the wall. She had done worse to herself shaving but the resulting trail of blood down the white wall made it look more dramatic than it was.

Straddling the wall, it felt that, for once this holiday, luck was on their side. A thick ledge ran along the wall, at points ballooning out into wider platforms where the guards could stand, the ledge allowing them to move from their spots if they saw something going out of view. They had hoisted her up next to one of the sentry spots along the wall, right where the tall wooden ladder rested against the wall.

The others were shouting up suggestions from below but this time she ignored them. She flipped her other leg over the wall, carefully lowered herself onto the ledge and disappeared.

40

Christina's confident mood was shattered by a loud scream from across the square.

She looked up in time to see the window across from hers explode in a blaze of light and shattered glass. Flames licked up at the curtains, leaping through the room and spreading out over the ceiling in seconds. More screams followed as smoke began to stream out of the window above as the fire relentlessly ate its way upwards.

It was spreading out of control and would soon take down the whole block. Residents poured out into the streets, hovering in the square, crying as they watched their homes burn before them.

From her office Christina watched in horror as the scene unfolded before her eyes.

The fire was so hot and caught so fast that she knew it had to have been the result of an infected catching. Carmen that lived in that flat, she and Christina had been friends since they were children and she often waved to her as she worked at her desk, reassured by the constant presence of her friend. It might have been Carmen she heard screaming but she couldn't be sure, she just prayed she had gotten out before the blaze spread.

The fire burned wildly, the speed and ferocity of its hunger threatening to take over the whole side of the square within minutes. Christina ran to the window, willing her friend to be in the throng of people below, safe from danger but a quick scan of the crowd offered her no reassurance. Christina was about to head downstairs but stopped as she spotted a man coming up a side street. He was walking towards the people huddled in the square, stumbling slightly on the uneven cobbles, reaching out to steady himself on the wall. Any other day she would have thought him drunk but she knew that look in his eyes.

Not far behind him she spotted another person heading toward the crowd.

In the square everyone was so staring intently at the blaze that no one saw them coming. Christina's warning went unheard, lost in the chaos of the fire. By the time the first one reached the edge of the crowd Christina knew it was too late.

He wrapped his arm around a crying woman, clutching her to him in a show of consolation. The sobbing woman didn't protest, she just sagged into his arms, overcome by the devastation before her. She clutched at his jacket, squeezing her eyes shut as she buried her face into his chest, unable to look at her burning home. He took her face in his hands, raising it gently up with a lover's touch.

Christina watched on, helpless, seeing the moment the woman the man she was holding was not the person she had assumed him to be. Her eyes widened as he pressed his mouth to hers, forcing the infection into her lungs.

A second was all it took.

He stepped back from her and drew his hand across his mouth, wiping her saliva from his face, his eyes glazed. She rocked slightly on the spot, watching the man walk out of town. There was no emotion on her face now, she was no longer devastated by the fire, she had a new focus now. More of the infected were approaching the square from all directions, attracted by the sounds of the calamity.

They had controlled the spread for so long now that the villagers had forgotten the horror of the contagion. They had normalised it by telling tales, romanticising it in the story until it had become a fairy tale. The handsome man that takes his beloved with him to the garden, both offering themselves for the sake of the village, unable to entertain the thought of a life without the other.

The truth was nothing like those tales.

She watched the infected working together, blocking the exits and circling around the distracted mass to herd them back towards the burning building.

Christina wanted to warn them, make them see that they were in danger, but already she knew it was hopeless. The arc of infected had now fully enclosed the hoard in the square. Even if she could warn them there was no way they could escape now, all it would serve to do was to alert them to her presence and make a target of herself.

No. They had panicked and run out into the square, she had warned them all and they had simply stood around and watched it burn, bleating as the wolves circled. She stepped back out of sight and watched the infected push forward, grabbing at those on the edge of the huddled mass, ripping them from the arms of loved ones and dragging them back, mouths locked over screaming lips. The speed in which the victims flipped was terrifying, shocked and screaming one moment then steely eyed and focused the next.

All she could do was watch as her people were decimated in front of her.

She should have felt horror at the carnage, screamed as she saw people fighting for their lives, fingers scratching at the faces of their former loved ones, screaming until the spores took over their bodies and minds in their relentless primal quest.

She should have tried to help them, should have called for help and led the charge to save them but all she felt was numb.

Everything had gone to shit.

The town was burning, people were turning and soon the life they had known for centuries would be nothing more than a memory for anyone that survived the cull. If they had any hope of surviving this, then there would have to be sacrifices. The people in the square had panicked at the sight of fire and now they were paying the price for their mistake. There was nothing she could do to help them now. Her focus had to be on getting as many people to safety as she could and stop the strangers from escaping.

Anything less would mean total failure.

41

'Jess!'

There was no answer to their calls and their friend was nowhere in sight. There had been no noise, she just vanished from the top of the wall.

'Lift me up,' said Shreya.

'It won't work,' replied Oskar, 'you won't be able to reach, you're shorted than Jess and she barely made it over.'

Shreya's face told him she didn't agree. They stood there and argued, Oskar adamant that Shreya couldn't make it while she protested that she could. Dean stood back and watched them as they bickered, a smile spreading across his face.

'What??' Shreya demanded as he began to chuckle.

'We could just use that,' he said, pointing to the top of the wall where Jess had pushed a ladder over the top and was now lowering it slowly down.

'Can't get rid of me that easily,' she said with what she hoped was a convincing smile.

Shreya climbed the ladder first, straddling the wall at the top before gently lowering herself onto the ledge at the other side. She shuffled over to the watch point and yelled over when she was clear. Dean followed, with Oskar bringing up the rear. He dragged the ladder back over with him and passed it down the line.

One by one they climbed down, finally free of the confines of the villa. There was no great celebration, the thin sense of freedom was an illusion, they were still trapped on the island and each of them knew it. Even so, getting out of the compound was the boost they had desperately needed.

Jess put the ladder back where she had found it, easily matching the ladder to the paint chips in the wall where it had clearly rested for years. Unless anyone saw the missing patch of broken glass at the top of the wall there was no way to know for certain whether they had escaped or were still in hiding on the compound.

'Right. Let's follow the wall around clockwise,' said Oskar, 'that should bring us to the main gates. From there we will have a clear view of the road down to the woods leading back to town. If it is clear then we run until we get into the tree line, if not we stay hidden and wait for a better moment.'

'Aye aye captain!' smiled Dean. For the first time in days the weak joke drew smiles from the others, their mood bolstered by escaping their confines.

They stayed close to the wall, keeping watch in all directions, alert for any sounds around them. They passed four sentry points before spotting the curved white line of the road ahead.

Amid the chaos, the island was still breathtaking. Their world had shrunk to the space inside the walls, staring at the vast expanse of trees and mountains surrounding them it was almost possible to understand why the locals would fight to protect their way of life. Almost.

Oskar motioned for them to stop, and they did, scanning ahead for any signs of life. A lone figure walked along the road, unaware of the cloud of dust it was kicking up underfoot as it walked. Her clothes were torn, bare flesh visible through the gashes, still bleeding from the obvious struggle and she dragged her right leg as she walked. Oskar was no doctor, but he suspected the bread knife sticking out of her thigh could be the cause. She hobbled closer, five hundred feet or so from where they hid. The curve of the sentry spot wasn't enough to hide the four of them, yet she gave no sign of having seen them.

'Get ready to run,' he whispered to the others. 'I want to try something.'

Before anyone could protest, he picked up a stone from the base of the wall and lobbed it to the road. They shrank back as it hit the ground clatter, coming to a just in front of the walking woman. She gave no reaction, just continued to stare ahead, undeterred from the mission that was propelling her forwards.

He gestured for them to stay hidden and stood up, walking towards her with his knife drawn. He was so close now that he could hear her laboured breathing. Blood bubbled from a hole in her chest with every breath she took. She didn't see him, or if she did, she had no interest in him. Oskar kept the knife raised and passed right in front of her. She paused as he blocked the gate from her sight but picked up her march again as he moved around her, clearing her path forwards. Shreya broke from their hiding spot and joined Oskar.

'She must have passed on the infection,' she said, watching the woman who had now reached the locked gates, pushing at the metalwork, trying to pull them open and failing. Undeterred the woman looked to her right and walked towards the sentry point, heading straight for Dean and Jess. At her approach they stood up and stepped backwards, not trusting her enough to turn their backs and run. Once again, she gave no sign of registering their presence, her only thought was to climb the ladder and get over the wall.

She pushed herself up onto the wall, broken glass slicing through her palms as she leveraged herself up. Blood spurted from her palms, crimson rivers flowing down the white wall, but she was oblivious to pain. Without a pause she swung her legs over and dropped from sight. All they heard was the thud of her landing and the crack of her tibia fracturing. She reappeared on the other side of the gate, swaying from side to side as she walked, but propelled forward regardless. She veered off the road and into the trees, pushing through the most direct route to the centre of the woods.

Shreya smiled as the woman vanished into the trees. 'This is good,' she said.

'It is?' asked Dean.

'Remember the ants? They were taken over for the sole purpose of spreading. The fungus programmed their brains to carry out a set routine to optimise the spread of the contagion. I think this is doing something similar. Ben was infected, then passed it on to Duncan before going back to the tree. It programmed him to spread the infection and then come back. It wants to feed from the bodies. Even Duncan started to head back to the tree before he…' Shreya stopped and looked apologetically at Oskar.

'Burned,' finished Oskar. 'It burned. It wasn't Duncan. No more than that thing was once a woman from the village.'

Shreya nodded. "If they are coming back this way we won't have to worry as they will be like her, reprogrammed for their final use.'

'How will we know if they are like her though?' asked Jess.

'We won't. But hopefully we can hide in the shadows until we are sure enough to get back on the road.'

It wasn't much of a plan but at this point it was all that they had.

They set off down the road, jogging towards the spot where the dark mouth of the woods swallowed the road. From their sunny vantage it was impossible to see anything inside the murky tunnel before them. Their eyes would adjust as they entered so they relied on blind faith as they ran into the shadows with their weapons drawn.

The contrast from light to dark was disarming. The second they entered the shadows they were blind, an easy target for anyone that lurked in the darkness ahead of them. Oskar pulled them to the side of the road, and they crouched down, waiting for their eyes to adjust.

Forms slowly appeared before them, inky shadows moving in the dusky hollow. There was a rhythm to their movement, the scratches of their feet on the road carving out a morbid beat. Dean grabbed a stick from the ground and threw it ahead. The rhythm of the march remained unaltered by the dull rattle as it struck the ground. Oskar rose, drawing the others behind him as they set back off down the road, sticking to the edge, ready to jump back to the trees at any sign of danger.

'Look over there,' whispered Jess, pointing at a weak blue light, pulsing in the trees.

'Where?' asked Shreya, peering into the gloom.

'There! The light in the trees.'

Shreya looked but could only see the deep, dark umbra of the woods. 'You must have caught a flash of the sun before we ran in, I can't see anything.'

'Yeah,' said Jess and let it drop.

Shreya pushed forward whilst Jess let herself slow down slightly, distracted by the light she could see running through the forest around them, deviated filaments linking it all together, getting brighter as her eyes adjusted. It was everywhere, in everything, a living network that stretched as far as she could see.

Dean took her hand as she slowed down even further. 'You okay Jess?'

'Yeah,' she said again, picking up her pace, 'just, you know…'

It seemed to be enough, and he gave her hand a squeeze.

'We can do this Jess, we really can.'

She smiled and squeezed his hand back.

Lone forms staggered past them, paying no heed to the four people passing by. Ahead Oskar counted another four visible forms approaching but still couldn't see any sign of the daylight beyond the trees. The trip through had seemed relatively short in the safety of the car, today though the road seemed endless, stretching out beyond all reason. He kept them moving, slowing down only as they warily passed the infected before once again picking up the pace. After ten minutes of walking against the tide of bodies Oskar finally spotted light ahead of them. The light drew them forward and they broke into a slight jog, eager to get to the end of this unnerving twilight world.

They bunched together as they jogged, huddled up to discuss their strategy once they got to the end of the tunnel. Oskar insisted they hide before the edge of the light as anyone on the other side would see them before their eyes adjusted back to daylight. As keen as they were to get out of the dark, they knew he was right. As the edge of the trees drew closer, they slowed down, dropping to a brisk walk. The daylight beyond the shadows beckoned them, the welcome respite from the shadow of the tunnel.

Dean marched at the back of the group, partly out of chivalry, but mostly because he was not built for flight. Working long days in retail left him with no desire to shop and even less time to cook. As Oskar slowed the group down Dean reduced his pace even further, not wanting to be panting when he reached Shreya. He walked behind them, hands on his hips to avoid a stitch just like he had been taught at school during the seemingly endless cross country runs they did for games. He concentrated on his breathing, taking deep slow breaths to try and slow his heartbeat down.

He didn't hear the figure behind him slip quietly out of the tree line.

A large hand wrapped around his arm, spinning him backwards as another hand locked over his mouth before he could shout. In seconds he was pulled backwards towards the trees, his feet dragging behind him as he vanished into the shadows.

43

From the door she could see that the steps from her office were clear.

Christina dropped down them two at a time and ran towards the back exit of the building. She gripped the handle and slowly pushed the door open, offering a silent prayer for a clear route out. The street behind her building was silent apart from the muffled trickle of water from the wrapped statue in the small square to her left.

She had always hated that damned thing.

After the successful completion of Batch 1, nearly six years ago now, she had decided to tear it down, but the villagers had rejected her proposal. To her it was a daily reminder of the dead that had been needlessly sacrificed, but they saw it as a totem to the island, fearing it's destruction would somehow anger some ancient power. She had finally gotten them to agree to moving it to this small square, a crappy compromise but at least she didn't have to see it every day. Last year one group had stumbled upon the fountain and had been unnerved by its alabaster maidens crying crimson tears. They had started to ask too many questions, the charade of the villa starting to unravel as their discomfort grew. That was the first and only time they had had to use force to get the Batch back onto the property. From that point on they had decided it would be simpler to cover it whenever there were strangers in town to make their lives easier. Now she looked forward to tearing the whole fucking thing down, pulverising every single figure until nothing remained but a pile of dust and rubble.

She ran to the crossroad, peering around the corner of the building to the main square beyond. The carnage continued unabated, but the crowd had dwindled down to a handful of people still fighting for their lives. A woman screamed, lashing out at the infected around her as they grabbed at her wrist, trying to pull them into their deadly embrace. She managed to slash one or two with her knife, but it was only a matter of time before she was outnumbered. Christina wanted to run but was transfixed, only breaking away when the woman's head was dragged down into the swirling mass of bodies. She ran across the road, not stopping until she was well past the square.

Iglesias De Santa Catalina was just on the edge of town, on the road to the docks. She had no idea how many people would have gone there as instructed. Having watched so many of them blindly flooding into the square she wasn't holding out much hope. The roads felt too quiet, she hoped people had already made their way to the church but suspected that if they weren't already dead most of them were still hiding in their homes. Let them hide, most of them would just end up as fodder for the island if they strayed into the open. She needed some bodies though as she had to ensure Batch 4 were hunted down and eliminated. She could rebuild the village once this outbreak died down but if any of them escaped, she couldn't stop what would come.

Each street she passed was empty. She peered into a few windows, but they are all deserted. If anyone saw her, they stayed hidden, no longer trusting anyone, not even her. Christina turned down a small side street, ducking off the main road to the port and approaching the church from the side.

It was a modest church by any standards, a chunky cuboid adorned plainly with white plaster, windows sparingly punched high up on the thick walls, allowing minimal light inside, just enough to pierce the gloom of the church to enable the original settlers to atone for their sins without distraction. Ironically, she had always found the church to be a godforsaken place, bleak and unwelcoming, the marker of a merciless God who believed firmly in the stick over the carrot. Today though the solid exterior was welcoming, a perfect fortress in which to hide from further attacks.

She hid around the corner, watching the church, waiting to ensure she had a clear route. For the first time that day Christina was pleased to see that the small square was deserted, giving her easy access to the wooden doors at the front of the church. Stepping out into the open she felt vulnerable but swallowed her fear and set off, running along the wall rather than cutting across the square. If there were any infected at the front, she wanted to keep some distance between them. Someone must have been keeping watch from inside the church as the thick door swung open just as it came into view.

Anita leaned out of the door, beckoning Christina over with a frantic arm wave. She took her cue and ran, crossing the distance and darting into the safety of the house of worship. The door slammed behind her, sealing her into the monolith's dank interior.

Anita rushed up behind her and drew Christina into her arms. She sagged into the embrace, allowing herself a moment of respite, the tears coming before she could stop them. Anita held her tighter, knowing instantly that Mateo and Mathias were gone. So many had died today but the loss of the boys cut her deepest of all.

Anita had never been blessed with children, but the boys had adopted her as their abuela, and she had treated them as her own. She would mourn them when this was over but for now, she knew she had to stay strong for Christina. Anita gave her another big squeeze and then held her face up, using her sleeves to dry the tears from her face. Christina swallowed her grief back down, the tight black knot sinking inside her, hidden but very much present. She gave Anita a quick kiss on the cheek and turned back to face the church, back in control and ready to lead the charge.

A couple of dozen people were all she found huddled on the dark pews. Christina's loss was reflected over and over in the faces staring back at her; husbands without their wives, mothers without their children - the infection had hit all of them deeply. Behind the fear and grief though she could also sense a building anger, a growing need for blame. Their relief at having a leader back was going to sour quickly unless she could harness their anger.

She whispered into Anita's ear and the older lady set off, lighting all the candles she could find in the church, pushing the gloom back into the rafters, replaced by the soft glow of candlelight. Christina walked through the small crowd, hugging people as she went, sharing their communal grief. Most were responsive but some she could feel holding back, responding to her stiffly, unable to look her in the eyes, barely able to maintain a forced level of civility.

Only Sister Sara turned from her approach, as stiff in her outlook as she was in her habit. The elderly nun turned on her heel, ignoring the mayor, instead turning to her sacred alter and dropping to her knees in prayer, smoothing out the blue fabric before clasping her hands in front of her.

Christina allowed her the pious moment, giving her a minute before she climbed onto the altar and facing her congregation. Sister Sara stood up and glared at Christina, hate burning in her eyes. Christina smiled back at her, gesturing for her to take a seat before she started speaking. The old nun skulked away, taking a seat at the rear of the church, arms folded in disgust.

'My friends,' she began, 'this is a dark day for our island. For generations we have lived in harmony with this land. We have always known that living here comes with a cost and we have dutifully paid that price.'

Her voice echoed around the sparse interior of the church, her words reverberating, lending them more gravitas than she expected. She paused, letting her words die out. She had to turn their anger and fear back towards Batch 4. It was them that had brought this terror to the island, not her, she just had to get them to understand that. They would help her to ensure 4 never left the island, they all had too much at stake to let them escape, but first she needed to refocus their anger, give them someone to blame that wasn't her.

She saw the questions in the faces huddled around her. No one knew what had gone so wrong this time. It had all unfolded in the hidden depths of the villa, they had only seen the fall out. It was time for the truth.

'We were… betrayed,' she continued, adding some theatrics for good measure.

A murmur ran through the crowd.

She could feel the mood changing around her, people were shifting in their seats, needing to know more.

'Eight years ago, God showed us another way to live in peace with this island. Now, it hasn't been easy, and we have all struggled with what we have had to do to save the lives of our children. But we are parents, it is our duty.' Nods around the church, at least two people that she could see in the crowd had not lost a child because thanks to Christina, so she knew she had support. 'Something went wrong last night. They set fire to the Heart Tree. We tried to stop them, but it was too late, my sweet boys died trying to save you, as did many of your friends and loved ones.'

Her voice caught as she finally acknowledged it out loud - they were gone. Every eye in the church widened in shock as her words sank in.

'They did it to save themselves, they don't care about your families, their lives mean nothing to Batch 4. Their only goal now is to get off the island and bring an end to our way of life. We are dying so that they can live. Even now they are making their way into town, mindless to the pain and suffering of our people, their only goal was to use our destruction to escape.'

Anger and fear rippled through the crowd. Christina watched it spread; a room full of lost soul's eager to have a focus for their rage. She had them now. Their instinct for self-preservation would push them to follow her and wipe out every member of 4.

'This is all LIES!' cried Sister Sara's angry voice from the back of the church.

Every head in the church swung around, snapped out of their anger by her fierce tone.

'You cannot blame this on anyone but yourself,' she continued. 'Your selfishness has doomed the island to this fate. You act like you have done this for the benefit of all, but the truth is that you were too weak. We have lived here for generations; all have known the cost of our lives here, but you decided to risk all our lives rather than pay the price you owed.'

She glared at the villagers huddled in her church, seeing nothing but a scared flock of sheep cowering in the dark. 'You have ALL become weak in the last eight years. Murderers each one of you, the blood of the innocents on each of your hands. You turned away from God the day you accepted the first strangers onto this island, you knew the evil of this plan but carried on out of selfishness.' She shook her head as she looked at them all. 'Today you seek shelter in His house, but He will offer you no protection here. This will not be your sanctuary any longer.'

A stunned silence settled over the church.

Heads turned in confusion, looking to Christina for guidance. She looked back at them and dug deep, finding a well of confidence that she hadn't known she had.

She'd never had her father's conviction for religion, but that hadn't stopped his words from searing into her subconscious. Heavily curated verses to justify every action in his life.

Sister Sara was the embodiment of everything Christina despised about the hypocrisy of religion.

She let the hate flow.

'"I desire mercy, not sacrifice. For I have not come to call the righteous, but sinners", isn't that what the bible says Sister Sara?' she demanded of the nun. 'And yet here you stand, telling us to leave this place because you feel we are unworthy? You presume to know the will of this God you speak of?'

The nun's face flushed scarlet, no longer hiding the rage that burned within her.

'You are not seeking the Lord's forgiveness; you are here out of fear. I have given my life in service to God, but you rejected Him years ago!'

'You have *hidden* here you coward. Brandishing your little book to justify your fear, using its words to protect your sisters. How many of you were ever sacrificed? None… You took your vows and were spared, too cowardly to do you duty. Such a coincidence that all the sisters here have been the first born in their families. Look around you Sister, every person here has known the cost of living on the island but you. Too long have we allowed clemency to those who chose to hide behind the veil, but it ends now.'

Sister Sara backed away, sensing the change in the crowd around her. She sank to her knees and clasped her hands around the small golden crucifix around her throat. '*My God is my rock, in whom I take refuge, my shield and the horn of my salvation. He is my stronghold, my refuge, and my saviour - from violent people you save me...'*

'Your only instinct has always been self-preservation.' Christina cut off her frantic prayers. 'My father told me how you found your calling mere months before you came of age, and now here you are again, throwing meaningless words up to the sky to save you once again. Don't you know that there has only ever been one God on this island, and it isn't to be found in the pages of your bible.'

Christina took a step down from the alter and made her way towards the stooped figure at the back of the room.

'You had your chance today; we came here seeking shelter, but you welcomed us with anger not with love.' She looked to around at the crowd surrounding her and nodded at two people. 'There is no longer any place in here for you Sister Sara, you had better hope your god will reward your faith by showing you his mercy outside these doors. Grab her!'

The two men nearest the nun jumped to their feet and took her by the elbows. Christina marched through the throng of people now raising from their seats and directed them to bring the screaming nun to the door. The nun let her body fall to the ground as she was pulled forward, forcing them to drag her forward by the arms, her legs trailing defiantly behind her.

Christina put her face to the small portal in the door and scanned the yard for infected. Confident there was no one out there she flung the door open, stepping back to watch them drop the nun's wizened body out onto the steps in front of the church. They jumped back in as the old woman sprung up, trying to get through the doors before they closed but her efforts were in vain.

Her gnarled fingers scrabbled at the door as Christina turned the key in the lock, forever banishing her from the church.

44

At the edge of the tunnel of trees Shreya crouched in the dark, watching the town for signs of life. The streets and buildings that had looked so quaint when they first arrived had now taken on a haunted appearance, devoid of life save for the occasional emergence of yet another lumbering figure making their way back towards the villa.

She watched silently as a woman stepped from the light into the shadow of the trees. Her left arm was slashed down to the bone, blood running down her hand leaving a trail of shiny red dots as it dripped from her fingers. There had been a good attempt at resistance, but she hadn't been able to overpower her preternatural opponent. The woman she had once been now gone, dead long before she would reach her final resting place. In her other hand she still clutched her lifeless baby. Even from this distance she could see the concave dip in its head.

Shreya shuddered and reached behind her, seeking a moment of comfort from Dean.

Instead of finding a reassuring hand her fingers passed through the air, waving back and forth in search of its mate. Her stomach dropped when it found nothing.

'No!'

She whipped around, finding the road behind her empty. She jumped to her feet and retraced their steps, Jess and Oskar joining her as soon as they realised what had happened.

'Where did you last see him?' asked Oskar, scouring the ground for any signs of a struggle.

'He was just behind us; I saw him seconds ago!'

'Here!' Oskar was at the edge of the road, pointing at what looked like drag marks. 'He's been taken into the trees. Stay here.'

Oskar ducked into the trees leaving Jess and Shreya alone on the road.

'Fuck that, I'm going in.' said Shreya, following Oskar into the trees, almost running into him in the dark of the canopy.

'Shhhh,' whispered Oskar. 'Listen, wait until you hear something.'

Together they turned their ears to the dark, hoping for anything that would lead them to Dean. Shreya heard something snap to her left and set off towards it. She couldn't be sure it was Dean but couldn't waste a second. As she leapt to the left Oskar sprang right, having heard something else in the other direction. There was no time for debate, she kept moving towards the sound she heard, hoping that at least one of them would find him.

There were more sounds from ahead.

This time she could have sworn she heard muffled shouting. She jogged through the trees, ignoring the pain as tiny branches pierced her while she ran. Her only focus now was Dean. She remembered the knife in her makeshift sock hilt she had tied around her belt and slowed down long enough to arm herself, ready to face whatever lay ahead of her.

The sounds of struggle were close.

Dean was meters ahead of her, a hand wrapped around his mouth, his eyes filled with fear.

'He's here!' she yelled behind her, hoping that Jess and Oskar would hear.

His eye's widened as he heard her voice. He thrashed in the arms of his attacker, for a moment his mouth broke free of the hand.

'Leave me, get away Shreya!'

She ignored him, closing the distance between them while he begged her to flee. The sound of his voice and his fear for her emboldened her, she was certain that he had yet to be turned, there was still hope.

Dean was still dragging his legs behind as his captor pulled him through the trees, trying to slow them down - his captor either unaware of her presence or uncaring. Shreya leapt forward, wrapping her arms around the top of his thighs, and tightening them around his knees as she dropped, dragging Dean from the arms of his infected captor.

The man slowed, confused that his prize had been stripped from his arms.

Dean scrambled to his feet, hauling Shreya up with him. The man turned and looked at them, tilting his head slightly to one side to appraise the situation. Shreya recognised him at once as one of the twin waiters from the odd pair of bars in town.

She didn't know why but it felt wrong that he was here.

Why had he tried to kidnap Dean rather than simply overpowering him straight away. This virus or whatever it was had only tried to spread so far but this felt different, and it scared her.

'You escaped,' the waiter stated. His words carried no emotion, just a statement of the facts. 'Where is the girl?'

'What girl?' asked Shreya, pulling a still panting Dean back through the trees with her.

'The one who knows us.'

It didn't take much to guess he was talking about Jess. 'I don't know, we lost her…'

'You lie. She is near.'

'Why? Why do you need her?'

'She will talk for us now.'

As the waiter spoke, she finally worked out what was so wrong with this situation. She was sure they had seen him up at the wall, one of the sentries at the gate when they had confronted Christina hours ago. If he had been there when the spores had spread, then he should have been infected last night. It must have been over twelve hours since they burned the tree. He should either have reinfected someone or burned long ago. Even if she was wrong and he had been in town then he should either be converting Dean or heading back to the villa, his job already done.

He shouldn't be here, shouldn't be communicating with them.

This had to be something different.

Thoughts raced through her mind as they pushed backwards, slowly followed by the former bar owner. It had adapted to fulfil another purpose and for whatever reason that now involved Jess.

Jess who even now was somewhere in the woods, blindly stumbling around and separated from the group.

They had been played.

'It's a trap!' she yelled behind them, 'get back to the road NOW!'.

They both turned and ran back the way they had come. She glanced back expecting to see Mateo/Mathias following her, but he still stood where they had left him, his hands wrapped around a nearby branch and his eyes closed in concentration.

Dean pushed her forward. 'Just keep running!'

Ahead of them leaves rustled, stirred by an invisible storm. Their path back was closing in on them, as trees knit their branches together, blocking their way back to the road. Shreya slashed out with her knife as they ran, zig zagging through the trees to try and outwit their omnipotent assailant. Daylight flashed through the leaves, and she pushed forward with one last cry, breaking through into the welcome warm sun.

Jess and Oskar ran over to her, dragging her away from the reach of the trees, out into the middle of the road.

'Where is Dean?' asked Oskar.

Shreya turned and looked around; certain he had been right behind her.

The trees had thickened already; the spot she had burst out of already covered by a wall of shiny green leaves that blocked her from running back in.

Beyond the verdant wall was nothing but silence.

45

Dean had been so intent on following Shreya that he never saw the long root rise out of the ground behind her as she ran. His foot caught it as he fled, sending him tumbling to the ground. He winded himself as he face-planted into the dirt. All he could do was lie there gasping for breath and hope that Shreya at least had made it out to the others.

He didn't care what happened to him anymore, his only desire was that she live. Panicked breaths wracked his body as he tried to draw air into his lungs.

Footsteps softly approached from behind, no urgency in their gait.

Dean turned over to face the waiter, still gulping for air.

Mathias reached out and grabbed him under the shoulders, dragging him to his feet.

Dean tried to resist, to keep his mouth closed as he was pulled forward, but his body demanded oxygen.

He tried to push away but it was too strong.

Mathias opened his mouth and locked onto Dean, forcing breath into the gasping man. His lungs inflated as the infection was passed from host to victim.

He begged his body to reject it even as he felt it working its way through him, probing at his mind, and digging through memories of the last few hours.

His body stopped struggling as Dean's thoughts were shut away.

The panting stopped. Control was restored.

His arm reached out to the nearest tree and wrapped around it.

Now they all knew where she was heading.

46

Inside the church there was silence.

No one moved whilst Sister Sara banged on the door, screaming words ill-suited to a bride of Christ. Decades of anger and frustration poured out of the nun, increasingly complex compound insults were hurled at Christina and her cowering flock.

Abruptly she stopped shouting, her last word faintly echoing around the church from the force of her vitriol.

cunt…unt…unt….

The silence shocked those in the church from their stupor. Christina ran to the high set window, already knowing what she would see.

The infected had heard Sister Sara's rage and homed in on the church. From all directions came a stream of bodies, a dozen or more once familiar faces stumbled towards the old woman cowering in the square.

'Run,' Christina whispered at the old woman, needing her to draw the infected away from their haven. 'Run you fucking bitch.'

But she didn't move.

Surrounded, her shoulders dropped, and she accepted her fate. She turned her head to the church and found Christina's face in the small window, raising her middle finger to her in a final act of defiance. As the infected advanced on her she raised her face to the sky, offering a silent prayer to her maker. A woman stepped forward from the pack, the ragged night dress that clung to her frame doing little to protect her modesty, but she was long past caring.

Sister Sara impotently raised her crucifix at her assailant, still certain that her love for the Lord would protect her, pressing it onto the skin of the woman as she was overpowered.

Death had come for her but all the nun felt was the flush of excitement as a woman's lips brushed her own for the first time, decades of repression cracking in one kiss, her last conscious moment one of wicked sin.

Then darkness.

The attack was over quickly.

Once the infection had taken hold of her the pack dispersed as the infected turned their attention to the church. Only Christina watched as the Fire took control of the host's old body.

Her body straightened up, the aches and pains of age no longer relevant. The former nun turned around and once again found Christina's face at the window, a grimace spreading over the wrinkled face.

Christina jumped as Anita gently laid a hand on her shoulder.

'Before you arrived, I collected up all the supplies that were brought and we have enough food to last us a day or two, maybe three if we can strictly ration it. The church has its own water supply so we can be safe here for a while if we need to hide.

She put her hand on Anita's cheek and smiled at her old friend. She had been her rock for as long as Christina could remember. Her father had hired Anita not long after her mother had died. He'd had neither the skill nor the interest to raise two children so bringing in a local woman was the natural solution.

She was the only maternal figure that Christina had ever known.

It was going to be hard to leave her behind.

'We cannot all stay here,' said the mayor. 'We have to stop 4 from leaving the island, if they get away then everything we have built here, everything we are fighting for right now will be gone.'

'No! They can't escape from the island, even if they did, they wouldn't get to the mainland. Please stay here niña, we can wait this out and then find them,' begged Anita.

'I must. It is too big a risk. I must make sure they don't get away. For Mateo and Mathias.' Tears welled in the old woman's face at the mention of the two lost boys.

Christina knew she wouldn't hold her back.

She wiped her eyes and composed herself, they needed to see a strong mayor, not a grieving mother. She turned away from Anita and addressed the small congregation.

'I need ten people to come with me. It is vital that we stop them from getting off this island. They will have a plan to escape, and we must stop them. I ask a lot of you, I know that, but this is for our future. Ten people, volunteers step to the rear of the church.'

The pleading started immediately as loved ones begged their partners to stay seated. Yet one by one people stood up until she had eleven men and women lined up at the back of the building.

'The rest of you will stay here in the church. Lock the doors behind us and barricade yourselves in. You have enough food to last a few days and there is plenty of water.' She squeezed Anita's hand as she walked to join the volunteers but was unable to turn to look at her. She had to be strong, and she knew she would crack if she saw the old woman cry.

The volunteers armed themselves with anything they could find; heavy candlesticks, knives from the vestry, a hammer someone found in a small toolbox, makeshift clubs made from chair legs. Anything they could swing became a weapon.

She huddled the group around her.

'The only way off the island is via the marina so that is where they will head. If you see them, take them out as best you can. Kill them, break them, anything to stop them getting away from here. But remember to keep quiet, we don't want to have to fight the infected as well.' The men and women around her were scared but she could also see a steely determination in their eyes. 'At most there are now four of them. We are twelve and we know this island. We have the advantage. We can do this.'

Confidence grew in the ranks; they were buoyed up and ready to fight. She had to get them out now before they had time to think any more about what they were doing.

Christina led them to the back door, checking that the rear of the church was clear. She jumped as a thunderous banging came from the front of the church. They all spun around fearing the worst but saw Anita hitting the doors with a chair, making noise to distract the infected mob outside, drawing them all to the front of the church.

Those staying behind joined in, shouting, and banging on the wall whist they waved to their loved ones at the back of the church.

Christina blew Anita a kiss then opened the back door and stepped out into the sunlight.

47

'He was right there. He was right behind me, he… he… Dean!'

Shreya scanned the green border but apart from the gentle rustle of leaves on the breeze there was no sign of movement.

'Look at me,' commanded Oskar, taking her face in his hands and forcing her to look at him. She slapped away his arms and ran back towards the tree line. 'Dean!'

Oskar caught up with her and dragged her backwards. 'Listen! If he were there and he was able to he would be calling for you, right?'

Shreya softly shook her head, spilling the tears that had been welling in her eyes. 'No…'.

'If he has gone then we need to go. Now. Dean knows our plans, so we have to assume they know them too.'

'No! We have to go back in and look for him!'

'Shreya…'

'He was right there, you saw him Jess, we have to get him back…' Her shoulders began to tremble, Oskar could see the fight draining out of her, the inescapable truth winning out over desperate hope.

'You said it was a trap. What did you mean?' asked Jess.

Shreya bit her lip. It would be so easy to stop and give up. Just walk into the trees and end it all now. They had been so close to being happy finally. She could still feel his hands on her body, pushing into her as they kissed. She had allowed herself to imagine a future with Dean, a chance to love and be loved.

Ten years it had taken for them to get their shit together and now she knew he was gone.

Taken from her.

Killed but not yet dead.

Anger stirred in her belly, a cold, white fury that burned upwards, pushing away all traces of fear and defeat. She wiped the tears from her cheek and pushed Oskar's hands away from her.

'They want you,' she said, glaring at Jess.

'Me?' Jess stared at her friend, trying to measure the words coming out of her mouth. 'But…why?'

'You tell me. It kept calling you *the one who knows us*. It has a connection with you, and you have already shown that it can communicate through you. She will talk for us now.'

Jess recoiled at the venomous edge to Shreya's voice but knew it would be easier not to challenge her friend right now.

Shreya retold the story of their encounter with Mateo/Mathias, how he had touched the tree and the woods had seemed to respond to him. 'I think they are all able to communicate.'

She also told them of her belief that he was acting differently to the others they had seen.

'From that the only good news I can see is that they must have to be physically in contact to communicate. Hopefully that means that the infected in town still don't know where we are going,' said Oskar, looking ahead towards the edge of the village. The only chance they had of getting to the shop unseen would be to approach it from the rear, try and find a back door they could use to gain access. 'Come on, we have to keep moving.'

He took the lead, running along the edge of the road, keeping to the side but no longer bothering to hide as the trickle of infected walked past them on their slow pilgrimage to the villa.

Shreya's words rang in his head as he jogged. Up until now they had assumed that anyone infected would act in the same way but what Shreya had seen with Mateo/Mathias had defied their limited frame of reference, his purpose at odds with the drones that now filed back along the road having fulfilled their primary need to spread. Now they wanted Jess, so they had adapted their programming to perform a specific purpose, they had changed the rules to suit their needs.

Dean and Mathias knew where they were heading but he had to assume now that anyone in contact with the trees could also know. Anyone that touched another infected could pass on that information.

He picked up the pace.

The sun cast an orange glow over the rooftops as is made its ways slowly behind the hills. They snuck though the smaller streets on the edge of town and made their way towards the town square, the changing light helping them to stick to the shadows and out of sight. They waited as a larger group of the infected walked towards them, eight of them this time, moving close together and away from the square.

Above the sky glowed in the dusk, the warm light getting brighter the closer they moved into town.

The sound of the fire stopped them before they even saw the flames.

It bellowed out of windows, primal and unconfined, consuming the one side of the square, room by room. They stopped, awed by the sight. It had torn up through one section of the building, powering its way through the floors and bursting through the roof sending plumes of smoke through the collapsing tiles. Unchecked it was exploiting gaps in the old building and spreading sideways, feeding off the whole side of the building, one section at a time, closing in on the shop in the corner.

'If we're going to do this it's got to be now, the shop will be gone in minutes!' Oskar shouted over the hiss and crackle of the inferno.

A nod from Shreya was all it took to spur him on. She had trudged behind them since Dean vanished, but the fire had brought her back to them, igniting the spark in her that she had lost. He just hoped it would last.

Oskar edged ahead and peered around the corner of the building. Happy that it was clear he signalled to them and disappeared.

The once pristine square now bore the signs of a recent fight. Blood had been spilt here, it splattered over the cobbles, small pools forming where harder fought battles had occurred. Clothing and personal treasures had been abandoned around the square. Photo frames spilt from torn bags, hastily gathered possessions strewn across the ground where they had fallen, forgotten in an instant as the horror of the flames had been replaced by the need to run.

There were no bodies on the ground, and no one gathered around to watch the fire spread. Judging by the glut of people they had passed on their way the battle was over.

Oskar felt nothing, all the battle meant to him was fewer people to get in their way. He grabbed the hammer from his pack and ran.

It sat awkwardly in his hand so he adjusted his grip until the handle sat snugly then swung the weighty metal head until it felt comfortable in his hand. The heat coming off the burning building next door was scalding, even from a distance.

The shop window was huge, and, from the look of the frame, it had been there for a long time. If he could manage to hit it in the middle, it should just shatter. He hoped. There was no time for more of a plan, he just raised the hammer and threw it with all his might. It sailed through the glass with a mighty crack. Huge fractures appeared all over the glass, but the hammer only punched out a small hole just off the centre, smashing into the storefront. He didn't want to kick the glass, knowing he would either end up slashing his leg on a shard of glass or…

A plant pot sailed past him as he pondered his options, taking half of the window with it.

Oskar looked behind him to find Shreya wiping dirt from her hands, a grim look on her face. The roar of the fire absorbed much of the sound of shattering glass but there was still a chance that the noise would attract someone.

He took off his backpack and swung it up at the few remaining shards dangling above the hole and hurried Shreya and Jess in through the gap. Next door the fire was already spreading, the heat in the adjacent barber's going up hundreds of degrees in mere moments. The window exploded outwards and cool air rushed into the shop, fueling the insatiable blaze.

'Quick!' yelled Oskar, pulling open drawers and emptying boxes, 'the second we see any sign of flames we are out of here, got it?'

They didn't waste time.

Shreya was already tearing through counter on the back wall, nothing was left untouched, dragging the contents of cupboards onto the floor and moving onto the next. Jess raced into the back, through the curtain where the old woman had first appeared that night, her startled face now burned on her mind. A simple kitchenette awaited her, equipped only for the meagre needs of one a lone person - a cabinet held a single mug and plate, a kettle and little else. Nowhere to hide a stack of passports.

She ran back into the showroom and was hit by the dramatic change in temperature as the heat coming from the adjoining wall increased. There were still no signs of the flames breaking through, but the paint bubbled and scorched on the wall. Things next to it were already beginning to lose their shape as their plastic components melted. A spinner filled with sunglasses sagged as she watched, lenses slipping out of frames that could no longer hold them.

All along the wall items were smoldering, an acrid stench growing in the hot room. Melting plastic and hot paper, teetering on the edge of burning. Fahrenheit 451 popped into her head, unbidden. She had read it as part of her GSCE English course. The details were hazy, something about a dystopian world where firemen were sent to start fires and burn books. The only thing she really remembered clearly was the fact that paper burns at 451 degrees Fahrenheit hence the title. It was of little comfort to know they weren't at that stage yet.

Oskar ran over to the counter, certain that if they were going to find them anywhere, they would be there, they *had* to be there. From the detritus strewn around it was clear that there was nowhere behind the counter that Shreya hadn't looked, no space unopened yet still she hadn't found them. Perhaps they were wrong, maybe they weren't stupid enough keep the only concrete evidence of their crimes. But if that were true then most things in the shop were a potential source of fingerprints and DNA. It was possible that they had stored them somewhere else but somehow that didn't feel right to either. Behind the counter there were no cabinets, just some stacked suitcases and a tiny lock box for cash. He tore through them all but found nothing.

There was nowhere else to look.

They would just have to work out another way off the main island if they got there. When they got there. He looked up to see the first flicker as a piece of paper caught on a table. One flame was all it would take, they had to get out, now.

He turned, about to run but his eye was caught by a yellow strap sticking out of a gap between the wall and the counter, tucked away, hidden from sight. He pulled it out and a little Fällraven rucksack hit the floor with a thud, oddly heavy for such a small, mauve bag. Even before she opened the zip, she knew that she had found them. Opening the bag, he had expected to feel elated but instead a wave of sadness washed over him as she looked down at the hodgepodge of blue, green, red, and black spines that were stacked inside, each one a life that had been stolen on this island.

48

They had been outside the safety of the church less than five minutes before Christina's mistake became obvious: the team of volunteers was far too large a group to get to the harbour discretely. The need for protection had been her primary aim but now they were outside in the bright sunlight she knew there were just too many of them.

The thin shadows couldn't hide all their group and crossing open space took too much time, each member checking they were clear, demanding that the forward part of the group idle until the last member had caught up. There hadn't been time for a more strategic approach but if she was to have any chance of stopping 4 escaping, she only needed to have a small group, just enough to overpower them.

She would have to split the group in two.

She watched each person as they crossed Plaza de la Solidaridad, looking for the strongest members, the ones who hesitated only enough to see the clear path before committing themselves for action. This was no time for sentimentality, only a strong team would enable her to stop them, the others she would have to divert away.

Once the last member of the group had crossed Christina gathered them around her once again.

'We have to stop those that have stolen the power of the island,' Her story in the church had given her an idea, 'But even with our numbers they will still be stronger than us. Our makeshift weapons will be no match against their newfound might.' She had already decided which were staying with her and she was reassured to see that the only ones nodding were the group she would be sending away.

The others were too quick to seek reassurance, not able to think for themselves. She had made the right choice.

'Back in my office there is a locked cabinet with several guns. I had it put in a few years ago in case we needed it. I don't know why I forgot about it when I was there before.'

This much at least was true.

She was a good leader despite the way things had unfolded. When she set out on her programme to import sacrifices, she had been prepared for the chance that something could go wrong although she had never imagined anything on this scale. If she had to send them off on a wild goose chase, she could at least give them a purpose that might help, should they succeed.

'The keys are in my desk. When I fled my office there was a fight in the square but that must be over by now. Half of you will go there and get weapons, the rest come with me to the harbour. We will head them off and try to stop them, at worst delay them until the others arrive with weapons.'

Nods from the slower members, the others stared at her, daring her to pick them for what they had quickly spotted as a doomed errand.

She divided them into the two parties.

'Javi, you lead the group, keep them together and try to be as quick as you can.' He puffed up his shoulders, buoyed by her confidence in him.

'Si senora el alcalde,' he replied formally.

She bid them a safe and successful journey and watched as Javi led his group back into town. They moved more quickly and with more confidence as a smaller group, she noted. She had hoped to divert half of their number but now she started to wonder if this other mission might succeed.

'Let's go,' she said to her new team.

Four men and one woman now escorted her.

She had known Pascal since he was born, as her boys had grown older Pascal become a regular visitor to their home. He had grown into a lively young lad who was still good friends with her boys.

Had been good friends with her boys.

Nicholás, Rodrigo and Carlota brought their numbers to five. The men were brothers-in-law in their forties and Carlota was an androgynous woman in her early thirties. All told it was a motley crew, but they were healthy, small, and speedy, that was all she needed for now.

There had only been one compromise in her new platoon. The final member, Tomas, Anita's husband. When he had stepped up to volunteer, she had been unable to refuse him. Any show of favouritism would risk the fragile grip she had been able to wrangle on those in the church. She had been forced to take him along, but she had told herself she would do everything she could to protect him, Anita would know that. He was still quick and agile for a man in his sixties but there was no doubt he might turn out to be a liability, even so she couldn't bring herself to send him off with the others.

Carlota joined Christina as they set off, the two women leading the men.

Christina was pleased to see that Nicholás and Rodrigo had flanked Tómas, with Pascal taking the rearguard. They had naturally assumed a strong formation, protecting their most vulnerable member but still able to move forward at pace. The marina was less than half a mile from their current location, with luck on their side she was sure they would be able to get there well before the members of 4.

There was still a chance that the group had already succumbed to the island. Obviously, there was no actual plan to steal the power of the island, they were just a normal group of holiday makers, so it was highly probable that they were already turning to mulch in the shade of the tree. In her heart though she feared the worst. If they had somehow managed to escape, they would be looking for a boat to get off the island, they had to be heading to the marina, it's where she would go if she were in their shoes.

She let Carlota assume the lead as they made their way out of town and along the single road that led down to the water, allowing herself the chance to formulate some semblance of a plan as they went. Surprise would be key if they were to stop them. 4 only knew what they had seen when they arrived which they had seen very little. She had made sure the trip between Tomas's boat and the villa had been quick and direct. She had also made sure that Carlo plied them with booze from the moment they stepped onto the plane until the time they reached the island, their memories would be hazy at best.

Ahead she could see a few masts rocking gently on the water, the sound of ropes dancing on metal soothed her.

Tómas picked up the pace as they approached the harbour. He had spent his life down in the marina, maybe he wasn't going to turn out to be such a liability after all.

49

Acrid smoke was already pooling at the ceiling, forming a dense dark layer that was growing as Shreya watched it.

'Out!' she yelled, 'Now!'

Behind her the fire raged, burning everything in its path. The secondhand furniture began to release toxic fumes as the ancient foam padding warped and contracted in the heat. Oskar grabbed a shirt from a stand as he made his way to the front of the shop, trying to cover his mouth but it was no use, he choked as the thick air filled his lungs. He was only a meter behind Jess and Shreya, but he was already struggling to see them through as they stepped through the broken window into the square. He could feel the air flowing against him as the blaze devoured the oxygen in the room, dragging in fresh sustenance from the world outside. He threw the rucksack ahead of him as he leapt through the opening and everything changed around him. Jumping through the glass he heard a soft *whoomp* as the chemical cloud ignited, flames engulfing every inch of the ceiling, flames licking at him as he threw himself into the cool evening air.

He made it to the middle of the square before he fell to the ground, gasping as he gulped clean air into his lungs, trying to expel the taste of the inferno. Shreya looped an arm in his and Jess did the same at the other side, dragging him to his feet between them.

'Over there,' shouted Jess, pointing to an open door across the square. 'Let's get him off the street and we can work out what to do next.'

They crossed the square, pulling Oskar along with them, dragged him through the doorway and pulled it closed behind them. The cool darkness inside the building was a welcome relief. There were no doors in the hallway, only a wooden staircase leading them upstairs. Oskar shook Shreya's arm from his and grabbed the banister, determinedly making his own way up the stairs, slowly but surely.

They took shelter in the first room they found. Chairs lined one wall and small desk sat tidily into corner giving it the unmistakable feel of a waiting room. Shreya took of the chairs by the window and kept watch, Jess and Oskar sprawled out at her feet with their heads resting on rucksacks, Oskar taking deep breaths as he tried to control his breathing until it returned to something close to normal.

A wild look took over Shreya's face as she watched the building burn. Dean was gone. She had forced herself to focus on escaping ever since he had vanished but here, watching the chaos unfold before, her she allowed herself a moment of anger. She willed the flames to spread, to destroy more of the homes and shops, raze the town to the ground - they deserved nothing better.

One way or another everyone here was complicit in his death.

50

When her boys were younger Tómas had brought them down to his boat most Saturdays. He took them out on his boat, and they would fish in the cool waters off the island. He taught them to respect the ocean, telling them stories the of volatile matriarch that shaped the lives of every person on Isla Manuta as they fished in the deep waters. Later, Christina and Anita would walk down to watch the boat return. She treasured the memory of her boys waving at the port side of the boat, silhouetted by the sun starting its low descent to the horizon.

Memories of those happy days assailed her as they approached the harbour. Mateo, the hunter, holding up his catches for her to admire - snappers in the winter months, Dorado and Spearfish in early summer and tuna as the months got hotter. Unlike his twin, Mathias had never taken pride in his catches, the more sensitive of the two he had always been conflicted between his love of the days fishing on the boat and the reality of taking the life of another creature. Instead, Christina had taught him about the circle of life and, with more than a little help from Anita, she had also taught him how to cook.

Together they showed him how to use every viable part of the fish to ensure nothing was wasted, that a life hadn't been taken for no good. On days when they had a particularly good catch this would mean hours of cooking for them, often moving the food out onto the square, creating an impromptu feast for anyone who hadn't eaten. Mathias had taken great pride in the looks on people's faces as they enjoyed his food and took pleasure in feeding his family and friends. It was those very days that led to Mathais opening the bar in town. He had been the real driver behind the project with Mateo tagging along for the ride initially but quickly finding his feet as the restaurant's outgoing front man.

Tómas slipped his hand into Christina's as they walked, jolting her from daydreams.

Those days were all gone now.

Her boys were dead. There would be no more restaurant, no more impromptu feasts in the square. All that was left now was to protect what remained of their way of life.

Walking into the harbour she was relieved to see no signs of life, just boats rocking gently where they were tethered. A quick glance revealed no obvious gaps, nothing missing, as far as she could tell all of the boats seemed to be accounted for but still, she had to be sure.

'Nicholás and Rodrigo, go and check the boats. There are thirty-eight licensed boats in the marina, count them all, and make sure no one is on board. We don't want to hand them a boat and a captain.'

'Yes ma'am,' they said together.

'Pascal, find a high spot with a good view of the road, I want to know the second you see anyone approach.'

The three men set off in different directions leaving Christina with Tómas and Carlota.

'What's the plan?' asked Carlota.

'I'm not sure yet,' Christina honestly replied. 'I'm trying to work out how we cover all these boats with just a handful of people.'

They looked out over the sea of bobbing masts, each one offering a viable means of escape. Carlota had never liked the water, a rarity in an island community like theirs. As far as Christina knew, she had never even left the island.

'I am assuming they don't sail?' she asked Christina.

'Not that I am aware of.'

'Then we need to focus on any boats with an engine, the simpler the better. I have never sailed so I would be looking for something I could just point and steer. The nearer to the harbour exit the better so that I wouldn't have to navigate my way out.'

Christina nodded her approval and saw the younger woman's neck flush.

'Supplies,' said Tómas. 'Water, food, fuel.'

He was a man of few words these days but when he spoke it was always for a good reason. He was right, they had to assume the survivors would not know where they were going or how to get there. They would need to ensure they took food and water with them if they hadn't already picked that up before they got here. That would mean they would head for the harbour master's store, taking them along the east side of the marina rather than the west. It would naturally follow that they would then continue along the eastern dock in search of a possible boat for escape. They wouldn't risk doubling back and the eastern side was closer to the open water.

As much as she hated the members of 4, she had to respect their resourcefulness and will to survive. She would send Nicholás and Rodrigo along the western dock in case she was wrong in her deductions, but she was now sure that any survivors would head down the other side as it gave them the best chance of escape.

Behind them Pascal had climbed onto the roof of the storage shed by the dry dock. He had a clear view of the road but kept turning back to keep an eye on the others on the dock. He saw Christina looking over and swiped his hand back and forth, low down with his palm facing down.

No one in sight.

Carlota led them along the dock, looking all the while for boats she would consider trying to use if she were trying to flee. She stepped cautiously along the slatted walkway, her heart pounding as she passed over the wider gaps in between the boards. She pulled her eyes away from the swirling green waters below. instead putting herself in the place of the group needing to get off the island. They would want a simple boat, no masts or complex mechanisms to daunt them, just something plain with enough space to shelter a few people from the sun if they ended up being at sea for a while.

Several options caught her eye as they walked along but none were ideal; the only thing that came close to fitting her needs turned out to be too big and daunting for a novice as they approached it. She was close to admitting defeat when she spotted a white bow hiding behind the larger vessel.

At around the twenty-five foot *El Hipocampo* was half the size of its neighbour, a polished wooden deck graced the stern leading onto a large, open backed bridge. Carlota could also see two portals below indicating further space below deck.

Goldilocks had found a boat that was just right.

She turned to Christina and pointed at her prize. 'This one.'

With Pascal on guard down the road Christina estimated they had at least fifteen minutes warning should anyone head to the harbour, there was still time to make sure this boat became irresistible.

Carlota stood out of the way as Tómas helped Christina to move the boat into a more favourable position, lengthening the bow line and shortening the stern line to shift it back along the jetty, revealing more of the smaller vessel behind it. Tómas leapt onto El Hipocampo and untied her. With Christina's help they were able to drift the boat out of its mooring and turn it around using the ropes, Carlota swallowing her fear to help her control the boat with another more line. By the time they were finished the boat was facing directly out to sea and clearly visible from the dock. It was perfect.

With the bait laid out it now became a waiting game, each of them strategically tucked away as they waited for their prey. For his own safety and as a linc of last resort she had Tómas hide below deck on El Hipocampo whilst she hid on a larger boat moored opposite. She didn't want them to get as far as the boat itself, her plan was to confront them on the dock with Carlota and Pascal coming up from behind to close the trap. As soon as they were surrounded Nicholás and Rodrigo would run to the east dock to pump up their numbers and outnumber them.

Considering she had created the plan on the hoof Christina was pleased with the strategy. If things went as expected she was confident that no one was going to be getting off this island. She sent Carlota to tell the others the plan before hiding herself behind the harbour master's store where Pascal would join her as soon as they came into view.

Christina found a comfortable spot on the boat and sank down to wait, thoughts of her boys flooding her mind and steeling her resolve to get her revenge.

51

Jess lay on the floor listening to Oskar breathing. He wrapped his hand around hers, holding it tight and she shut her eyes to the flickering orange light on the ceiling.

She had had to lie back at the villa. Telling them she didn't know what had happened at the tree was an easy deception, justifiable even. The hours between her going into the woods and waking up back in the sheet-lined room had been a blur, a strange mixture of dreams and clarity swirled into a confusing daze. Was it even lying if you were just being selective in what you told? There *had* been a dream about burning the tree, she may have glossed over some parts but the core of what she told them was true… mostly. They hadn't needed to know what else she had seen. Nor did they need to know about the deep itch she had felt in her throat since she came around or the feeling that she was no longer alone in her own skin. They would only have panicked and left her behind. She wouldn't have blamed them either, it would be the sensible thing to do, the *only* thing they could do.

Increasingly though it was becoming harder for her to hide the truth.

There was an *otherness* now, something new inside her, connecting her to the island in a way she couldn't explain. It was getting stronger too, the filaments of light she had seen in the trees had been no trick of the light, it was the flow of energy that linking the island together; millions and billions of connections that ran through every branch, root, and leaf on the island. A mighty network connected them all, communicating and nourishing everything from the Heart tree to the grasses that bound and shaped the sands of the vast coastal dunes.

It had always been this way, long before people had arrived on the island - the mighty conquistadors in their tall ships and frock coats - blindly destroying its riches in their quest to claim new lands for their Queen. There was no hierarchy on the island, instead everything was drawn together, one thriving system in which everything played its own part.

She had seen how the dying trees, felled by the invading humans, had pumped chemical warnings into the sky, the same alarm simultaneously dispatched underground through the web of mycelia that bound them all together. A silent bell, already tolling for the oblivious humans, no change in balance would go unchecked.

Now she was a part of it, she could feel it all out there and it was intoxicating.

There was no need to focus on the cost of this knowledge, she told herself, not yet anyway. She wasn't even sure she believed it herself yet so for now it was safer to just go with it, test the waters to see if what she was being shown was true.

She wanted to believe there was hope but part of her was scared that there could be. To accept there was a way off the island also meant accepting the sacrifice she knew was needed to ensure survival - and the price of freedom wasn't cheap.

Jess lay still and opened her mind, calling her decision out into the void.

Eager green tendrils snaked out of the darkness, leafy digits wrapping around her legs and arms, pulling her down into the lush embrace of the island.

Jess's mouth moved silently, intently.

Oskar tried to shake her awake, but she was unresponsive, her lips just carried on working, continuing their mute conversation.

'Jess…' whispered Oskar, squeezing her hand, 'Jess…'

His tone changed, growing more urgent as she shook her harder. 'Shreya, she won't wake up,' he said, panic rising in his voice.

'Let's get her up,' said Shreya, hooking her arm under Jess and dragging her up to a sitting position with his help. 'Come on Jess, wake up babe.'

They shook her harder but still she wouldn't wake, her mouth kept on its seamless communication as her head lolled from side to side. Shreya lowered her back down to the floor and stood up, pulling Oskar away with her.

'I think she's communicating with it,' she whispered.

Oskar looked back at the prone figure of his friend, head tipped to one side, dead to the world apart from her animated mouth.

'With what?'

'With *it*, with *them,* the island, whatever the hell it is.'

She was annoyed with herself for not suspecting it sooner. They had known that Jess had forged some kind of connection to the island. Ever since she went to that damned tree, she had been a little bit different, not enough to make them worry, just enough to move them along. It had been *her* that had come up with the plan, taken control of the situation when they had been lost, gotten them out of the villa compound.

That should have been Shreya's first clue. Normally Jess was the last to step up and take the lead, preferring to let the group decide and then go with the flow. It had been so easy to ignore the clues when they were helping, but now she was turning into a problem. If she *was* having some communication with the island, then she was effectively a fucking transmitter to the enemy. Any plans they had would be useless now.

'No, she can't be,' said Oskar.

'Look at her! She is not just asleep. She is unconscious but very clearly communicating with someone or something and we both know that she has not been herself since she came around earlier. Look, maybe I'm wrong, but if I'm not then we've got to assume that anything she knows, the island knows too.'

Oskar leaned against the wall and stared at the prone form of his friend, wishing he were in a place where Shreya's argument was harder to believe.

'What do we do?'.

'Well, they seem to be able to reach her when she is unconscious, so we need to wake her up and break the connection. If we can do that, then we tell her we have a new plan to get away. We don't have to have one, we just need her to believe we do in case she falls unconscious again.'

'That's the best we have?' he asked.

'Unless you can come up with an actual new plan while we try and bring her round then I don't see what other choice we have.'

'What are you girls whispering about?'

Shreya whipped her head around to find Jess was awake but groggy, still leaning against the wall where they had left her. She couldn't have been awake for more than a second or two so Shreya decided to call her bluff on the change of plan.

'Oskar had a great idea while you were asleep,' she said, hoping he would play along, 'let's get out of here and we'll fill you in as we go.'

'We didn't want to wake you,' Oskar added feebly.

Jess stood up and looked at them both in turn. Shreya could be the best liar in the world, but Oskar was never going to convince anyone.

'Here's the problem,' she said, challenging her friends, 'there is no new plan to get off the island. We couldn't think of one before and I am pretty sure you didn't brainstorm a new one in the five minutes I have been asleep.'

No one spoke, but she could see in their eyes that she was right. The silence stretched on. Shreya finally cracked and looked at Oskar, seeking some kind of answers in his impassive Nordic face.

He sighed, out of ideas.

'Fine. You were talking in your sleep, and we couldn't wake you up. I'm not going to abandon you now just because we think the island may have some kind of hold on you, but I have no fucking clue what we do now.'

Jess felt herself flush, partly in relief that they weren't going to abandon her but partly in shame as she had doubted them.

'I think we just carry on as planned. We've been over the options dozens of times and the only way off is by boat and the only place we know they have boats is the marina. The plan has to stay the same – we've got nothing else.'

'What about the other thing?' asked Shreya.

'You mean the whole Jess-is-talking-to-the-trees conspiracy?' This time it was Shreya's turn to blush. 'Look, I don't know what is going on here, I think it's safe to say that this whole thing is a bit of a mind-fuck for all of us. But you *know* that I will do whatever it takes to get you away from here, trust me on that.'

'I do,' said Shreya, wanting herself to believe it.

'Let's keep going as planned but go quickly. The rules seem to be changing around here so we can't take anything for granted so we stay out of the trees and away from anyone, infected or not.'

Oskar nodded. 'We stay in the shadows and stick to the streets.'

Shreya opened her mouth to agree but was cut off by the creak of the heavy door opening downstairs, quickly followed by footsteps as a group of people walked into the building, making their way up the same stairs they had climbed fifteen minutes earlier.

If someone had spotted them on the way in, then they would have come for them before now.

Jess pointed behind the desk and the three of them silently moved behind it, crouching low, ready to spring up and run if they had to. The stairs creaked as people climbed them, muttered conversation drifting up the stairwell as they ascended.

If they were looking for them then they weren't being subtle about it.

Jess braced herself to run but the footsteps moved to the right of them, opening another door somewhere on the landing and filing into different room, closing it softly behind them.

'Let's go,' whispered Oskar.

They unfurled from behind the desk and walked to the door as softly as they could, following each other's footsteps for fear of treading on a noisy board in the creaky, old building. Oskar eased the door open, ready to pounce, but found the hallway empty. Whoever they were, they had all vanished into the other room en masse. Creeping along the corridor towards the stairs they heard a satisfied exclamation from behind the door.

If they had found what they had come for, it wouldn't be long before they left again.

They had to get away quickly.

A small commotion ensued as the hidden locals sprung into motion in the other room. It was enough to mask any sounds from the stairs, so Oskar picked up the pace, taking the stairs two at a time and waving back to the others to follow. He closed the door behind them as they fled the building and they found themselves back in the unbearable heat of the burning square. A second side of the square was now aflame; it wouldn't be long before the whole square was burning. Oskar spotted a small alleyway, further along from the door they had just run out of, a tiny snicket between two rows of buildings. He ran to it, checking for signs of life, there would be no room to fight in the trapped confines of the dark alley. Nothing moved in the darkness, so he took the plunge, leading them away from the searing heat of the square.

Doors ran at intervals along the walls of the alley, the fetid smell of rubbish and the bins next to each door. Oskar stopped in the middle to give them a chance to catch their breath, but Jess pushed past him, taking the lead in the group. She grabbed her knife from her backpack and brandished it in front of her.

She could sense them around her, the dull pull of the infected as they moved around. Rather than fearing the power she embraced it, opening herself up to the sensation, using it to try and guide them safely through the streets of the old town. There was so many of them, but one was close, too close. She dropped behind a bin and waved at the others to follow her lead.

At the end of the passage an infected local veered into sight. The graceless plod of its footsteps moved along the street as it dragged one leg behind it. The sound grew distant and finally vanished as the host disappeared. After a minute of silence Jess got back up and pushed forward, towards the end of the tunnel, sensing the others staring behind her. The infected woman had disappeared around a corner leaving the rest of the street empty.

'We've got a clear run,' she said to Shreya and Oskar who were now staring at her, unaccustomed to seeing this was a side of their friend. 'We need to be quick, less caution and a lot more speed.'

Oskar was about to ask her the question, so she didn't give him the chance.

Jess ran out of the alley and darted left, knowing that Oskar would follow her without question and that Shreya would just have to follow or be left behind. Muffled cursing behind her was quickly followed by footsteps. Jess smiled as she ran, feeling in control for the first time since everything had gone to shit.

At the next junction she didn't bother stopping to look, she knew the way ahead was clear, so she just pushed herself forward, ignoring the sound of her footsteps bouncing off the walls around her. She did allow herself a quick glance back and was reassured to see that the others were keeping pace with her.

This new resilience was all well and good, but it had done nothing to improve her sense of direction. The roads stretched out around her, each looking the same, none of them familiar to her having paid no attention on the drive from the boat to the villa. Now she was running blindly. Even though she was sure she was heading in the right direction, she couldn't risk leading them away from the harbour. She stopped and waited for the others to catch her up. They were still a few hundred feet away; she must really have been pelting it along the streets.

Too late she felt the presence in the side street.

Before she could yell out it stepped out of the small side street and grabbed Oskar, pushing its face into his as it tried to pull him down to the ground.

Shreya's knife lashed out instinctively, taking it by surprise as the blade slipped through the calf, catching on the bone behind the muscle then slicing through fat and tissue as she dragged it through his leg. The attacker felt no pain, it didn't yell as the metal sliced through the host's body, but the torn ligaments were enough to make it stumble.

Shreya watched as Jess charged, smashing her weapon - a small cast iron frying pan she had scavenged from the villa - into its face as hard as she could. Bone crushed under the weight of metal, cheekbones crunched inwards as the top of the nose popped forwards, dragging its eyeballs out of their orbits.

The thing turned in circles, unable to see them as its eyeballs bounced against its cheeks.

Jess got back to her feet and yanked Shreya's knife from its leg, leaping back as it swung around wildly. It began to screech, a high-pitched throaty wail crying out into the night. They backed away from it, glancing around the empty street hoping it had been alone.

Above them a sash window slid open, and their heads snapped up, seeking out the source of the noise. Across the street a little girl, barely ten years old, glared down at them. Tears lined her face, but her eyes were filled with rage. Whoever she was, it was clear from the way she stared at them that she saw them as the cause of her misery. The girl vanished inside, reappearing at the window seconds later with a long, green plastic horn.

If she hadn't been running for her life Jess would have laughed at the ridiculous sight. Instead, her stomach dropped and panic set in. Any chance they had of sneaking through the town undetected would be gone the second the girl blew into the vuvuzela.

There was no time to beg her to stop, the girl spat down at them and raised the horn to her lips and it blared out it's angry, apian sound echoing all over the town. If anyone was nearby, infected or otherwise, they would soon be descending on this street.

This time no one had to say it. They ran.

Oskar took the lead, pushing them back towards the main road that cut through the town. Once they hit that it was a simple straight path out to the marina if he remembered rightly. Had that journey into town just been a few days ago? He was a different person now from the carefree man that had arrived on the island. Hardened by the loss of Duncan he was now determined to get the others away from this hell hole.

With stealth now out of the equation he just hoped they could get out to the docks before anyone caught up with them.

He was leading them back into town, the road he needed wasn't far, he just hoped he recognise it, things had a habit of looking different in this crepuscular light. He spotted the route he needed as the sun vanished from sight. It was closer than he thought - he had to take a sharp right, barely slowing down as he turned the corner in a wide arc. Shreya and Jess staggered around the corner behind him, their forward momentum dragging them in a wide arc as they turned, the sudden change of direction taking them by surprise.

Ahead of them the road ran through a scattering of houses, the last habitations before the road opened out, then dipped, winding its way down towards the harbour.

Oskar began to feel optimism rising inside of him. Getting onto a boat and off the island was only the first step in the perilous journey ahead of them but if they could just get out to sea, they would be free. They would have beaten the island, beaten Christina.

He had to believe they could make it.

Shreya and Jess followed behind him as night took hold. There was no sign of anyone following them and the lights of the town soon fell behind them. They slowed down as the shadows embraced them, hiding them from view.

Alone in the darkness they regrouped on the road and hugged.

52

The mournful sound of the vuvuzela blared out over the town.

The infected instantly turned their heads towards it, drawn by its cry. They swarmed together, pushing down streets and alleys, trying to find the source of the droning.

People, hiding in their flats and houses heard it and argued over what it meant. The discussion raged in attics and basements, one young couple holed up in a small cupboard of their newly bought home decided to ignore it whilst their more elderly neighbours ventured out from their bathroom for the first time in hours, certain that they were being called out of hiding, that the nightmare was finally over.

In the Mayor's office Christina's other team paused as they headed down the stairs. They were on their way to meet up with the others at the marina, but the noise called to them, emboldened as they now were with guns in their hands. If someone was in trouble then they were duty bound to help, to shoot any infected they saw, even if it meant saving just one uninfected person.

The girl in the window watched as people began to appear. She knew she the three people had been in the street below. Kids weren't supposed to know what happened at *Arboleda del Dios* but they weren't stupid. The best way to inspire kids with a thirst for knowledge is to tell them they are too young to know. They hadn't been locals so she had known exactly who they must be and tried to warn people where they were.

And now she could see doors opening below; men and women tentatively poking their heads out before stepping out and heading in her direction. She knew she should stop, but instead blew harder on the vuvuzela, the long note cracking in her excitement that help was coming.

More doors opened as people risked leaving the safety of their hideouts in the hope that the call signalled the end of the horror. There were already a few people starting to gather in the road below her. She lowered the trumpet from her lips, tears running down her face as she saw that she wasn't alone anymore. She had been alone since her mother had taken a phone call and run outside to collect her grandmother and bring her here to safety. *Momentito* she had whispered as she closed the door behind her, waiting to hear the key being turned in the lock before she ran down the stairs.

For hours she had been sure that everyone else must be dead, or worse, turned into the monsters she had seen walking down the street. An hour ago, her teacher had walked past, she had been about to call to him but there that something was different about him. Even from her lofty heights she could see that his limp was gone, the cane had had always needed discarded as he walked upright, no longer concerned by the pain he had always droned on and on about in their classes.

The feeling she had seeing him walking normally was nothing to her shock moments later as she saw him force himself onto a young woman in the street. She fought him, trying desperately to push him away but he pushed his mouth down onto hers until her arms gave up their fight. In cartoons True Love's kiss was a blessing but this was no fairy tale. The would-be prince pushed away from the woman and walked off, leaving her in the street, hungry to find a mouth of her own to claim.

But now there were others still out there, people who could help her, she was no longer alone.

She pulled the vuvuzela back through the window. One street over she spotted still more people walking towards her. Everyone she had seen had been nervous, looking all around them as they made their way to her street, but this group moved with purpose, sure of their direction, pushing each other out of the way to get there first.

Too late she realised what she had done. This group wasn't coming to help her; she had drawn them to her with her alarm call. She wanted to shout down, warn the people below; but when she opened her mouth no sound came out.

Terror and guilt froze her to the spot, unable to call out.

As the infected crowd neared the square, she saw another group arrive at the top of her street, holding their arms out, weapons drawn as they approached the people below. One woman lowered her arm as she saw her sister standing in the crowd, seconds before the first of the infected poured into the street, swarming over the milling crowd.

Shots rang out, the shooters panicking as they saw people dragged to the ground in the melee, arms flailing at their assailants, too late to stop the assault. People started to drop as the bullets sailed into them, uninfected innocents falling at the hands of the armed mob, unable to distinguish the good guys from the bad.

The conflict was short lived.

Untrained, the shooters fired off ammunition until they ran out of bullets, one by one lowering their useless guns, hoping they had done enough to save themselves.

The girl looked down from the window and watched in silence as the infected pulled themselves out of the pile of bodies and turned on the group of shooters.

She reached out and grasped the handle of the window, drawing it towards her slowly, the noise from the street disappearing as she pulled it shut.

The girl backed slowly away and nestled back into her hiding place behind the sofa.

She pulled a blanket over her head and lay there, tears silently flowing.

53

Christina's head snapped up as she felt herself drifting towards sleep, lulled by the gentle rocking of the boat and her own exhaustion. She had been awake for over twenty-four hours, but this was no time to let her guard drop.

Pascal was still crouched on the roof in wait.

She stared at his unmoving shadow, willing the boy to be awake still, otherwise they really were in trouble.

After long minutes of stillness Pascal swiped at something buzzing around his ear, readjusting position as he did so.

Thank God one of them was still alert.

The spot she was huddled into was far from comfortable, nothing was on these fishing vessels. They were geared to practical needs, not comfort, function over finesse. The smell alone should have kept her awake but moments later she felt herself losing the battle as her eyelids once again drooped, her body willing her to sleep. She had to stay awake, had to fight it, but before she could offer any resistance her eyes closed.

A sudden mournful droning shocked her awake.

The noise was familiar, but she couldn't place it, whatever it was though, she knew it wasn't good. She leapt from her hiding place, cursing herself for falling asleep again.

It blared out for several minutes, the staccato blasts oddly jarring in the tranquil setting of the harbour. She prayed that it would stop, knowing the sound would draw people out of their houses. The longer it went on, the more would be at risk. The relief she felt as the noise died out was short lived.

A volley of gunfire pierced the sudden silence, the shots sounding reactive and uncontrolled.

It wasn't hard to work out what was going on somewhere in town. The others had found the weapons cache in the office and then been drawn to the noise. It would have drawn villagers out of hiding but it would also have attracted the *others.* Christina knew that having a gun is one thing, but knowing what to do with it was completely different. The scene played out slowly in her mind, she imagined the armed but untrained group firing wildly as their attackers swarmed towards them. They would barely have managed to hit the quickly moving targets and, even if they had, the chance of a bullet stopping the infected in their tracks was slim. They were no longer human, pain meant little to them, she had seen that firsthand. Unless they had managed to blow out their brains or shoot through a leg they would have kept charging forward, driven by their relentless need to spread the contagion that controlled them.

One by one the guns fell quiet.

The sound of the last bullet ricocheted around the roofs and silence finally returned to the village. There was no way to know for sure what had happened, but she imagined the worst.

On the warehouse roof Christina could see that Pascal's body language had changed, he was tense and alert, staring into the distance. It could only mean that someone must be approaching from town.

Her focus had been so intent on stopping 4 from leaving the island that she hadn't even considered the possibility that the infected might reach them here. If this wasn't the survivors of Batch 4 trying to flee the island, then she had just trapped them all at the end of the docks.

A small light was shining in the direction of the water, flashing on and off as Pascal waved his phone from the roof of the warehouse. Clever lad, they hadn't even discussed how he should signal them, but she hoped it meant what she thought it did. Pascal dropped out of sight, appearing moments later on the dock, running along the boards to hide behind the store with Carlota.

There was no way to see the road from where they were, the first time she would see the approaching group would be as they got to the edge of the docks.

There was no going back from that moment, this would end here.

Her heart beat hard and fast, adrenaline pumping in anticipation of their arrival. She no longer worried about dying, there was nothing left for her here on the island. It was her duty as mayor to try and save her community but in her heart, she knew she no longer cared about most of them. Revenge was her motive now, she just wanted them to pay. Her words back in the church had been exaggerated but her message had been true. 4 killed her boys by their actions and she would have her revenge. She had already forgotten the horrors of her brief dream, the only thing she held on to was the feeling of those young boys clinging to her as they watched a film together. She held on to that moment, letting it fuel her anger as she waited for them to arrive.

Looking around her, she saw that most of the equipment hanging around the cabin would be a hell of a lot more effective than the makeshift weapons they had cobbled together back at the church. She laid down her small knife and ran her hands over the hilts of the profession gear on the wall, finally selecting a nine-inch Bubba Blade filleting knife. She had been around fishermen her whole life and had seem them use knives like this to slice into the brain of a stunned tuna, pushing it around until the fish stopped moving before slicing under the gills to make it to bleed out. These knives slid through their skin like butter, splaying their bellies open ready to have their insides torn out. They would doubtless do the same to her sons' killers.

Movement drew her eyes back to the docks.

There was someone out there now, moving slowly, constantly checking their surroundings as they went. From its cautious behaviour she was sure this was not the actions of an infected, it had to be one of the group.

The shadow moved along the quay, heading straight for the shop just as they had predicted. A sharp tinkle of glass breaking drifted across the water and two more shadows ran over to join the first.

Three survivors, was that all? This was better than she had hoped.

She gripped the hilt of the knife, liking how it felt in her hand.

54

The link was no longer uncomfortable, the creeping digits caressing the edges of her mind were almost soothing.

Jess could feel them dancing all around her, ever present but no longer probing at her, an equilibrium now established.

The result was overwhelming. Where she had once just seen trees, she now saw complex, thriving citadels - beyond the trunks, branches and leaves hung bright clouds of moss, teeming with life; swathes of lichen glimmered in the dark, silver-plating bark as far as the eye could see. Even within the lichen she could now see the layers of fungus and algae, their beautiful alchemy of colours creating the metallic hue of the bark's crust. Her link was deepening, showing her all the complex secrets of the island, the dark of the night eliminated by the light of the life surrounding them.

She would have counted her new sight as a gift were it not for the visions that were being show to her as they fled from the town, a freak show being projected onto the back of her eyeballs. Glancing at her friend's faces the flickering images blurred into their features and she was unable to discern either clearly. But when her eyes caught a patch of darkness the pictures sharpened, an 4K Ultra HD horror show that she couldn't ignore.

Shreya lying in the water, her once beautiful face now a bloated, fleshy mask that now that had slipped across her skull, her lips obscenely parted to reveal her chin. Oskar lying face down on the slatted docks, his arm draped over the edge, Shreya's hair wound his fingers, anchoring her body to him.

His blood sluiced over the wooden deck - so much blood - dripping between the slats and into the salt water below.

She saw herself kneeling in front of the Heart Tree, her eyeballs wrinkling as they dried out, her leathery skin clinging to her bones as every ounce of sustenance drained from her body and into the ground.

It took all of her will power to try to ignore the images, staring straight through them, focusing instead on the newfound beauty of the island. The technique worked so well that she was almost able to ignore them until the real Shreya turned to look at her and smiled. Her happy, healthy face was overlaid perfectly with the macabre death mask, her healthy features peering out through the decay that now covered them. Her delicate little nose hanging loose, the skin having sloughed to the side, slipping away to reveal the cartilage below, the black depths of her nasal cavity…

Bile rose in Jess's throat, and she feared she might faint but caught herself, passing it off as a stumble on the uneven road.

The island didn't do subtle. It knew her now, had seen everything about her, knew which buttons to push. These warnings were more than a threat, the images showed her what would come to pass if she ignored its offer.

Life for life, that was what it demanded.

Death masks flashed before her, Shreya, Oskar, and her own desiccated face, blurring as they spun in her mind, flickering into motion as they sped up until they became a macabre zoetrope, one face smiling at her in death.

Jess didn't know she had stopped until Oskar and Shreya began to jog back towards her.

'Are you ok?' he asked, wrapping an arm protectively around her.

'Sorry, just… it's nothing, just a stitch.' She stood up straight and took deep breaths like she had been taught at school, arms on her sides to stave off the pain on the dreaded cross-country runs. She saw Oskar and Shreya exchanging worried looks but she knew that they had little choice now. Her act wasn't convincing anyone but at this stage it was too late to go back. 'Come on, let's keep going.'

The three set off again, slowing down now that they were out of sight of the town. The images had stopped now, and she was left alone with her thoughts and her friends. All that remained of the merry band that had arrived on the island days before.

There had to be another option, another way that could get them *all* off the island but if there were, she couldn't find it. Unfortunately, she had never really been one for the ideas and now she was out of time.

A sacrifice was unavoidable.

Oskar slowed to a stop and pulled them together, from where they stood, huddled on the gentle slope of the road, the full layout of the marina was visible just below them. 'If we manage to get a boat, we need to be prepared for the fact that we may be at sea a while. We can work out how to sail but neither one of us can navigate our way out of a paper sack.'

'Bag,' Jess corrected absentmindedly, 'navigate our way out of a paper bag.' The others looked at her, given their predicament this perhaps hadn't been the best time to correct his turn of phrase. 'Sorry.'

'I think that must be the harbour store over there,' he continued, pointing to the right of the dock. "We grab anything we can, water, snacks, anything. Then we find a decent boat and get the hell off this island."

Jess managed to muster an enthusiastic nod, but her eyes turned to the end of the dock, scanning the shadows.

She knew what would happen at the docks which could only mean that they were already out there, waiting for them, poised and ready. One way or another this was where it would end. The others were walking blindly into an already sprung trap, only she could lead them away from the steeled blades that dangled over them.

All along the marina lights were strung around the waterline, their soft glow illuminating the wooden docks that stretched out into the water. As best she could tell their path was clear all the way to the store; Jess was sure they would get all the way to it without being jumped on. She would wait until they were safely inside and then warn them.

They would believe her but then what? There was no plan B to get them off the island. They could hope that the other side of the docks was unguarded but somehow, she doubted it would be. If they had learned one thing from all of this, it was that Christina was resourceful. It was no easy feat to keep an operation like this quiet for so many years. The last thing she would do was leave one escape route wide open. Whatever they did now, it would inevitably lead her to the fork in the road that she knew was coming.

Better to get it over with quickly.

There was no option for stealth, no shadows to hide in along the dock so they opted for speed, running along the slats in a tight huddle. Oskar hit a small pane of glass in the door with his elbow, reached through the gap and turned the lock. Textbook breaking and entering. She was half expecting him to do a roll over the desk, jumping behind it to cover the door as the girls followed. There was always humour to be found in crisis, at least there was to her. If only she could find the solution as quickly as she could find the laughs.

Oskar had been right about the store and was already filling his rucksack with bottles of water and packets of food, clearing the shelves as best he could. Shreya had picked up a fishing rod and some tackle. She picked out several different flies from a large display, feeling the weight in her hand and holding them up to the light, checking their reflective qualities.

She had always been full of surprises.

'It's another trap.' The words popped out of Jess's mouth before she had the chance to think them through.

'What is?' asked Shreya, rejecting one of the flies in favour of a more elaborate one that looked like a fluffy shrimp.

'I was infected back at the tree… I have one of them inside me.'

Her confession hung in the air. Oskar and Shreya stopped filling their bags and stared at her. The silence was unbearable. Quickly she recounted the tale of her link with the island, selecting the best bits of the story and holding back the parts that they didn't need to know. She told them that she *knew* that Christina was waiting for them right now, somewhere on the pier ahead of them.

Oskar deflated before her very eyes as her words sank in.

It was Shreya that broke the silence.

'I don't suppose it told you how the fuck we can get off the island, did it?'

'No,' she lied.

Shreya perched against the cash desk and sighed. 'Ok. I don't know what to do about… that,' she said, pointing at Jess's throat, 'so all we can do for now is to adapt our plans with this *new* information. If Christina has anticipated our moves so far, then we need to do the opposite of what she expects. Double back and go to the other pier. She may well have that covered but if we assume she thinks we will head towards her then the other way should at least have less cover.'

Oskar looked about as convinced as Jess felt.

At most that would buy them a few short moments before Christina realised and they had gone the other way and came after them. Without knowing how many people were hiding out there either pier would now be tantamount to suicide.

'No. We have to go back and hide,' said Oskar. 'They can't stay out here forever. We take all the supplies we can carry then find somewhere nearby to shelter, keep an eye out for a chance to sneak away, grab a boat and go.'

Jess was less than enthused by Oskar's plan but at least it kept them alive longer and took them away from the water, away from the rotting faces floating in the harbour. It would have to do for now.

All three jumped as the door to the shop swung in, the remaining panes of glass smashing as the door slammed into the wall behind it.

Four angry faces stared through the door.

They had just run out of options.

55

This wasn't part of the plan.

Christina watched as Pascal and Carlota emerged from the shadows moments after the three survivors of 4 walked into the shop. Pascal had once again used his phone to signal to Nicholás and Rodrigo, drawing them over from the other pier. As soon as they reached them Carlota stepped forward and kicked the door in, the four of them crowding around the doorway, blocking Christina's view.

It was simple and effective, why hadn't she thought of it?

They were now trapped in the shop, with no windows or doors at the back so there was no way for them to escape, unless they forced their way through the crowd at the doorway, but she was certain they weren't going to try that. Carlota stood back, the others following suit, forming a line along the dock, blocking the exit.

Her team led the three figures out of the shop and along the pier towards them. The two women walked at the front; the man was positioning himself wide of the others. His body language was clear even from this distance, his right shoulder dropping as he reached down to grab the knife from the side pocket of his cargo shorts. Before she could scream out any warning she saw Carlota's arm jab out, there was a flash of metal and the man stumbled forwards. The girls grabbed him and helped him to his feet, helping him on wards as his hand clutched his side.

The attempt to break free had been feeble and short lived.

Now there was no attempt to run, they just allowed themselves to be herded along the pier.

Seeing them defeated like that, free of hope or fight, made her uneasy. She felt her own fight ebbing away as the reality of taking their lives kicked in. She was going to have to kill them.

She had been responsible for scores of deaths as mayor but that was all strangely passive, bureaucratic almost. It was one thing to coordinate the leading of the lambs to slaughter, but to take a life with her own hand was very different. What if she couldn't go through with it? Mateo's cheeky laugh rang out in her mind, and she felt his loss cut through her again. The last thing she had done to Mathias was to drive away, abandoning him to his fate.

She left him to die alone at the wall.

Her anger rose again as she thought of them both dying alone.

Her legs wobbled slightly as she got off the boat and stood on the docks to meet them. Less than an hour on calm water and already she had sea legs. She had never been good at sea which is why she had always been so glad the boys had Tómas to take them fishing.

On the island she had always referred to the villa guests with letters and numbers, stripping them of any identity to make it easier for the islanders involved in the process. Only a handful of people ever knew their names, it was better that way. Christina remembered the name of every single person that had ever come to the island and given their lives to save her boys. She knew exactly who the three people were walking towards her.

Jess

Oskar.

Shreya.

Jess was the one she was nervous about, but she didn't know why. There had been something about her when Jess had confronted her at the gate, a spark that had unnerved her then and still did. This group had torn apart everything Christina had built in a matter of days, if anyone in the group had masterminded it then it was her, Christina was certain of that.

The girl turned her head, looking around as she walked. She looked out to sea and her head froze. She had seen something out in the dark seascape, something that made her smile.

Christina gripped the knife in her hand, flexing her fingers over the hilt. This had to be quick. For all their sakes. The islanders had fallen behind her lies about the evil nature of 4, she couldn't let them see that the blame was hers.

Oskar was still leaning against Shreya, his face pale, blood seeping through the fingers that pressed against the stab wound.

'Your faggot boyfriend didn't make it I see.' She goaded him. 'I can't say I'm surprised; he was probably on his knees begging for something down his throat.' She didn't give a damn about his sexuality, she just needed to get him angry, get some fight in him to make it easier for her to kill him.

She was disappointed when her words didn't rouse him, instead his shoulders sagged and he, oh no, now he was crying. It would have been much simpler to fight him if he had been angry, but how was she going to bring herself to stab the pathetic sack of bones before her, head bowed as he sobbed and sank to the ground. Although, from the looks of him Carlota might already have done the job for her, she could see blood starting pool as his friend propped him against one of the piles supporting the walkway.

Shreya stepped away from him and ran forward, brandishing her knife.

'You fucking bitch!' she screamed, rage twisting her features as she lunged at Christina.

The older woman spun away from her attacker, instinctively turning away from the blade. It caught her elbow as she moved, the knife jerking out of Shreya's hand as its point stuck into her joint. The pain was exquisite but was soon numbed by the adrenaline rush she felt from the attack. Christina swept out her leg, catching Shreya's foot as she tumbled past her, sending her crashing headlong into the deck.

It was good to feel the killer instinct rushing through her veins once more.

She watched as the Indian girl tried to push herself up, still dazed from the fall, a new-born lamb struggling to stand for the first time. There was no indecision as she swooped down and grabbed the knife from the boards. She saw her blood on the tip of the blade and touched her fingers to her elbow. There was no pain now, just a slow crimson drip from the small wound.

She threw the kitchen knife into the water. One stab with her Bubba Blade would be all it took to finish off the girl kneeling on the pier, she was so slight that the steel would probably cut right through her.

A scuffle broke out behind her as she walked towards Shreya, her knife raised ready for the kill. She risked a quick glance, enough to see that Oskar had found some fight, but not soon enough. Pascal and Carlota were dragging him backwards, his arms locked in theirs.

Jess still stood free but made no move to help her friends.

She still stared straight out to sea, unaware of the fact that her friend was moments from death.

Rodrigo and Nicholás closed in on her, approaching her warily, as unnerved by her odd behaviour as Christina herself. She turned back to the prone woman in front of her, trusting her men to grab Jess if she snapped out of her trance and tried to stop her.

Shreya's eyes locked on the curved blade of the nine-inch knife in Christina's hand. She raised it up, showing her the point, turning it so she could see how thin, and razor sharp it was. Somewhere inside a voice was yelling at her to step away and spare the girl, telling her the girl had a family, that she was an innocent in all of this. But that voice was overwhelmed by the anger and hate that raged through her, drove her to walk forward and stamp on her shoulder, forcing the girl flat to the pier once more. She slid her foot upwards, pushing her heel into the dip of the girl's neck, trapping her on the floor. With Shreya immobilised Christina looked back along the pier once more.

Something was happening with 4-J, she could feel it. The codename popped back into her head, somehow more appropriate now, more detached given what she had to do.

No time to worry about that now, she had to finish the one in hand first.

She yanked up Shreya's shirt, revealing the soft skin below. The girl's shoulder blades were clearly defined, her panicked breaths heaving them up and down as Christina ran the knife below them, feeling out the soft flesh beneath. She was no butcher, but she was certain she could pierce the heart if she avoided the ribs, an easy thing to avoid given how skinny this one was.

'This is for Mateo and Mathias,' she said, touching the knife between two ribs.

She felt her boys with her in that moment, close to her, urging her to revenge their deaths.

It felt right.

Standing alone on the pier Jess finally understood.

Images had been bombarding her since they had been forced out of the shop and along the pier. Snapshots curated from the minds of those now linked to the hive. Images of parents weeping as they took children out to the area she recognised as the villa they had been taken to.

In some the villa was a rundown shell of a building, abandoned and ramshackle, in one flash the roof was sagging, in another flash it was gone.

Grief linked all the images.

The same scene repeated time and again, with only the faces changing. The sad history of a population forced to give up its children to appease an unseen, primitive force.

A new image.

People running in fear as the glowing spores filled the night sky, lighting the village below. There was no explanation to the images, but she knew this was what happened if the sacrifices were stopped. The hunger she had felt before came through with the image. The memory of an island overlaid with the memories of the people it took. The villagers gave up their own to keep the hive at bay, feeding it as infrequently as possible to keep the balance.

She stared out into the dark as the images sped up, forming a juddering montage all focused around one subject.

Christina.

A young girl walking along the street with a stern looking father.

The same man sat at a desk, a position of power in the village, the girl sitting quietly in the corner.

The girl now lying across his legs, skirt hiked up and his trousers dropped.

Christina ages as the thoughts flick past, her features strengthening as she gets older, rarely a smile to be seen. Her clothes get baggy, hiding the ever-growing bump.

A funeral. The girl's father. She sits in the front row, no longer trying to hide her belly, no longer afraid.

She is smiling.

The montage leaps back to the villa which is now alive with motion. Jess watches men scurry over the roof, bent over, tiles balanced on their backs. It is starting to look like the villa she remembers. In the background she sees Christina standing away from the work, watching the action but tilting her head towards the trees, lost in thought. Behind her identical looking two boys run around, laughing at some imaginary game they have created.

"This is for Mateo and Mathias". These words are not from the vision, they are being spoken now.

Christina is poised over Shreya, pressing a knife into her back.

'I CAN BRING HIM BACK!'

The words come out of Jess's mouth without thought but she knows it is the truth.

She can feel the network all around her, feel the electricity flowing through the flora all around her, willing her on, promising her the world if she will stay.

Behind the promise there is no compromise though, she knows that now.

It is in all of her.

She was always more than a host.

She *is* the sacrifice.

The islanders have become greedy, believing that they can control the power of the island, tame it like a stray dog. But it can no longer be sustained by the scraps they feed it; balance must be restored. She cannot leave now, and she no longer wants to. The magic of the island and the power on offer to her are hypnotising. The idea of trying to flee to a normal life feels absurd. Nothing waits for her back at home, but the island needs her.

A new ruler, linked to the island and feared by diminished local population.

Christina's rule over the island is over, she just doesn't know it yet.

She jumps up at Jess's words, turning to confront her.

'You can't give me anything, everything I need has already been taken from me.'

Jess smiled at her. 'I can bring back your son.'

She reached out to the island, testing the powers she now knew she wielded. Christina may have had a weak connection to the hive in the past, Jess could feel that, but it had been nothing compared to hers. She sent out new orders, pushing her thoughts out through the chemical web of the island.

They were near, she could sense that, now they turned at her command, stepping out of the shadows and into the marina.

There was no need to look around, she trusted the island. Jess simply raised her arm slowly, gesturing behind her as two men walked onto the dock.

Jess saw all fight drain out of Christina as the woman watched Mathias walk towards her. She forgot everything else in an instant, abandoning Shreya as she walked towards Jess, her momentary elation sinking as the truth hit her.

Shreya lay on the dock, eyes wide as Dean stepped towards Jess. There was nothing behind his eyes, he just stared into the dark, unaffected by the scene before him as he walked forward.

But he was *here*. He was still alive. Hope surged through Shreya.

'No. No, no, no. That is no longer my boy,' cried Christina, 'He died the moment that thing entered him.'

Jess took pleasure in the woman's grief, drawing the moment out, making her suffer longer than she had any need to.

'He tried to kill you, didn't he? How did that feel as a mother? To have your boy turn against you?'

Christina sobbed, 'Mathias would never turn against me, you made him like this. You did!'

'Huh, I guess I did. Just like you wanted to do to us. So, what will happen now do you think?'

Christina knew the answer to this question. She had seen it again and again since the tree caught flame. They sought a new host, spreading the infection before returning to the villa. Or worse, they failed. The was link severed and the spore combusted, beaten by time. The process never varied.

'Don't you think it is a little odd that your precious boy is still here?' taunted Jess.

Jess watched as the woman thought it through, her brow furrowing as the questions the popped into her head, her confusion that none of the usual outcomes had happened in the hours since Mathias had been turned. She waited until she was sure the penny had finally dropped.

'You didn't know the rules could be changed?' Jess asked, giving her a pitying look. 'Mathias is no longer looking to spread the spores into new hosts, he has a new job, don't you Mathias?'

The surviving twin stepped up behind her, slipping into place to her right as Dean fell into her left.

'I think I might keep him, he's quite cute, isn't he?' she said, appraising Christina's son as she watched on in confusion. 'Not as cute as his brother though, that one had a different spark, a whole different energy. Weird how twins can be so similar but so different at the same time.'

'What are you doing?' she begged, barely daring to hope.

'Your ancestors kept the balance on the island, but you have proven yourself unworthy. You couldn't do what had to be done, you changed everything to suit your own needs and look what you did'. Jess raised her hand and stroked Matthias's cheek as the flames picked out the skyline in the village behind her. 'It's time to bring back the old ways, give the island a leader that can restore things to the way they have always been. I don't know why but it wants me to be that power. It will do anything it can to get me to stay, Christina, I just need to ask.'

She let the words sink in for a moment, giving her opponent the chance to think about what that meant to her.

'Anything?' Christina looked hopefully at her son.

Jess nodded slowly. 'Anything.'

'What do you want in return?'

'You walk away right now and let my friends leave. Simple as that. They get off the island and they get home. They will keep their mouths shut and I will stay behind in their place and ensure that no more people will be brought to this island, ever. The burden will once again fall to the islanders. My friends will keep your secret to protect me.'

The words hung in the air. Jess knew that the implications of victims escaping the island were huge, but she also knew that Christina would do anything to get her son back.

'Give me my boy and you have my word.'

Jess paused, as if considering the deal, killing time momentarily.

In truth there was no deal to be made. The island had already taken more than it needed, she could see it spreading out from the Heart tree, nutrients flowing out to the furthest reaches of the network, the equilibrium on the island finally restored. The human population had been depleted to acceptable levels, now the island had to protect what remained. Already bodies were piling up around the tree, any more would be wasteful.

Within moments any spores still active in viable hosts would be reprogrammed to simply expire, leaving the human carriers left intact.

She hadn't demanded the island release Mathias; she had simply taken advantage of the situation she was presented with.

The moment was approaching.

She raised her arms theatrically, squeezing her eyes shut in mock concentration. Seconds passed but nothing changed. She redoubled her efforts, swaying on the spot, willing time forward as she gave the performance of a lifetime.

Either side of her the men slumped to their knees. There was no spark, no theatrics, they just collapsed as the infection in the bodies died, returning control to their unsuspecting bodies.

'Dean!' cried Shreya, springing to her feet the moment she saw him fall. She scooped him into her arms and held his head against her as he came to.

The sight of the two men being released sent the rest of Christina's band scurrying back to town, desperately hoping that the miracle would be repeated, and their loved ones returned to them. Pascal quickly hugged Mathias before joining the others as they ran back up the road.

Christina walked slowly up to Mathias, looking for signs that her boy really had been returned to her.

'Mama? What happened?' he asked, reaching out for her.

She ran to him, pulling her tight to her chest.

'Oh, my baby, my beautiful, beautiful boy.'

56

Oskar watched the spectacle as he lay on the dock.

Ever since everything had gone to shit, he had managed to keep a clear head. There had been no time to stop, he hadn't let there be. He'd taken charge where he could, keeping them on the move, pushing them onwards towards the safety of the dock, focused on getting everyone home.

Then he felt the burn of the knife in his side and his world had shrunk around him.

This was no silent void he found himself in, instead his new world roared with Duncan's absence, pulling at him, begging him to stop, screaming that there was no need to carry on now. Memories from a decade of loving Duncan were all he had now. He had spent the last twenty-four hours blocking all thoughts of his dead lover from his mind and now he was all he could think about. Holidays they had taken, exploring museums and castles, still hungover from the night before. Both laughing, thriving in their own company. Two souls merged into one perfect unit.

Even in their quietest moments, lazing in bed on a cold winter's morning they were always in tune. Oskar trying to read with Duncan lying next to him, pressing his finger against Oskar's nose, sliding the tip into his nostril until they both shook with laughter, his book falling closed on the duvet.

Being stabbed was almost a blessing, he had no idea how to live after half of his soul had been ripped from him.

The absence was surreal to him. It wasn't a bad dream, there was no hope that Duncan would come running to his aid, he knew he was gone, it just didn't make any sense.

He was barely aware of the activity going on around him. He knew they were surrounded on the pier but that became an abstract concept to him. A play being performed in the background of his grief.

Only Christina's words had broken through.

She had called Duncan a faggot.

The rage he felt in that moment made him silent with fury.

He had wanted to run at her, tear her fucking head off with his bare hands but he had already known that he didn't have the strength. The rage gave him a strange comfort and drew it into himself as he slumped down on the ground.

He was aware of a fight and now Shreya was lying on the floor with Christina on top of her.

What was going on with Jess? Words were flying from her mouth, but he couldn't make sense of them.

He drifted back into his memories as he continued to bleed out.

He had no idea how long he had been lying there but at some point, the stage came slowly back into focus. Christina was hugging one of the waiters from the bar and now she was crying.

She was crying tears of joy.

The pier had emptied behind them; their captors were gone. Jess was picking him up, trying to get him to his feet, telling him they could go home. Shreya was at the far end, hugging Dean, stepping onto a boat with the help of an old man.

They had done it. Jess had done it. And now they were going to take him away, make him leave the island, make him leave Duncan.

He eyes focused on Christina, crying as she clung on to her beloved son.

She had done all of this; this was all her fault. How dare she stand there happily holding her son to her. He wanted her to feel the black despair that was dragging him down to the depths, engulfing him in its cold, thick embrace.

She didn't deserve her happy ending.

Jess dragged him upright, taking his face in her hands.

'Oskar! Can you get to the boat?'

He wasn't following her words, but he nodded, needing her to stop talking.

She pushed him gently forwards, pointing to the boat where Shreya and Dean were beckoning him over.

He had no intention of getting on the boat but took a slow step forward anyway. He stumbled with his second step, falling to one knee before Jess scooped him back up.

Back on his feet he walked forward with confidence, he could almost feel Duncan helping him along.

57

Shreya hadn't let go of Dean since he had been brought back to her. She sat on the deck of the boat, still clutching him to her as she watched the scene on the dock unfold with horror.

Oskar had barely been able to walk but after he stumbled his whole body had changed. For the first time in days the loss that had been etched on his face was gone, replaced instead with a look of grim determination. She could have sworn he was smiling.

He hadn't been holding a knife a moment ago but now she could see it in his hand as he lunged forward, plunging it deep into Mathias's back, using all his strength to force the blade as deep as he could.

A confused look crossed the young man's face as he felt the tug of the knife pushing inside of him. He coughed, then yelled as Oskar dragged the cold steel through him, forcing the blade through his flesh until it caught on a rib.

Christina blinked as her son coughed blood over her face. There was a moment of stunned silence before her scream pierced thought the night. Shreya knew she would never forget that primal sound of a mother holding her son as he died in her arms.

Oskar staggered away from them, leaving the knife still lodged in his back.

He watched Christina struggle to hold her son in her arms as he began to lose consciousness. Blood pumped out of the deep wound in his back and her hands until she could no longer grip him. Mathias slipped through her arms and dropped to the pier, never to get up again.

Christina fell to her knees and pulled him up into her arms, resting his head on her breast, feeling the life flowing out of him. Losing him all over again, no hope of a miracle this time.

Oskar staggered towards the boat as Christina screamed again.

Shreya and Dean leapt up at the same time, the sight of their bleeding friend finally snapping them from their shocked trance. They yelled his name and reached out their hands to urge him on, but never got there. Instead, Oskar sat on the dock and gave them a final wave goodbye.

He leaned back against the wooden post and smiled.

Duncan was coming.

Epilogue

After the last of the staff had left Dean pulled the shop doors closed behind them, locking himself in the empty store.

He flicked off the lights behind the tills and walked through the silent shop. Out of habit he tidied up a few displays as he went, straightening books on shelves and tucking magazines back into their acrylic holders. This was his favourite time of day. The store took on a sense of calm and he allowed his mind to drift.

His memories of the night were hazy at best.

He remembered fleeing the villa and reaching the road that led back through town, the next thing was seeing Shreya lying face down on the dock.

Whatever had happened in between was gone.

Tómas had gotten them off the island, too scared of the repercussions to do anything else. He had untied the boat as they watched Mathias and Oskar bleed to death, starting the engine before Christina had time to stop them.

It felt like a dream now.

Shreya had called out for them to wait, begging Jess to get on the boat but Dean knew that she had never intended to leave the island. He didn't know what had happened during the hours he lost but whatever it was, she had been at the heart of it.

In the end she had sacrificed herself to save them, Jess, of all people.

In the stillness of the empty shop, he could still see them, Jess holding Oskar as he died, waving to them, showing them it was all ok.

The following weeks were thankfully a blur. There had been no simple way to explain what had happened, no one would have believed the truth. Faced with their story anyone would assume they were lying and then wonder what they were trying to hide. Instead Tómas had told the officials on Gran Canaria that he had found Dean and Shreya at sea, rescuing them from drowning after a freak accident with a rented boat. The right people on the mainland had been bribed and the appropriate paperwork issued.

The official story was that Jess, Duncan, Oskar, and Ben were all missing at sea, presumed drowned.

Weeks had passed and gradually their families gave up any hope of the four being found alive. Empty coffins were buried, and the tragic tale of the drowned holiday makers eventually disappeared from the papers.

He often thought about Jess, wondered if she was still out there, bridging the gap between the island and the people. He could still see Christina's face as they sailed away from the dock, and he knew there was no way she was ever coming back from her grief. He doubted she would have lasted long, she had been broken by losing her son twice, she didn't have the strength to live with that.

He crossed the shop floor and punched in the four numbers to unlock the door to his office. Sitting down after a day running around the shop was always bliss. He reached down to the safe under his desk, four more numbers and the heavy door sprung open. Kicking off his shoes he took out the small, maroon rucksack and commenced his nightly ritual.

Kobayashi, Keiko

Registered domicile - Kumamoto
Date of birth - 24 Aug 1976

He rubbed his thumb over the image in the girl's passport, her face now familiar to him as his own.

She had gone missing along with three other Japanese nationals whilst on a holiday in Morocco in 2010. The official cause of death was unknown, he had found few stories in English to enable him to understand what reasons had been given. He opened all four of the group's passports, one by one, remembering the sparse details of their lives before closing them and returning them to the lock box.

Over the months he had gathered information on every one of the twenty-eight passports Shreya had managed to smuggle back with them.

Most of the people in the passports had gone missing by themselves, drowned, kidnapped, or simply missing; three - including Keiko and her friends - had been smaller groups that had fallen victim to *misadventure*; four of the victims had disappeared without comment, erased from the world without a care.

Every night he had returned the bag to the safe and locked it, biding his time until he could work out what to do with them. Tonight, though he packed the passports back into the ruck sack, next to the bottle and slipped the postcard between them.

Dean looked at his watch and grabbed his coat from behind the door, setting the alarm as he left the shop. He'd promised Shreya he would be home in time to give little Jessie her bath before bed and didn't want to be late. He pulled his jacked up over his ears, protecting them from the worst of the icy breeze as he trudged his way to Hendon Central station. They were predicting snow in the next twenty-four hours, and they were both excited that Jessie's first Christmas might be white. She wouldn't remember it but these days they clung onto the little things, taking joy in the moments that had often passed by unnoticed before.

Walking up the road he could see Shreya looking out of the window, staring into dark winter evening, praying he would make it home. They didn't often talk about what happened on the island, but their scars still revealed themselves in the detail. Every night she kept a look out, dropping back when she spotted him so that he didn't know she had been watching for him, just has he pretended he hadn't seen her or felt a surge of relief that she too was safe.

They knew all about survivor's guilt, an army of armchair experts had warned them about it, trying to help them overcome a boating accident that never happened. For a time, the island had been all they could talk about, agonising over each detail, second guessing everything that had happened.

Like her namesake, it was Jessie that saved them.

She had worked her magic on them from the moment they found out Shreya was pregnant, bringing them together, united in the shock of their love for her. Day by day they put the island behind them, talking about it less and less until they fooled each other into thinking they had moved on.

He put Jessie to bed and clicked on the baby monitor, giving her one last look before he pulled the door to.

Shreya hugged him as he came into the kitchen, and they sat down to dinner. Dean talked about his day at the shop and Shreya caught him up on the latest gossip from the baby yoga group. After dinner they sat in the lounge and watched the TV, the log burner blazing and the lights twinkling on the Christmas tree. The was already an obscene pile of presents under the tree, all with Jessie's name on them.

They had a couple of glasses of wine, and it wasn't long before Shreya fell asleep on the sofa, blanked pulled up around her neck and a red wine smile on her face. He watched her lying there, not getting up until he heard her softly snoring.

When he returned from the kitchen with the Fallraven rucksack in one hand and a bottle of scotch in the other. The bottle had arrived several days ago, dropped off at the store by a harassed Amazon driver who had clearly not been happy at having to wait while someone found him to sign for it. He had started opening it on the shop floor but stopped the moment he saw the small silver horse glinting at him through the box, recognising it straight away, even after all these months. Back in his office he had searched the packaging for a card or a message but there had been nothing. Until today. The postcard had been in the stack of post brought to his desk, its lurid colours a stark contrast to the mundane correspondences from the head office in Swindon.

Dean sat cross-legged in front of the fire, opened the bottle, and read the postcard again.

Weather amazing, wish you were here… not.
Island life coming together. No regrets.
Make it count.

J xx

He smiled as he read the words. Typical of her to joke after nearly two years of silence. The card was a reminder of what she had done, the bottle was an order.

Drink. Remember. Move on.

There was nothing that would bring back to the victims of the island now, exposing the truth of the island wouldn't help their families now, it would just reopen old wounds. Jess had given up everything to make sure that he had been able to escape the island with Shreya and he knew she would never let anyone from outside the island be taken ever again. It was time to return the favour.

A soft whoosh of air came from the wood-burner as he opened the glass door, hungry flames sucking down more oxygen.

He checked that Shreya was still asleep then quietly unzipped the bag. Without looking he reached in and pulled out the first one he found, throwing it onto the burning logs. The dry pages of the passport caught instantly, the blue jacket turning black as the flames ran along the front, eating away the golden lettering.

His face burned from the surge of heat as the pages burned but he didn't move away.

He took a sip from the bottle and reached back into the bag.

Printed in Great Britain
by Amazon

43179155R00205